DARK AWAKENING

NEW WORLD

THE CHILDREN OF THE GODS
BOOK EIGHTY-SIX

I. T. LUCAS

***Dark Awakening: New World* is a work of fiction**! Names, characters, places, and incidents are products of the author's imagination or are used fictitiously and are not to be construed as real. Any similarity to actual persons, organizations, and/or events is purely coincidental.

Copyright © 2024 by I. T. Lucas

All rights reserved.

No part of this book may be reproduced in any form or by any electronic or mechanical means, including information storage and retrieval systems, without written permission from the author, except for the use of brief quotations in a book review.

Published by Evening Star Press, LLC.

EveningStarPress.com

ISBN: 978-1-962067-47-8

1

JASMINE

First kiss.

Jasmine had had many of those, and most had been exciting, but none compared to the one she had just shared with Ell-rom.

None even got close.

Perhaps it was the exhilaration of finally reconciling the elusive prince her tarot had promised with the flesh and blood male she'd saved from wasting away in a nonfunctioning stasis chamber.

A stasis chamber that had been inside a crashed escape pod, which had been ejected from an exploding alien ship. It could be a great script for a sci-fi movie in which Jasmine was the star, but ironically, she had never even auditioned for one of those.

The closest she had gotten to playing a part in a fantasy or a sci-fi production was when she had gotten a callback for a zombie apocalypse film. In the end, she had not gotten that part, which she hadn't been too sorry about.

Zombies freaked her out, and she wasn't a fan, but she had watched all the big sci-fi movies. All the *Star Treks*, *Star Wars*, *Stargate*, and *Independence Day*.

The last one was her favorite, especially the president's speech. But while most remembered the famous line, *we will not go quietly into the night*, Jasmine favored a different one—*you will be fighting for our freedom not from tyranny, oppression, or persecution but from annihilation. We are fighting for our right to live, to exist*.

Jasmine chuckled.

The speech was epic, but in that film, the aliens were the enemy, and humans cooperated to save the planet, while, in reality, it was the opposite. The aliens were trying to save humanity, while humans were more divided than ever, and World War III was brewing.

Well, at least she was aligned with the good guys and was now part of an alternative reality that had been running parallel to the one that had prevailed throughout human history.

Until a few short weeks ago, Jasmine had no clue of its existence, and the most out-there thing she had ever done had been to join the Wicca community and practice a bit of harmless witchcraft. In her wildest dreams, she couldn't have imagined that it would lead her to kiss an alien prince who was part god, as in the mythological gods of yore, and part a completely alien race, the Kra-ell, who drank blood for sustenance.

It wasn't Ell-rom's alien origin that had made the kiss magical, though. It was the fact that it had been his first.

Ever.

Her prince had been a priest in training when he had been smuggled onto the settler ship, and Kra-ell priests were celibate. Ell-rom was a virgin, an innocent she had tempted with forbidden fruit…

Jasmine's fingers flew to her lips. "Oh, dear Goddess. What have I done?"

Ell-rom's eyelids, which had been at half-mast until she'd spoken, popped wide open. "What's wrong? Are you not allowed to kiss me?"

The guilty look in his eyes made it evident that he had been aware he was not supposed to get intimate with a woman, and yet he hadn't stopped her.

Jasmine wanted to believe that he had been overcome by desire or didn't care about his religious obligations because he couldn't remember them, but it was more likely that he felt indebted to her.

After all, she had saved him and his twin sister from death and then pulled him out of a coma by talking and singing to him for days.

No, it couldn't be gratitude.

Ell-rom still looked dazed and euphoric from the kiss, so it had to be lust or maybe even some tender feelings that Jasmine didn't dare hope for.

Nevertheless, she should have been mindful of his situation and not tempted him. He shouldn't succumb to desire until he remembered more about his past and figured out where he stood concerning his religious convictions.

"I'm so sorry." She took his hand. "Well, that's a lie. I'm not sorry that I kissed you. I'm sorry about you being a celibate priest and for tempting you to do something that you were not supposed to."

As Ell-rom frowned, guilt made Jasmine shift her gaze away from his handsome face and look at the wall behind his hospital bed. The unadorned, cream-colored walls and medical equipment were a reminder of his vulnerable condition. She had just taken advantage of a male who, only a day ago, hadn't been able to remember his own name.

"I don't recall what being a priest entailed," he said. "I don't even remember what I was taught about spirituality. The only reason I know I was a priest is that you, Jade, and Annani told me about it." He rubbed a hand over his jaw. "Jade said it was my mother's way to protect my sister and me. We didn't look Kra-ell, and we were in mortal danger if we were discovered. They didn't tolerate hybrids where we came from. The only way she could hide us was to put us in the temple where we were protected by the head priestess and the robing that veiled us from head to toe. It wasn't our choice to join the priesthood. Do I have to follow a path I didn't choose?"

Jasmine wanted to say that he didn't have to do anything he didn't want to or didn't feel duty-bound to do, but the truth was that neither of them knew what his life had been like in the temple. What if he had found it satisfying to dedicate himself to serving the Mother of All Life and helping others with their spiritual journey?

Despite her love of carnal pleasures, Jasmine could understand how giving it all up could be fulfilling when it was done in the service of others.

To internalize people's plights and offer genuine compassion, it was necessary to give up something meaningful or experience hardships.

Being a spiritual leader was about more than just leading prayers and rituals.

"Perhaps we should wait until you remember your choices," she said, even though it pained her. "I don't want to lead you astray from your beliefs. When you remember more about who you are, you might realize that you loved dedicating your life to the service of others."

"What others?" Ell-rom asked.

Jasmine looked up at him. "Jade and her people might need a spiritual leader."

He looked at her for a long moment, his piercing blue eyes holding hers captive. "I may not remember my past, but I know how I feel right now, and I know that I enjoyed that kiss far too much to give it up." He took her hand and brought it to his lips for a sweet, feathery kiss. "I enjoy *you* too much to give you up."

It was a relief to hear him say that, but it didn't assuage her guilt. She still felt responsible for leading him away from his faith. "I was hoping that would be your answer. Indeed, I hope it will still be your answer after your memories return. But I don't want to become your regret."

"Never." He pulled her toward him. "But just to be sure I'm making the right decision, I'll need another kiss."

His humor surprised and delighted her. It must be innate because he hadn't had enough life experience since he had woken up to learn and emulate it, and his memory loss meant that he couldn't have remembered it from his past.

Ell-rom's face fell. "I see that you don't want to kiss me again. Was my first attempt so inadequate?"

"Oh, Ell-rom." Jasmine cupped his cheek. "Of course, I want to kiss you again." She leaned in and brushed her lips over his. "It's just that my mind tends to race, even when it's not supposed to."

He frowned. "In which ways was it racing?"

She shrugged. "Just a lot of silly questions that you can't answer."

"Like what?" He leaned into her palm, his eyelids going to half-mast.

"Are you tired?" She brushed her other hand over his nearly bald head.

"Not too tired to hear you talk. I love the sound of your voice."

Jasmine chuckled. "You just want another kiss."

"Yes, that too. But I want to know what's on your mind." He lifted his head and smiled at her. "You seem to have thousands of thoughts swirling around at any given moment, and I want to know all of them."

That made her laugh. "Believe me, you don't want to look inside my crazy, busy head, although you probably can."

He frowned. "What do you mean?"

"The immortals can look into the minds of humans, and since you share ancestors, you should be able to do that as well."

"It doesn't seem right to me." He tapped his temple. "Even though there isn't much anyone can gain from looking into the fragmented pieces of my mind, I wouldn't have wanted anyone invading my thoughts without my permission."

"They can't do that to you. You are one of them."

He looked confused. "Can they only read the minds of humans?"

Jasmine nodded. "But they don't do it unless it's necessary." She looked up at the camera installed near the ceiling and lowered her voice. "But I have to wonder how many do so despite the prohibition. It's not like anyone can find out. And without enforcement, most people will ignore it and do as they please, especially when there is so much to gain and so little to lose."

Ell-rom pursed his lips. "What about honor? If they vow to uphold the law, that should be enough."

"Not all are equally honorable," Jasmine whispered. "I can't speak about the immortals because I haven't been part of their community for long, but since they are part human, and humans are not all honorable, I have to assume that the same is true of the immortals."

Ell-rom's expression darkened. "Did any of them enter your mind?"

Jasmine suspected that one of the gods had bitten her to speed up her recovery after she'd twisted her ankle, and then had made her forget it. But even if she was right, the gods were not part of the immortal community, and therefore not bound by the same rules.

Should she confide her suspicions to Ell-rom?

It felt right to share everything with the male she was falling in love with, but he was still so weak, and it wasn't fair to burden him with too much too soon.

On the other hand, she didn't want to hide things from him, and the way he looked at her expectantly, her only choices were to tell him what she suspected or lie.

"There was this one incident during our trek through the mountains when we were looking for you."

A growl emanated from deep in Ell-rom's throat. "Who did that?" he hissed.

His sudden vehemence was in such stark contrast to his otherwise affable demeanor that it was quite jarring.

Jasmine raised a hand. "Hold on. Don't get mad yet. I twisted my ankle and was in a lot of pain. I fell asleep while taking a short rest, and my ankle felt much better when I woke up. I suspect that one of the gods thralled me to go to sleep, gave me a dose of his venom to heal me, and then thralled me again to make me forget it."

Ell-rom's brow furrowed. "What do you mean that he gave you a dose of venom? Where did he get it from, and why did he hide it from you?"

"Oh boy." She let out a breath. "There is so much you still need to learn about yourself. You know that you have fangs, right?"

Jasmine had felt them elongate when they kissed, but she hadn't been surprised or alarmed. Being with Edgar had taught her how to navigate around them to avoid getting nicked.

Ell-rom lifted a finger and touched his canines, which were back to normal by now. "Isn't that part of my Kra-ell heritage? They need fangs to drink blood. I don't, but I still have them."

Jasmine scrunched her nose. "Not exactly. They are also—"

Her words were cut off as the door to the room swung open, and Bridget walked in.

The medic paused in the doorway, taking in the scene of Jasmine perched on the edge of Ell-rom's bed, their hands intertwined. "Am I interrupting?" she asked, a knowing smile playing at the corners of her mouth.

Jasmine let go of his hand. "I was just about to explain to Ell-rom about his fangs and what they are for, but you can probably do a better job of it than me."

Bridget regarded her with a twinkle in her eyes. "I can explain while I do my checkup. Why don't you get some fresh air while I'm at it? Maybe grab a cup of coffee?"

"Good idea." Jasmine shifted her gaze to Ell-rom. "I'll be back in a few minutes. Do you want me to get you something from the café?" She turned to Bridget.

"Can I get Ell-rom coffee? He's probably never had it."

Bridget shook her head. "You can give him a tiny sip of yours to taste. But you can get him some more vegetable soup."

Jasmine arched a brow. "I didn't know they had soup there."

"They do now." Bridget turned to her and smiled. "Since the clan owns this building and the café belongs to us, we can ask them to get whatever we want."

That made sense.

The clan owned half of the high-rises on this downtown Los Angeles Street, and the humans renting apartments and offices in the buildings above had no clue that their landlord was a clan of immortals.

They also didn't know that there was a vast underground complex sprawling beneath them.

2

ELL-ROM

As Ell-rom watched Jasmine leave his room, his body and mind were still ablaze from their kiss.

Perhaps he was lucky that he did not remember his celibate life and the sacrifice of intimacy he had been forced to make. He did not know how old he was, but he knew he was not a boy. He was an adult male who should have enjoyed the pleasure of a female partner for many years. Instead, he had been forced to play the role of a priest and forgo touching and being touched.

What a terrible loss that had been.

Whatever he ended up remembering about himself and his convictions, religious and otherwise, he was never going back to being celibate. If the Mother of All Life had a problem with that, she would have to appear to him in person and argue her case to convince him to return to that miserable existence.

The chief medic approached his bed with an amused expression on her face. "How are you feeling, Ell-rom?"

How should he answer that?

That he had been transformed? But how could he claim to have been remade if he did not know his old self?

"It has been a long and momentous day," he said instead. "So much has happened."

"Indeed." She handed him an odd-looking device.

It was a compact, sturdy tool with a handle to grip and a small screen on top.

"What is this?" he asked.

"It's a device that measures the strength of your hand grip. It assesses your muscle function and helps us monitor your recovery by tracking changes in your strength over time."

Ell-rom regarded the device with suspicion. "What am I supposed to do with it?"

"Place your hand around the grip handle, and when you're ready, squeeze it as hard as you can. Try to apply maximum effort, and don't be afraid of breaking it. William calibrated it for an immortal male's strength."

He hesitated before doing as she instructed. "Does

that mean that human males are weaker than immortals?"

The medic nodded. "Immortals are about three to five times stronger than humans, and Kra-ell are about three times stronger than immortals. Since you are a hybrid, you are probably somewhere between the two on the strength scale, but that is in peak state. Presently, you are far from it, but this gadget will help us monitor your progress during your recovery."

Bridget sounded earnest, but he still wasn't convinced that her motives were purely therapeutic. These people had heard rumors about him and his sister, accusing them of being abominations and possibly incredibly powerful.

What if the rumors were true?

Jasmine was human, which meant she was much weaker and more fragile than the immortals, who were supposedly weaker than him. If he wanted to keep kissing her and maybe put his arms around her and hug her too, he should know his strength so he wouldn't harm her by mistake.

With that in mind, he squeezed the device as hard as he could and waited to see the result flash on the small screen. Except, he had forgotten that he couldn't read the language it was displayed in.

"What does it say?" he asked.

The medic took the device from him, looked at the display, and nodded her approval. "Right now, your grip strength is forty-five pounds, which is what I would expect from an elderly human female."

He winced. "That sounds terrible."

"It's very good, given the state you were in when you were brought here. Your muscles were completely atrophied, but you are growing stronger quite rapidly." She gave him a reassuring smile. "We will keep checking daily. At your current recovery rate, you will be as strong as a human in a week or two, and as soon as we can get more food into your stomach, you will improve even more rapidly."

She pulled out a small tablet from her coat pocket and wrote something on it, probably the results of the measurement she had just taken.

"How are your memories?" Bridget asked without looking up from her tablet. "Any new recollections?"

Ell-rom frowned, scanning the fragmented landscape of his mind. "Nothing concrete. Just feelings. Impressions." He sighed, frustration creeping into his voice. "I was told that I was a priest or at least training to be one, but I can't remember what that meant to me. Was it just a sanctuary to hide in from those who would have killed my sister and me, or was it my calling?"

Bridget put the tablet back in her pocket. "It will come back to you eventually. Don't force it, and don't stress over it. Just let it flow."

He winced. "I am impatient, and I am also apprehensive. What if that is all I'm going to get? Some fragments of memories, some impressions, and the occasional dreams?"

She smiled fondly. "The fact that you are getting those so soon after waking is a good indicator that you will get all of it back. Just as your body cannot recover its full strength overnight, your mind can't either. These things take time."

He stifled a frustrated groan. "Is there a way to speed up the process?"

"Of course." Bridget walked to Jasmine's chair and sat down. "Tomorrow, I will start you on physical therapy. I ordered a walker to be delivered, and you will begin by walking down the corridor outside the clinic. Jasmine can watch over you while you are at it, but if you are embarrassed about her seeing you struggling, Julian or Gertrude can assist you."

"Why would I be embarrassed?"

A smile tugged at the medic's lips. "Evidently, losing one's memory is not all bad, especially for a male." When he frowned, she chuckled. "Males like to portray strength, especially when trying to impress a female, but those who are smart realize that there is a caretaker inside most females and that they love nursing a good male back to health."

"They do?"

Bridget pursed her lips. "Well, I don't think that is true for the Kra-ell. Their females are not typically nurturing; the males would rather die than admit weakness. For them, getting killed in battle is the only honorable way to die."

Something about what she said resonated with him, more like a distant memory than something he believed in. "They sound like warmongering people."

"That's how they used to be." She sighed. "Tribal wars were a way of life for them, and duels to the death were commonplace. Nature compensated for the high male death toll by giving them a gender distribution of four males born for every female, but then a progressive queen disturbed the balance by stopping the tribal wars and outlawing deadly duels. A new system had to be devised with males outnumbering females four to one. They are not monogamous, and their family units include several males to one female who heads the household. Things got even more out of whack when they landed on Earth and had to survive, but I digress. I just hope that the Kra-ell who joined our community will adopt our values, at least to some extent, and learn that compassion and kindness are not weaknesses but strengths."

Once again, something about what she'd said resonated with him, but as before, he didn't know whether it was because he agreed with her or for some other reason. Compassion and kindness were excellent qualities, but they should be applied cautiously and only to those who had earned and deserved them. Otherwise, they could be manipulated by the unscrupulous to trap and destroy the well-meaning people.

How did he know that?

Was it innate knowledge or something he had learned?

"You look troubled," Bridget said. "Did something about what I said jog your memory?"

He shook his head. "It's a feeling. A warning sensation that goodness could be one's downfall."

"That's a very good instinct, Ell-rom." She pushed to her feet. "Whoever provided your education did a good job. Compassion and charity need to be backed up by strength, or they will be exploited." She patted his shoulder.

Was she planning to leave already? He wasn't done with his questions.

"Can you stay a little longer? I have another question."

"I'm not leaving yet," she said. "There are a few more tests that I would like to run on you."

3

ELL-ROM

Asking the medic about his fangs was going to be so embarrassing, but Jasmine had left him no choice.

"Um, it's about my fangs," Ell-rom said. "Jasmine said that you can explain what they are for."

Bridget's lips twitched, but she stifled the smile and retained her professional demeanor. "Ah, yes. I can certainly help with that. What do you know about your physiology?"

"I know I'm half Kra-ell and half god, and I know the Kra-ell drink blood, but I don't. The idea of consuming blood repulses me. I don't know whether my fangs are just a remnant of my Kra-ell genetics that is not needed or if they serve some other function." He cleared his throat. "I've noticed that they elongate in response to certain stimuli."

"In that respect, you take after the part of you that is half god. Your fangs aren't for feeding; they're for... well, let's call it sharing."

"Sharing?" Ell-rom echoed.

Bridget nodded. "Both Kra-ell and gods have glands that produce venom. The Kra-ell use it mainly to immobilize their prey and to heal its wounds once they are done drinking its blood. The venom actually makes it a pleasurable experience for the prey. This ability is much stronger in gods, naturally or genetically enhanced, but only the male gods have fangs. The females do not."

That didn't seem fair, but the Mother of All Life knew what she was doing, so there was probably a good reason for that.

"In what way is the gods' venom different?" he asked.

"To start with, their venom is much more potent than the Kra-ell's," Bridget said. "In a fight, it can incapacitate an opponent or even stop his heart, which is one of the few ways to kill a god or an immortal. Aggression triggers the production of this dangerous type of venom. The production of the other type, which is used to pleasure sexual partners, is triggered by arousal. Your fangs will elongate in response to either trigger, but the composition of the venom will depend on the situation."

That explained why his fangs had elongated when he kissed Jasmine.

"Is it dangerous?" he asked, suddenly worried. "Could I hurt Jasmine?"

Bridget shook her head. "Not with the venom. Your body knows what type to produce for her benefit, which is not limited to enhancing her pleasure. She will feel stronger, healthier, and more energetic. If she has an ailment bothering her, your venom will help cure it or at least alleviate its symptoms. So, you shouldn't worry. But as you get physically stronger, you will need to be mindful of your superior strength and of her human fragility. Also, her sexual stamina cannot match yours. While you will be able to perform consecutively without rest, she will tire long before you are satisfied, but you will need to follow her lead in this."

Bridget had delivered the explanation in her usual dry and factual tone, but the effect of her words on Ell-rom was instinctive and visceral. All that talk about climaxing and satisfaction was making him respond most embarrassingly, and he crossed his legs under the blanket to hide the evidence.

"Does that answer your question?" the medic asked.

All he could do was nod.

"Very good." Bridget moved to stand close to where he did not want her to be. "Let's check your mobility. Can you sit up for me?"

He was happy to comply and further hide the evidence of his arousal. Pushing himself into a sitting position took less effort than it had taken earlier that day.

As Bridget guided him through a series of simple exercises, testing his range of motion and strength, his arousal subsided to a level where he was no longer embarrassed. Then, his mind just had to wander back to the kiss, and he had to force himself to think about his past before the situation became awkward again.

"Can I ask you something?"

"Of course." Bridget didn't look up from her tablet, her fingers flying over the screen.

"I was told that I was a priest in training and that the Kra-ell's consecrated clergy are supposed to be celibate."

She lifted her head from the tablet and leveled her gaze at him. "That's what Jade told us, but I don't know much about it."

"I know, but all I'm asking for is your opinion. Do you think I should ignore the past I can't remember and follow my feelings for Jasmine instead?"

Bridget hesitated. "I can't comment on your religion or your individual beliefs. All I can say is that from a medical standpoint, your connection with Jasmine has been beneficial to your recovery."

"I understand your reluctance to opine about something not in your field of expertise, but I don't have anyone else I can talk to."

Bridget sighed. "This is something that you'll have to decide for yourself, but in my opinion, I think life is too short—or in your case, too long—to deny yourself happiness based on a past you can't remember."

Relief washed over Ell-rom. "That is what I thought, but since I lacked any meaningful reference, I didn't know whether I was just telling myself what I wanted to hear or whether it was the right thing to do. Thank you for easing my mind."

The medic nodded, patting his shoulder. "Any time. Now, let's get you up and walking a bit before Jasmine gets back with the soup."

With Bridget's assistance, Ell-rom swung his legs over the side of the bed and slowly stood up, his legs trembling slightly under his weight. Still, he remained upright and took a step forward, then another.

"Excellent." Bridget held on to his arm with surprising strength for such a petite female. "You're making good progress."

As they made a slow circuit around the small room, Ell-rom's thoughts once again drifted back to his conversation with Jasmine and what she had said about immortals' ability to read minds. He was particularly concerned about her suspicion that one of the gods had used venom to heal her during their mountain trek. He didn't have a problem with them doing that, even if it required some level of arousal, but he had a big problem with them doing so without Jasmine's consent.

"Hold on," he said, pausing to catch his breath. "I need a little rest."

"Of course." Bridget helped him to lean against the bed. "If you are tired, we can stop and continue tomorrow."

"No, I just need a few seconds to rest, and then I can continue."

"No problem."

"I have another question."

She smiled. "Ask away."

"Is it true that immortals can read human minds?"

The medic's expression tightened. "It's not mind reading exactly. We can't read thoughts. But we can read impressions; when they are very recent, that's as good as reading thoughts. It's like seeing a movie of what has just happened in that person's life. Why do you ask?"

"It's another thing that Jasmine mentioned to me. I don't know if I have the ability, and if I do, when it's okay to use it. I don't think it's acceptable to invade someone's mind without their permission."

Bridget smiled approvingly. "You are right. We have strict rules about it. It's only allowed to hide our existence from humans, which is an existential risk for us, and to save lives. Sometimes special permission can be given by our judge if she's presented with a compelling argument for it."

"How is compliance enforced?" He pushed away from the bed, and the medic helped him take a few more steps around the room.

Bridget sighed. "As you can imagine, it's impossible to enforce. We drill this into our children's heads and hope it sticks."

That was what he had suspected, and there wasn't much else that could be done about it.

"Is there any way to know if someone has invaded your mind?"

Bridget helped him back to the bed before answering. "Not really, but you don't need to worry about it. I doubt anyone other than the gods can invade your mind, probably not even them."

"I see." Ell-rom settled back against his pillows. "Are the gods bound by the same rules as the immortals?"

Bridget's hesitation was answer enough. "The gods operate under their own code, but from what I have seen of them so far, they are honorable people. I don't think they would violate the privacy of anyone's mind unless it was absolutely necessary for security reasons or to save someone's life."

4

JASMINE

As Jasmine crossed the lobby toward the café, she again experienced the disconnect between the secret world of immortals that existed underneath the luxury residential highrise, and the world above.

Standing in line, she felt odd to be surrounded by humans suddenly. It wasn't that the immortals or even the gods looked markedly different than the people around her—well, except for being unnaturally good-looking—but then this was Los Angeles, and there were plenty of good-looking people around.

The main difference was in her, though, and what she knew now that she hadn't before. She was privy to the best-kept secret in the world, and none of these unsuspecting humans could even imagine that it existed.

Then there was the kiss that had changed everything and yet hadn't.

It had only proved that the tarot had been right all along and that the prince they had shown her had not been just a prince of a man, although Ell-rom was that too. It had always been about the prince being her one and only, her destined mate.

So why wasn't she giddy with excitement?

Because nothing was ever that easy, and Jasmine knew with absolute certainty that many obstacles would materialize on her and Ell-rom's way to happily ever after.

It was just the way it was. Nothing good ever came easy.

It could be his religion once he remembered it. Or it could be his sister once she woke up. Or it could be something unexpected.

Jasmine had done a tarot reading the night before, and the cards had been encouraging, hinting at new beginnings and deep connections, but they'd also warned of challenges ahead and difficult choices to be made.

That had fueled her worries. After all, if the tarot had been correct before, there was no reason to doubt them now.

Still, she was grateful for the chance she'd been given

and the wonderful male the Mother of All Life, or the Fates the immortals believed in, had sent her way.

Who would have thought that she would find his innocence and inexperience so endearing?

Perhaps that was why the Fates had prompted her to be so easy with her affections. It had all been a part of their grand plan. Ell-rom was the novice, the apprentice, and she was the expert, the master, and it was up to her to teach her virgin prince everything she knew about carnal pleasures, which was quite a lot.

The prospect of introducing him to all the marvels of sex was so exciting.

"Next in line, please," the barista called, jolting Jasmine from her reverie.

She ordered her usual latte, adding a blueberry muffin on impulse and a cup of soup for Ell-rom.

Waiting for her order, she wondered if there was coffee on Anumati. The gods had drunk plenty of it on their trip through the Tibetan mountains, but they might have developed a taste for it during their time on Earth.

She should call Margo and ask her.

"Order for Jasmine," the barista called out, sliding a cardboard tray across the counter.

Jasmine collected the tray, but instead of heading straight back, she chose to enjoy her coffee at a small table by the window.

Bridget was probably still in Ell-rom's room, and the doctor didn't like being crowded when she performed her examinations. She should give her a few more minutes.

Besides, after being cooped up in a room without windows, Jasmine enjoyed gazing at the outdoors.

It was getting dark outside, but traffic was still congested, and Jasmine watched the cars passing by. People were heading home to join their families, eat dinner together, or engage in whatever drama was currently consuming their lives. Each individual was a microcosmos, each with their own issues, aspirations and hopes, triumphs and disappointments.

As her phone buzzed, she pulled it out and smiled when she saw the message was from Margo. Her friend must have felt that she needed to talk to her.

Good evening, my darling. How's your Prince Charming doing today? Any more memories surfacing?

Jasmine stared at the screen with her thumbs hovering over the keyboard and wondered what she should tell Margo. Should she tell her about the kiss?

At her age and with the number of sex partners she'd had, it seemed silly and immature to brag about a kiss, but the truth was that it was a big deal.

How many women could boast about kissing a celibate alien prince?

Nevertheless, it wasn't something to convey in a text message.

In the end, she settled for a simple reply. *He's doing better every day, but today was a big day for Ell-rom. He got to meet Kian.* She knew she wasn't supposed to tell her about the goddess's visit, and she needed to remind Ell-rom not to talk about it either. *I'll fill you in later, okay?*

When? Margo replied.

When Ell-rom falls asleep, I'll come upstairs. Are you there tonight?

Where else would I be?

Jasmine smiled. *Partying or clubbing with your god.*

My god is spending most of his waking hours tinkering with the salvaged equipment as if the secrets of the universe are hiding somewhere in there.

Jasmine typed back. *Who knows? They may be. BTW, any progress with spying on Lynda?*

I'll tell you when you get here.

Was that Margo's payback for Jasmine's cryptic reply?

Probably.

As her thoughts returned to her prince, she took a bite of her muffin and washed it down with a sip of coffee.

Hopefully, she wasn't leading Ell-rom down a path he wasn't ready for. Perhaps it wasn't fair for her to encourage his feelings when he was still piecing together his own identity.

Maybe she should slow down and wait until he knew who he was and what he wanted.

She had no easy answers. All she knew was that her feelings for him were real and growing stronger.

5

ELL-ROM

As Bridget continued to measure the length and circumference of Ell-rom's atrophied leg muscles, he struggled to keep his eyelids from drooping. The few steps he had taken around the room had robbed him of the last dregs of energy he could muster, and if he weren't eager to see Jasmine return, he would have gladly succumbed to sleep.

When the knock came and Jasmine peeked in, he couldn't help the grin spreading over his face.

She held a steaming cup in one hand and a covered bowl in the other. "Is it okay to come back in?" she asked, her eyes darting between Ell-rom and Bridget.

"Perfect timing," Bridget said, gathering her things. "I was just finishing up. He's all yours."

As Jasmine walked in, Bridget headed for the door but paused in the doorway, looking back at Ell-rom.

"Remember what I said. Don't push yourself too hard."

He nodded.

When the door closed behind the medic, Jasmine set the two containers on the bedside table. "Hungry?" She removed the lid from the bowl, and given the smell, it was his soup.

He tried to stifle a grimace. "Frankly, I'm a little nauseous after all the physical activity Bridget made me do."

"What did you do?" Jasmine perched on the side of his bed.

"I just took a few steps around the room, and it exhausted me." He didn't want to mention the device that had measured the strength of his grip and the results that were in line with that of an elderly human female.

Jasmine eyed the soup. "It's a shame to let it get cold. Also, Bridget said that you need to eat to get stronger."

That was the convincing argument.

He definitely wanted to get stronger as soon as possible.

"I'll try some." He leaned over to take the bowl, but Jasmine stopped him.

"Let me feed you. You're tired."

Recalling what Bridget had said about females enjoying the role of caretakers, Ell-rom didn't argue. "I like it when you feed me."

Jasmine's bright smile turned her face from beautiful to spectacular. "And I love feeding you." She lifted a spoonful into his mouth. "I have to wonder, though, how you are going to grow back your muscles on vegetable broth. You need to eat protein, but since you don't consume meat, I guess it would have to be tofu or beans or maybe a protein shake. Can you tolerate milk or cheese?"

"I don't know. Maybe?"

"Let's give it a try." She put the soup on the side table and picked up the other container. "This is coffee with milk. Do you want to give it a try?"

The idea of drinking something that was meant for baby animals did not appeal to him, but Jasmine seemed to enjoy it, so maybe it tasted good.

He nodded. "It doesn't smell offensive."

"I think it smells really good." She brought the cup to his lips and gave it a little tilt so he could drink. "So, what do you think?"

"It's good." He licked his lips.

It was sweet, but that wasn't because of the milk. "Did you sweeten the coffee?"

"Yes." Her eyes remained glued to his mouth as she murmured, "Do you want more?"

He felt his fangs elongate. "I do, but not coffee. I want to kiss you again."

Jasmine swallowed. "Did Bridget explain the fangs and the venom and all that?"

"She did." He lifted his arm and was proud of himself when he managed to wrap it around Jasmine and pull her to him.

Not that she offered any resistance. With how weak he was, he wouldn't have been able to do anything to her without her full cooperation.

"Be careful around the sharp points," he murmured before he fused their mouths together.

She kissed him lightly this time and leaned back. "I know my way around fangs. You are not the first immortal I've kissed."

Ell-rom smiled. "It's obvious that you have more experience than I do. I'm operating on pure instinct. I just hope not to fumble too badly."

"You're doing great." Her smile was tight for some reason.

"What's wrong?" He kneaded the soft skin at the back of her neck. "Suddenly you seem tense."

"Aren't you going to ask me who I kissed?"

He frowned. "Should I?"

She seemed frustrated. "Doesn't it bother you that I had sex with other males?"

"Why should it?"

She shook her head. "You are right. It shouldn't, but my previous partner was such a jealous guy that I'm surprised to find you so indifferent. Don't you care about me?"

"Of course I care. How can you say that I don't? If you want me to display jealousy, I will."

"But you don't feel it. I don't want you to fake it."

He kept massaging her neck even though it was becoming difficult for him to keep his arm up. "I would not be happy if you showed affection toward another male now, but what was in the past has no bearing on the present or the future." He finally let his arm drop away.

She pouted. "What if I was a terrible person in my past? Would you forgive all of my past transgressions?"

"Yes. But I'm sure there is nothing to forgive. You are pure of heart and strong of spirit, my lovely Jasmine."

6

JASMINE

Jasmine wasn't sure that she deserved such unconditional acceptance, especially given how little Ell-rom truly knew about her. Not only that, she was the only person he knew other than the doctors and the nurse.

When he got exposed to more people, he might not like her, especially after he got to know her better. Not that there was anything inherently wrong with her, but she was a nobody with average intelligence, better-than-average looks, a better-than-average voice, and a mediocre acting talent. She also had a witchy ability that she was still exploring.

Not bad for a random human, but Ell-rom was a prince, and once he remembered what that entailed, he might realize that he needed a female of a higher caliber than her.

"You think too highly of me." Jasmine averted her

gaze. "I'm not as pure of heart or as strong of spirit as you believe. You don't know anything about me."

"I know that you are a wonderful singer and storyteller, and I know that you went searching for me and my sister despite the journey not being easy. You saved both our lives. Then you sat by my side day and night. That makes you pure of heart and strong of spirit in my eyes."

She leaned over to the bedside table and picked up her latte to buy herself a moment to think.

Honesty was important in a relationship, but they didn't really have one yet. They were in the courtship stage, and during such a vulnerable and impressionable time, it was better to throttle the insecurities and doubts while inflating all her positive attributes. It was the selling stage, not the settling stage, and being an actress, Jasmine was an expert at selling herself.

Still, a little self-deprecation was always a good strategy as long as she didn't overdo it.

"What you feel is gratitude." She took another sip. "But you forget that I wasn't the only one there. The three gods, Julian, Edgar, and their mates, were there too."

He arched a brow. "Did all of them go trekking through the dangerous mountains to look for our pod?"

"Only the gods and I went trekking, but the mountains weren't all that dangerous. I twisted my ankle because I'm a clumsy city girl who is not used to hiking, trekking, or any of those outdoorsy activities. If it were Jade instead of me, I'm sure nothing would have happened to her."

He chuckled. "I'm sure of that as well, but that makes your sacrifice even greater. You volunteered to do something that you were not good at, something you did not like and that was potentially dangerous to you, and you did that because you wanted to save lives. That's admirable."

"I was searching for my prince," she reminded him. "The prince that the cards promised me."

"Oh, yes. The foretelling cards. I am still waiting for you to show them to me." The smile died on his lips. "Perhaps you can do a reading for Morelle."

Her eyes widened. "Why didn't I think of that sooner? I should go get them."

He put a hand on her thigh. "Not yet. I'm so tired that once you leave, I'm going to fall asleep, and I'm not ready to part with you yet."

Goddess above, that was so sweet.

Out of all the nice things he had said to her so far, that was the sweetest.

Putting her latte back on the side table, she kicked off her flip-flops and lifted her legs onto the bed. "Bridget will probably have my ass for this, but it's worth it." She stretched out next to him on her side and leaned to brush her lips over his. "This is probably the first time you've had a woman in your bed. Do you want me to take a picture?"

Without waiting for his answer, she pulled out the phone from her jeans pocket, activated the forward-facing camera, and lifted it over the two of them. "Smile!" she commanded while beaming at the screen.

Ell-rom did as she asked, but his smile looked more like a grimace. Nevertheless, she snapped several pictures before putting the phone on the side table. "Why did you make a face at the camera?"

"I saw my reflection on your device, and it looked terrible. I have no hair on my head, but I think that I'm starting to grow hair on my face. My jaw looked dirty in the reflection."

Frowning, Jasmine leaned closer, cupped his cheek, and rubbed her thumb over his skin. "You are right. It's still just hair follicles, so I can't feel the stubble, but you are starting to grow facial hair. I thought that you didn't have any."

"Why? Kian has facial hair, and so does Julian. What about the gods? I don't remember if Aru had hair on his face. And what about the Kra-ell?"

"Aru either shaves or has stubble. I've only gotten to see the Kra-ell males that Jade brought to carry the stasis chambers to the catacombs. They all looked clean-shaven, so maybe the Kra-ell don't have facial hair, but we can ask Jade the next time she comes to visit."

"If she comes." His eyelids drooped, but he forced them to open.

"Right."

Lying so close to Ell-rom and not getting any reaction from him was a little disappointing. His fangs were still dormant, and his eyes weren't glowing.

He tried to shift to his side, but he ended up needing her help. "I walked today. I should be able to turn on my side."

"You are exhausted. Don't be so hard on yourself."

He looked down at the teardrop hanging from her neck. "I guess being hard is one of the idioms that don't translate well to Kra-ell." He lifted his hand and brushed her hair aside, exposing her ear. "Do you experience the same in reverse? When these devices translate what I say for you?"

"Rarely." She brought the hair forward to cover her ear again. "I forget that they are there. Kra-ell probably doesn't have many idioms and is more straightforward than my language."

She still hadn't told him that the earpieces were doing more than translating Kra-ell to English for her and that they were filtering compulsion.

He must have misinterpreted the guilty look in her

eyes. "Tell me why you think that you are not as pure and courageous as I think you are."

Listing her shortcomings was not something Jasmine wanted to do, but it was better than telling him what the earpieces were really for.

"I am an actress. Do you know what that is?"

He nodded. "A performer. You sing and tell fictional stories."

"I also enact fictional stories. I don't know if you have movies or theater on Anumati. The gods do, but maybe the Kra-ell stay away from such entertainment. Here on Earth, it's a highly desirable profession, and many hope to become a star, a face that everyone recognizes." She looked into his eyes. "Are you following so far?"

"I think so. What qualifications do you need to become a star?"

Ell-rom was a smart guy, and he was grasping concepts with surprising ease.

"Good looks are important, and many use surgical means to enhance their appearance, but I'm proud to be all natural. Acting skills are required as well, the ability to memorize scripts quickly, being easy to work with, which means taking directions well and not being overly demanding or fussy."

"You seem to have all those requirements covered."

"Thank you." She smiled. "I do, but that's about it. I'm good, but I'm not exceptional. It's not easy to get rejected over and over again and still go on auditions hoping that a miracle will happen and I will fit the director's vision for a breakthrough part. There are two ways to get great parts. One is to be already famous, and then they want you because you have an audience that will come to see you no matter what the movie is about, and the other is to fit a role so perfectly that the director will be willing to take a risk on a no-name."

"Sounds tough."

"It is." She sighed. "At times, I pretended to be attracted to males to gain favor, hoping it would help me get chosen for a part I wanted." She shivered. "It's a nasty business, and many young people are exploited. I should have given up on dreams of fame and fortune as soon as I realized how sleazy it was, but I convinced myself that if others could do that to get ahead, I could do it too, and that it wasn't a big deal." She smiled nervously. "I bet that didn't translate well to Kra-ell either."

"No, I got the meaning." He lifted his arm with effort and wrapped it around her. "I'm sorry you had to go through such unpleasantness."

The guy was a born diplomat. To call her basically whoring herself out for parts an unpleasantness was a masterpiece of understatement.

"It wasn't as bad as it sounds. I don't like sleeping alone, so I would have probably picked up some loser who I didn't care for anyway. At least by seducing casting directors, I got a few parts."

Jasmine fell silent, memories of lonely nights and hollow victories washing over her like a wave of muddy water.

Ell-rom squeezed her hand. "Nothing of what you told me contradicts my assessment of you being pure of heart and strong of spirit."

"You are pure sweetness." She leaned to plant a soft kiss on his lips. "I've never met anyone like you."

He smiled. "And I have not met anyone like you."

She rolled her eyes. "You don't remember meeting anyone at all."

His smile wilted. "From the little I remember, my sister and I were alone most of the time. Our mother was too busy to visit, and the head priestess who knew what we were under the veils was not the kind, loving type."

As tears prickled the back of Jasmine's eyes, she kissed him again to hide the pity she felt for him and his sister. What a horrible way to grow up.

Ell-rom returned the kiss, his touch gentle but filled with so much passion that it made her heart race.

It was like being fourteen all over again and stealing kisses with Jason Moreno behind the bleachers.

Jasmine had lost her virginity young and hadn't looked back, but she had to admit that the change of pace was nice, and taking it slow was kind of charming. Why did everyone rush into sex before getting to know each other?

If she had done her due diligence instead of jumping straight into yet another relationship, Jasmine might not have gone with Alberto to Cabo. But then she wouldn't have met Margo, wouldn't have ended up on the *Silver Swan*, and would never have found her prince.

7

KIAN

Shai poked his head into Kian's office. "Brandon is here to see you."

"Excellent. Show him in." Kian rose to his feet and walked toward his guest with an extended hand. "Good morning, Councilman."

Brandon flashed him a smile full of teeth, but it lacked the usual spark. "Good morning, Regent." He shook Kian's hand while doing the one-armed bro hug and clap.

Kian responded in kind and then motioned to the conference table. "Please, take a seat."

"Can I get you coffee, gentlemen?" Shai asked.

Kian wasn't comfortable sending Shai on errands of that sort, but it was early, he had a feeling that his talk with Brandon would take some time, and he wanted his guest to feel comfortable and stay as long as was needed.

He looked at his guest. "Coffee?"

"Sure." Brandon smiled apologetically at Shai. "I should have grabbed three cups at the café for us, but my head was elsewhere."

Shai waved a dismissive hand. "Don't worry about it. I was planning to go anyway. Do you want pastries as well?"

For a moment, Brandon looked like he was going to refuse, but then he shrugged. "Oh, hell. Why not? I would love a Danish."

"One for me, too," Kian said.

When the door closed behind Shai, Brandon leaned back in his chair and crossed his arms over his chest. "You said something about needing my movie magic expertise. Can you elaborate?"

"You are aware that we have the royal twins in the keep's clinic, right?"

Kian had sent all the council members a memo, but Brandon did not live in the village, and he avoided council business when he could, so Kian wasn't sure he had read the updates.

"I am aware. How are they doing?"

If he had read the last memo, he would have known, but it seemed like he hadn't.

"As you know, they were in terrible shape when we found them. It was just in the nick of time. The medical team tried to wake them both up from stasis, but so far, only the prince has woken up. He had lost his memory and didn't even remember his name until two days ago. The team is slowly bringing them both back to health, and the prince is about to start physical therapy."

"What is his name?" Brandon asked.

"His name is Ell-rom, and his sister's name is Morelle. He only remembered both their names after he was brought into her room. Seeing her triggered the recollection. They seem very close, and he feels responsible for her."

"That's natural." Brandon uncrossed his arms. "What about the immense powers that he was supposed to possess?"

Kian smiled. "For now, he seems as harmless as a kitten, and I'm positive that he's not pretending, but I wouldn't be surprised if those powers manifest once he gets physically stronger and regains his memory. It could also be that the sister is the dangerous one."

"I assume that you have guards stationed near the clinic."

Kian nodded. "Two Guardians and two Kra-ell hybrids are manning the security office at all times. I have them working in shifts and monitoring the surveillance cameras from the clinic. That way, the prince doesn't feel like he's a prisoner under guard, which my mother would have never approved of, but

I don't need to worry about his powers suddenly manifesting, either. Also, everyone wears the compulsion filtering earpieces around him."

"Good," Brandon said. "So, where does my expertise come in?"

"We need to stage their deaths. We are waiting to perform the funeral rites for the Kra-ell who perished in that pod, until the twins regain enough body mass to look like their fellow Kra-ell, and we want to film it. Aru will send the recording to his commander, and ultimately the evidence will reach the intended audience, meaning the Eternal King. It is essential for the king to be convinced that everyone inside the pod is dead. The problem is that Anumati tech will immediately recognize digital or computer manipulation. We need to do this the old-fashioned way, with movie magic. We will probably also use Bridget's poison trick to induce a death-like state for the twins, but adding a convincing funeral pyre would help."

He didn't need to explain why it was important for the Eternal King to think the twins were dead. That had been covered in a council meeting that Brandon had actually attended in person.

The media specialist chuckled. "These days, everything is done with CGI, but I know a few old timers who still remember how things used to be done before that. If they are still around, they are probably working for theme parks. They are a dying breed."

"How convincing can they make it look?"

Brandon shrugged. "For regular moviegoers, they can make it very convincing. I don't know if they can fool superior technology, though. Perhaps you should think about a better solution that will not require movie magic."

"Like what?"

"I can't think of something off the top of my head, but I'll give it some thought. When do you need to do this?"

Kian was about to answer when Shai walked in with a tray of coffees and a bag of pastries.

"Here you go, gentlemen." Shai put the tray and the bag down on the conference table, took one of the paper cups, and turned around. "I'll be in my office if you need me."

"Thank you," Kian said, and so did Brandon.

Kian picked up one of the cups and took a sip. "The twins are not camera-ready yet. They are no longer as emaciated as they were when we brought them in, but they are still very thin and pallid. In contrast, the dead Kra-ell look healthy because their bodies did not eat themselves and were perfectly preserved in the sealed stasis chambers. The twins also lost most of their hair, and it will not grow as fast as it would have if they were physically well. Regrowing hair is not their bodies' top priority while they rebuild weakened muscles and organs that were on the verge of collapse."

Brandon leaned forward. "We can get creative with wigs and maybe some subtle prosthetics to fill out their features. Careful lighting and camera work can hide imperfections as well."

Kian smiled. "I'm glad to see you getting excited about the production. You've always loved the creative side of the business."

To Kian's surprise, Brandon's expression turned serious. "I still do, but I reached a point where I can no longer stomach the rest. I'm done with Hollywood."

Kian blinked. "What happened? You used to boast about beating the sharks in their own infested waters."

Brandon had been instrumental in propagating the clan's narrative through films and television. Equal human rights independent of race, gender, and religion had been an uphill battle that owed its success in no small part to the councilman in charge of informing and enlightening human culture through media.

Brandon ran a hand through his hair. "The industry has changed dramatically in recent years. It's becoming increasingly difficult for us to exert our influence in the ways we once did."

Kian raised an eyebrow, prompting Brandon to continue.

"The rise of streaming services, the consolidation of major studios, the shift in focus to woke issues, and the influx of high finance—all led to lesser focus on good storytelling," Brandon explained. "Writers, the very people we used to work closely with to shape narratives, are being marginalized with less creative control and lower pay."

"Surely, that makes them more susceptible to our influence?" Kian countered.

Brandon shook his head. "Not when they're constantly worried about their next paycheck or jumping from project to project without fully understanding the bigger picture. And don't get me started on the obsession with remakes and seemingly perpetual franchises. It's limiting the scope of stories being told."

Kian's brow furrowed. "I see. So, what's the solution?"

"Social media. This is where modern narratives are being shaped, and it's where the public attention has shifted to." Brandon's eyes lit up with excitement. "Platforms like InstaTock are shaping culture faster than any blockbuster movie ever could or did. We can reach millions instantly, without the bureaucracy, financial constraints, and the big egos of Hollywood."

Kian considered the implications. The clan had always adapted to changing times, and this shift seemed particularly significant.

Not for the first time, he wondered how much longer they could maintain their influence hidden in an increasingly connected world.

"Very well," he said. "Whether it's a silver screen or a smartphone screen, our goal remains the same—to guide humanity away from the shadows." He didn't add that it was growing increasingly more difficult lately.

Kian had a strong feeling that their archenemy had made a secret move on the eternal chessboard game they had been playing and that he was getting ahead of the clan. Wars were once again sprouting everywhere, human rights were diminishing, and darkness was once again spreading, but this time, it was happening at an alarming pace.

"I'm glad that you are so understanding about it." Brandon sighed. "I'm so fed up that I'm selling my condo in Brentwood and moving to the village full-time. I need to hit the reset button and devise a new strategy."

"What do you have in mind?" Kian asked.

"I'd like to talk with Kalugal and brainstorm some ideas and see what we can do to take it to the next level. Movies are dying, Kian. The future is in interactive, immersive experiences. That's where we need to be."

There was nothing more interactive and immersive than Perfect Match, but it was not ready for general consumption yet. For now, InstaTock was all they had to work with.

Kian leaned back. "I will arrange a meeting with Kalugal."

"Excellent, thank you." Brandon pulled a Danish out of the bag and took a big bite. Once he was done chewing, he used a paper napkin to clean his lips. "So, what's the next step with the twins? I mean, in addition to staging their deaths?"

"I'm sure my mother would demand that we bring them to the village. She's already told Ell-rom that he and Morelle are her half-brother and sister. The truth is that I'm not even going to fight her over this. Moving them both to the clinic in the village will make life easier for everyone. Bridget and Julian want to get back home to their mates." He chuckled. "They have been creative, with Turner sleeping with Bridget in the clinic and Ella staying some nights with Julian in one of the penthouses. They are being good sports about it and not complaining, but there is no reason to make their lives more difficult than we need to."

Brandon seemed skeptical. "That's not like you, Kian. You still don't know whether the twins are threats or assets. Don't you want to find out first how powerful Ell-rom will get before you move them to the village? We can't have everyone wearing earpieces all of the time."

"Of course. I'm referring to the future after we know everything there is to know about the twins' powers. Right now, Ell-rom doesn't even know what compulsion is, and my mother will have to coach him on how to use it for us to assess it."

Brandon frowned. "Is that smart?"

"If he has the power, he will discover how to use it sooner or later. I'd rather it didn't happen spontaneously. Ell-rom is improving rapidly, but Morelle is still unconscious. She might be the dangerous one. What if she's hostile? What if she has abilities we're not prepared for?"

"Those are all valid concerns," Brandon said. "Perhaps you need to call a council meeting and brainstorm this together."

"That's a good idea. I'll call a council meeting soon. We need to make a decision as a community. But first, I want to see how Morelle progresses. And I want to get a better read on Ell-rom. In the meantime, I want you to work out a solution for faking their deaths."

"Give me a week to make some calls, feel things out. I'll have a preliminary plan for you by next Friday."

8

MARINA

The morning rush at the café had subsided, leaving a comfortable lull in its wake. Marina was glad of the break in the hectic pace, humming happily as she wiped down the counter.

"What's that tune?" Wonder asked. "It sounds so lively."

"It's a Karelian-Finnish polka." She smiled. "It's very popular with Finnish accordionists, and we had a lady in the compound who could play it, and we all sang along."

"Do you speak Finnish?" Aliya asked.

"Just a little, but I understand most of it."

"Funny," Wonder said. "It sounded like Russian music to me. I guess the two cultures influence each other."

"We have a customer," Aliya said. "The honorable and admirable Lusha." She made a mock bow.

"Lusha?" Marina turned around. "Dear Mother of All Life, it's great to see you. How have you been?"

"Great." Lusha grinned at her. "Welcome to the village. I meant to come say hi, but I was busy working on a big project, and I didn't want to upset my boss by asking for lunch breaks."

Marina wondered if there was really a job or if Lusha just didn't feel like welcoming her to the village. After all, she and Lusha were acquaintances rather than friends.

"Who's your boss?" she asked.

"Come have a cup of coffee with me, and I'll tell you all about my illustrious career in the village."

The invitation was a pleasant surprise, but Marina had already taken her break earlier.

"I don't know if I can." She cast a hesitant glance at Wonder.

"Go." Wonder shooed her away. "We are not that busy. I'll bring you your coffee to the table."

Not for the first time, Marina got teary-eyed in response to Wonder and Aliya's kindness and friendliness. She had known them for such a short time, and they had already become as dear to her as Larissa.

"Thank you."

Lusha put her hand over her heart and bowed. "You have my gratitude as well. Please put it on my tab."

"You don't have a tab." Wonder chuckled. "But that's okay. It's on the house this time."

"You are the greatest." Lusha blew her a kiss.

Marina hadn't known Lusha well, and they hadn't been friends in the compound, but there was only a handful of humans in the village, so becoming friends with the attorney was a good idea.

If she would be agreeable, of course.

As the daughter of a hybrid Kra-ell father and a human mother, Lusha had always belonged to a slightly higher social strata than Marina, and when she'd been sent to college to study law, she'd moved even higher on the social ladder. But that was nothing compared to becoming famous for defending the Kra-ell males who had faced execution and having successfully reduced their sentence to community service instead.

"So, how have you been?" Marina asked when they sat down.

"Great. I'm enjoying the village much more than Safe Haven. I think Safe Haven is better for the older humans, and the village is better for the young ones. That's why I decided to move here permanently after the trial."

Marina frowned. "I think it's the other way around. Those who live in Safe Haven can meet other humans they can marry and start families with. That's not really an option here."

Lusha lifted a brow. "You seem to have found an immortal to settle down with."

"And you found a Kra-ell," Marina countered. "I heard that you and Pavel got close during the trial and have stayed together ever since."

A mischievous grin spread across Lusha's face. "Oh, you know. We're just friends with benefits. It's not serious." She leaned in conspiratorially. "To be honest, I'm more interested in catching an immortal's eye. How did you manage that?"

So that was why Lusha was suddenly interested in becoming her friend.

"Here are your coffees, ladies." Aliya put down a tray with two cappuccinos and two chocolate croissants.

"Thank you," Marina said. "I've been planning to have one of these all morning."

"I know," Aliya said. "I saw you salivating when you served them. Enjoy." She turned around and walked back behind the counter.

Marina tore a piece of the warmed-up croissant, making sure she got some of the gooey chocolate, and popped it in her mouth, buying herself a few moments to think and decide what to tell Lusha. She didn't owe her the truth, but she didn't want to lie either. Perhaps something in the middle was the way to go. She could tell the truth, just not the whole truth.

"It started as a casual thing, you know, a vacation serial hookup." Marina took a sip from her cappuccino. "I didn't plan on Peter being such a wonderful guy and falling in love with him. What was even more astonishing was that he fell in love back." She paused, her next words still feeling surreal. "He even proposed."

Lusha nearly choked on her cappuccino. "No way," she sputtered. "You said yes, right?"

Marina couldn't help the giddy laugh that escaped her throat. "Of course. But we haven't made any concrete plans yet. It's crazy, and I question both our sanities for even thinking about getting married." She snorted. "In our case, until death do us part means something very different to each of us. From an immortal's perspective, I'm not going to be around for long."

Lusha frowned. "Why do you say that? Are you sick?"

"Yes. My disease is called mortality, as opposed to Peter's immortality."

"Oh, yeah. I get it." Lusha took a sip from her coffee. "I hope my father's genes will help slow my aging process." She leaned over the table to get closer to

Marina. "Pavel's venom helps to keep me young as well, but an immortal's venom is much stronger. That's why I want one." She tore a piece off her croissant. "Peter's venom might prolong your life expectancy as well. Have you discussed it with the clan doctors?"

"No," Marina admitted. "It's uncharted waters for them because no immortal clan member has had a long-lasting relationship with a human before, so they wouldn't know. I'm the first."

Lusha chewed on her croissant for a long moment and then washed it down with some coffee. "You should talk with them, nonetheless. They should monitor you so they'll know the answer for the next human who enters a long-term relationship with an immortal male."

For a moment, Marina considered arguing with Lusha and telling her that there was no point because there would be no other couples like her and Peter, but that wasn't necessarily true.

As Peter had said, they were trailblazers, and others might follow.

"That's smart. I'll do that. Thank you for the advice."

"You're welcome." Lusha lifted her arm and looked at her watch. "I have to rush back to work, but I want to continue our chat. When are you getting off?"

"I'm here until closing."

"I'll stop by, and we will have another cup of coffee."

Marina wanted to get home as soon as possible after work, cook dinner, and spend time with Peter. She didn't want to stay after hours to chat with Lusha.

"Maybe you can come back tomorrow at the same time? It's usually quiet here after the morning rush is over."

"Sure." Lusha pushed to her feet and collected her cup and what was left of her croissant. "I'll see you tomorrow." She smiled. "There aren't many humans in the village. I hope we can become friends."

Lusha sounded genuine, and Marina felt guilty for brushing her off.

"You know what? How about you come over to my house for dinner tonight? I mean Peter's house. Our roommate Alfie is going to be there, and you said that you wanted to meet a nice immortal male."

"That sounds lovely. What time?"

"I usually serve dinner at eight, but if you don't mind sitting in the kitchen while I cook, you can come earlier."

Lusha's eyes sparkled with excitement. "I can do better than that. I can help. You know, chop vegetables, clean the dishes, and stuff like that. I'm not a great cook."

"Sounds like a plan to me. Seven?"

"I'll be there." Lusha leaned over and surprised Marina with a kiss on her cheek. "Thank you for inviting me."

9

JASMINE

Jasmine sat on a chair next to Ell-rom's bed and sipped her morning coffee while he ate breakfast. The tray held a modest assortment of foods that were easy to digest and provided proper nutrition but didn't look overly appetizing.

Where did Gertrude get that breakfast from?

Had she ordered a delivery? Or had she cooked it herself in the keep's kitchen?

The café didn't serve oatmeal or eggs, and given Ell-rom's expression, he wasn't overly enthusiastic about either of those items.

"You need to eat," she said.

He grimaced. "I don't like the smell of that yellow thing, and I don't like the texture either."

"Those are eggs, and they are very nutritious. If you

refuse to eat, Bridget will feed you through a tube. You don't want that, right?"

He cast her a mock baleful look. "Of course I don't." He grimaced. "I'm just deliberating which of these delicacies I should try first."

She was discovering that her prince had a dry sense of humor, and it tickled her silly every time he deployed it.

The small bowl of oatmeal, which was topped with a few slices of banana and a light drizzle of honey, would have been Jasmine's choice, but maybe he preferred the clear vegetable broth, which he was already used to. The scrambled eggs looked a little greasy, and the two slices of wholegrain toast were a little burned, but they were buttered, so they should still be tasty. There was also a glass of apple juice.

"Do you want me to explain what is what?" she offered.

"Gertrude already did." He lifted a slice of toast. "I'm curious about this thing. I don't think I've ever tasted bread." He took a bite and chewed slowly.

"So? Is it good?"

Ell-rom nodded. "Not bad." He put the toast down and looked at the oatmeal. "What are those white round things floating on top?"

"Banana slices. Bananas are fruit."

That got a smile out of him. "I remember liking fruit. And what is that golden liquid thing on top?"

"It's honey. It's sweet."

He reached for the spoon and dipped it into the oatmeal, lifting it to his lips with a deliberate slowness. He tasted it, paused, and then took another spoonful.

Jasmine was relieved that he was eating. "I see that you like that."

When he nodded and took another spoonful, she decided to stop nagging him about every morsel he put in his mouth and leaned back in her chair. When Ell-rom had fallen asleep last night, she had fallen asleep with him, and she hadn't gone up to the penthouse to talk to Margo as she had promised.

It had been strange to wake up on the narrow hospital bed, wrapped up in Ell-rom's arms. Good, but strange.

Bridget hadn't commented on it, so maybe she hadn't known. Gertrude had been in charge of the night shift, and she had known for sure, but she might have decided not to tell the doctor, though Jasmine doubted that. The more likely scenario was that Bridget had pretended not to know so she wouldn't have to admonish her for compromising Ell-rom's comfort.

"We fell asleep before we had a chance to do a card reading last night," she said. "After the physical therapy, I'll get them, and we will do a reading." She smiled. "It will be your reward for all the hard work you are going to put in."

He put the spoon down and wiped his mouth with the napkin. "I was hoping for a different kind of reward." The glint in his eyes didn't leave room for interpretation.

"Then you can look forward to a double reward. A reading and a kiss." Jasmine grinned. "It's going to be a wonderful day."

Ell-rom lifted three fingers. "I need to ask for one more reward."

"Name it."

"I want to see my sister and sit by her side for a bit. Maybe she is not waking up because she has no one talking and singing to her. The sound of your voice pulled me out of the abyss, and it might do the same for her."

Jasmine swallowed the lump in her throat. "We will sit at your sister's side for as long as you want, and I will sing and talk until my voice gives out."

"Thank you, but I don't want you to hurt yourself."

"I won't." She put the coffee cup on the side table and rose to her feet. "It was just an expression. I am a trained actress, and I can go for hours without my throat giving out."

Thankfully, she didn't have to worry about the prince misconstruing her words and turning them into sexual innuendo. Sometimes, it was good that things got lost in translation.

She leaned over Ell-rom and brushed a kiss on his forehead. "I'll go see if Bridget got the walker."

He caught her hand. "Can you eat the eggs for me? I don't think I can stomach them, and I don't want Bridget to put the tube in me again."

Jasmine laughed. "She won't. I was just teasing. Tell her that the eggs make you nauseous, and she will get you something else next time."

Ell-rom sighed in relief. "Thank the Mother of All Life. The smell alone upsets my stomach."

10

ELL-ROM

Ell-rom watched Bridget enter the room with a strange contraption and followed her movements as she set the device near the foot of his bed. It was a metallic structure with four legs, each ending in a cap that was made from some sort of rubbery material.

Jasmine followed, but she stayed by the door to give the medic room.

Bridget eyed his half-eaten meal and frowned. "I see that your appetite is still diminished."

"I have an aversion to eggs," he admitted. "The smell is nauseating to me."

Bridget's eyes widened for a moment. "Right. You have an aversion to animal products. Since the gods don't have that problem, I thought that it was a conscientious choice that your body somehow remembered, but it seems that your aversion is very deeply rooted."

He knew what eggs were, but he didn't remember whether he had ever eaten fowl or their eggs.

"I liked the oatmeal and the banana slices with the sweet liquid over them."

"Good. I'll get you more fruit for your next meal." Bridget positioned the device next to the bed. "So, this is the walking assistance device I told you about. It's called a walker, and it will help support your weight and provide stability as you walk while you build up your strength."

Ell-rom eyed it warily. "How does it work?"

"First, let's get you sitting up on the edge of the bed."

With her assistance, Ell-rom swung his legs over the side and sat upright. The room tilted slightly, and the contents of his meal threatened to come out the same way they had gone in.

"One moment." Gripping the edge of the bed, he breathed through the nausea.

"Take your time." Bridget placed a hand on his shoulder. "Let me know when you are ready to continue."

"I don't know why I'm reacting this way. I was fine yesterday when you helped me walk around the room."

"It might be the food," Bridget said. "Your body is so weak that even digestion is a stressor. We will need to divide your daily calorie intake into smaller and more frequent meals."

It was disturbing to think that eating a relatively small meal could put such a demand on his energy reserves, and it didn't seem logical to him, but he didn't have enough information to doubt Bridget. She seemed like a competent senior medic, so he should trust her assessment.

Taking a deep breath, Ell-rom focused on the floor beneath his feet, and when the room steadied and his stomach settled, he looked up at Bridget and nodded. "I'm ready."

"Good." She positioned the walker in front of him. "Now, place both hands on the grips here." She demonstrated, wrapping her hands around the handles.

Ell-rom mimicked her actions. The cool material under his palms felt foreign, but the stability of the walker was reassuring.

"Now push down slightly on the walker as you stand up," Bridget instructed. "Use it to support your weight, and I'll be right here to help you."

Bridget's hand was at his elbow as he pushed against the walker, guiding and steadying him as he rose to his feet.

The world wobbled momentarily, but the walker held firm.

"Excellent," Bridget encouraged. "To move, lift the walker slightly and place it a small step ahead of you. Then, step forward with one foot at a time."

Ell-rom focused on her words, lifting the walker as she instructed. It felt awkward as he moved it forward and took a tentative step with his right foot and then his left.

"You're doing great," Bridget encouraged. "Make a few more steps around the room."

Ell-rom repeated the process, finding a rhythm in the mechanical motions. Lift, step, lift, step. With each repetition, his confidence grew, though the process still felt awkward to him.

"How does it feel?" the physician asked. "Are you still feeling nauseous?"

"Not at all. I feel good." He cast a sidelong glance at Jasmine. "I'm ready to venture out of the clinic for the first time."

"We have a slight problem." Bridget looked down at his feet. "You don't have any shoes, and I'd rather not give you hospital booties. They're too slippery for your unsteady steps."

As Ell-rom followed her gaze to his bare feet, a flush crept up his neck.

It suddenly dawned on him that he had nothing. He didn't even own clothing or shoes. He was completely and utterly dependent on these people, and not just until his health was restored.

The prospect of being a beggar in his half-sister's community filled him with shame. Perhaps the Kra-ell who lived among them needed a priest?

Would he ever remember what that entailed?

And even if he did, how was he going to perform his priestly duties while having a relationship with Jasmine?

Would the Kra-ell accept a priest who was half god and who was not celibate?

Ell-rom didn't remember a thing of what he had been taught, but he knew that everyone needed a purpose. For most, providing their family with a roof over their heads, clothing for their bodies, and full bellies was enough, but some needed to do more to feel like they were contributing to the greater good.

Right now, he wasn't capable of providing even the basics for himself, let alone someone else, and to realize his full potential, he first needed to find out what it was.

11

JASMINE

Jasmine didn't need to be a mind reader to recognize the embarrassment in Ell-rom's expression, and her heart went out to him. She should have thought about buying him shoes, and she would do that at the first opportunity.

Once he fell asleep again, which would no doubt happen after his therapy session, she would go online and order him shoes.

They could be delivered as early as tomorrow.

First, though, she needed to get the address, and second, she needed to measure his foot to know what size to order.

Using the credit card Kian had given her to buy things for Ell-rom didn't feel right. Even though she knew Kian would be okay with it, she still couldn't use her own cards because he had told her not to.

In a way, she was only slightly better off than Ellrom.

Everything she owned had been collected from her apartment and put in storage, and her car was supposedly in the clan's private parking level. She hadn't gone to check, but she had no reason to doubt that it had been done. Jasmine had some money in her savings account, but it wasn't enough to keep making payments on her car and also put a deposit on a new place. Rent had gone up so much that if she had to fend for herself, she wouldn't be able to afford to live on her own, not even in a tiny studio apartment like the one she'd been renting for the past five years. She would have to share a place with a couple of roommates, and who wanted to do that at her age?

Kian had promised her an allowance until she started working for Perfect Match, but Jasmine didn't know if he'd made good on his promise, and if he had, how she could access the money. Maybe he would deduct what she bought with his card from that?

"It's probably better if you walk barefoot for now," Bridget said. "Just make sure you wash your feet before getting back into bed." She patted him on the back.

"Yes, definitely." He was still looking down. "I wouldn't want to dirty the bed."

"You have very nice feet," Jasmine said, hoping to defuse the tense moment. "People don't appreciate the beauty of feet enough."

Bridget's lips twitched. "I have to admit that I have a weakness for shoes. Stilettos, in particular." She waggled her brows. "And before you say anything about the lack of practicality of such footwear for a physician, let me remind you that as an immortal, I don't get calluses."

Ell-rom's expression changed from embarrassed to confused. "The translator did not know the Kra-ell word for the kind of shoes you mentioned."

Jasmine opened the door. "Let's start walking, and I will give you a crash course on the different styles of shoes that are popular on Earth and why."

As they headed out of the room, Ell-rom's grip on the walker was tight, his knuckles white with the effort, but he pressed on, one shaky step at a time.

Jasmine kept a watchful eye on Ell-rom. "Ready to hear about the different kinds of shoes?"

"How many are there?"

She laughed. "A lot, but I will only mention a few. The ones Bridget likes have a very tall and thin heel. They make a short female look taller, and since they elongate the legs, they make them look shapelier. They are considered sexy."

Ell-rom frowned. "They sound very uncomfortable and impractical. I can't reconcile a no-nonsense female like Bridget with that sort of footwear."

Jasmine laughed. "Didn't you hear her explanation? She doesn't get calluses."

"But she can feel pain. Why put herself through this?"

"Not everything we wear is practical and comfortable. People are willing to suffer in constrictive clothing to look desirable."

He shook his head. "I don't understand this."

"You will, once you learn a little more about human culture." She shook her head. "Looking at it through an outsider's eyes, the picture is not flattering. But enough about that. Let's get back to shoes. Males are lucky to be spared the fashion torture females endure, and I can get you very comfortable shoes with rubber soles that are not slippery. After I measure your feet, I can order them for you." She stopped and looked at him. "In fact, we can do it together. We can shop online."

"What's that?"

"I'll show you when we get back to your room." She cast him a warm smile. "I'm so excited about introducing you to my world. You are like a blank page that needs to be filled."

He grimaced. "I don't even know what that means."

"Right." She needed to remember to stop using idioms.

They didn't translate well.

Showing and not telling applied to Ell-rom's situation even more strongly than it did to fiction.

Jasmine gestured towards the double doors they were approaching. "That's the kitchen." She pushed one side open and held it for him to enter.

Ell-rom's eyes widened with interest as he took in the gleaming stainless-steel appliances and the enormous prep counter that ran in the middle of the space.

"This is where food is prepared, but it's way bigger than what people have in their homes. This is a commercial kitchen, which makes me think that there must be an event hall somewhere down here."

Another possibility was that it had been used to feed an army of Guardians before they had all moved to their new location.

How many Guardians were there?

There couldn't be too many if most of the clan could fit onboard the *Silver Swan,* which was a mid-sized cruise ship that could house a thousand people at the most.

Edgar had told her that in the past, the keep was the center where most of them lived. That's why Kian and his sister had penthouses there. Then, everyone moved to a new location, and most of the apartments aboveground had been leased. The clan still used the underground facility for training and other things. They also had a catacomb level, which she hadn't seen and didn't want to visit. It gave her the creeps, and she preferred not to think about it.

"What else is down here?" Ell-rom asked.

"I haven't had much chance to explore. But maybe we can find out on these walks." She led him out of the kitchen. "There are many levels in this underground, and we can explore all of them, a little bit at a time."

Jasmine hoped that Kian would be okay with that. No one had told her that there were places she wasn't allowed in, and so far, her thumbprint had allowed her access to all the levels she had wanted to get to, but she had tried only three, so there might be others that were restricted.

A smile spread across Ell-rom's handsome face. "I would like that. I'm curious about this world, and this structure is a good place to start learning about it."

As they continued their slow progress down the hallway, Jasmine peeked into the various rooms they were passing by through the small square window at the top of each door.

"What are you looking for?" Ell-rom asked.

"Somewhere down here, the gods are working on the equipment they salvaged from your pod."

His eyebrows rose with interest. "I didn't know they did that. I also don't know what they did with the pod itself. Is it hidden?"

"Yes. They toppled half a mountain on top of it." She peeked into the next room. "These all look like classrooms, which makes them perfect for spreading out the equipment, but maybe they are on one of the other levels. I would love to surprise them with a visit. I'm sure they'd be happy to see you up and about."

A shadow crossed Ell-rom's face. "I doubt it. It's not like I can be of any help to them. Even if more of my memories returned, I probably wouldn't know the first thing about Anumatian technology. I was raised in a temple, remember? My education was most likely limited to spiritual matters."

"I wouldn't be so sure about that." She cast him a sidelong glance, making sure that he didn't look like he was about to keel over. "In human history, monks and priests were often the most educated people. They were the ones who learned how to read and write, so they kept historical records. Your education might be more comprehensive than you suspect."

12

ELL-ROM

"I hope so."

Ell-rom hoped that he had been taught skills that could be useful in this world. He didn't want to be a burden on his sister.

Annani had promised to come see him again, but no one had told him to expect visitors today. She was probably busy with more important things than visiting her half-brother, who had turned out to be a big disappointment.

Instead of the powerful compeller she had expected, she had gotten a weakling who needed to be nursed back to health and kept her medical staff away from others who might need their services.

"What's that glum face about?" Jasmine asked.

"I hate being weak and dependent so fully on others. I can't even go to the bathroom without Julian's help. I try to inconvenience him as little as possible, and I only call him when I can't hold it anymore, but even that is too much."

"Oh, Ell-rom." Jasmine stopped, forcing him to stop as well. "It's okay to need others from time to time." She cupped his cheek and looked into his eyes. "Helping you is making me feel like a better person, and it does the same to everyone else who's involved with your recovery. So, in a way, you're helping us feel good about ourselves and become better people. And one day, when you are back to being strong and your memories have returned, you will find ways to pay it forward." She chuckled. "I know you don't understand the expression. It means that you will help others, giving back to the universe in payment for what you have received."

He tilted his head. "It's a beautiful sentiment. Is this part of the spiritual teachings you grew up on?"

She snorted. "Not at all. I did not grow up with any spiritual teaching. My father was a devout atheist. When I became an adult, I found my path to the goddess, and I learned that in order to receive good things from the universe, you need to send out positivity first. It doesn't need to be anything big. It can be as small as smiling at someone for no reason and brightening their day a little. Or it can be sitting with a friend and letting her vent her worries without passing judgment. There are many ways to do good."

"That is a beautiful philosophy." Looking into her eyes was mesmerizing. There was a hypnotic quality to the gold flecks swirling around her irises, and he found himself lost in them.

"Ell-rom," she said softly. "Are you tired?"

"No. I was just thinking that sitting by an unconscious male and singing and talking to him to pull him out of the abyss is also one of those positive deeds."

"Yes, but that was not as selfless as all that." She cast him a bright smile. "You are my prince. I found you, and I hoped you would wake up, take one look at me, and fall hopelessly in love with me."

"Then you have gotten your wish."

"Oh, Ell-rom." She leaned toward him and brushed a soft kiss on his lips. "I love to hear you say that, but I don't want to take advantage of you, and right now, it's gratitude talking. You don't even know what love is."

"Then you need to tell me. You are the one with all the life experience that I lack."

A shadow passed over her eyes. "I'm not sure I am qualified. Maybe we will figure it out together."

She resumed walking, and he had no choice but to follow. "Have you never been in love before?"

"I thought I was. Many times, but I always realized that it was just an infatuation. I've never really been in love." She slanted a look at him. "You are going to be my first."

His heart squeezed so hard that, for a moment, he couldn't catch his breath. "Going to be? Don't you have feelings for me now?"

"Of course I do, silly. But we have just met, and even though the seeds of these feelings are strong and robust, they need time and space to grow. Do you understand what I'm trying to say?"

He nodded. "You are right. I'm acting like a young boy."

"I think it's sweet." She leaned over and planted a quick kiss on his cheek. "I love that you are so inexperienced, so innocent. Teaching you is exciting."

She'd called him innocent, but was he?

He might have never been with a female in a carnal way, but he might have done bad things that he couldn't remember. It wasn't that he felt unexplained guilt because he didn't, but there was some unease. He knew that hidden among his memories would be things he would have preferred to forget.

When they reached the end of the long corridor, and he turned the walker around for the return journey, the exertion was starting to take its toll on him, but he tried to hide it. If he wanted to get stronger fast, he needed to push himself.

"Where are the living quarters?" he asked. "Are they on those other levels you mentioned?"

He knew that Jasmine had a bedroom in the building, but he didn't know where it was.

She shook her head. "Maybe a few are on one of the underground levels, but most people live on the floors above, the ones that have windows to the outside. Many of Kian's people used to live in this building, but they moved to a different place a while ago."

13

JASMINE

Ell-rom looked tired, but given the stubborn expression on his face, he wasn't about to admit it or quit before he fell on his face.

Jasmine needed to coax him into returning to bed. She tucked a strand of hair behind her ear. "The truth is that I've never been to their new location, but there is a whole beautiful world out there."

Perhaps as nature went, it was still true, but the state of humanity was a different story. The world wasn't as beautiful as it had been just a few years ago, with wars raging and hatred seeming to spread like wildfire. But Ell-rom was still too fragile, physically and emotionally, to be burdened with the harsh realities of the world he had woken up in.

She could shield him from that for a little longer.

"I'd like to see it," Ell-rom said. "I don't like being

underground, and I miss seeing the sky and breathing fresh air."

Jasmine patted his arm. "You will. As soon as I can, I will sneak you up to the penthouse, and you can sit outside on the terrace and enjoy the Los Angeles smog."

He frowned. "The angels?"

She hadn't known that the Kra-ell religion had angels. Perhaps the teardrop translated the word to the closest thing it could find in Kra-ell.

"Angels are supposed to be God's servants. What do they mean in your language?"

He thought for a moment. "Good spirits. Metaphysical guardians who watch over warriors."

"That's similar enough. Many people believe that there are guardian angels watching over them. Anyway, the city we are in is called Los Angeles, which means the city of angels. It's a nice name, but it's not indicative of the people living in it."

"Are they wicked?"

"No. Most people are good or rather neutral. But deftly directed propaganda combined with the herd mentality of the masses often results in people promoting evil causes with no self-awareness." She sighed. "Or maybe there is a seed of evil inside all of us, just waiting for an excuse to germinate."

Ell-rom halted, leaning heavily on the walker. "I don't believe that even for a moment. There is none of that in you, Bridget or Julian, or any of the people I've met so far."

She tilted her head. "What about Jade?"

He closed his eyes. "I'm not sure about her. There is darkness in her."

He sounded so sure of his assessment that Jasmine was tempted to believe him. "Maybe you have a special talent for seeing the light or darkness in people."

"Doesn't everyone?"

"Not at all." She smiled sheepishly. "I thought that I was a good judge of character, but I let myself get blindsided by a charming guy who had very nefarious intentions. After Alberto, I don't trust my own judgment."

Ell-rom's eyes started to glow. "You told me about his subterfuge, but you didn't tell me what happened to him."

"I don't know. He's probably still serving the cartel boss, but instead of doing his evil bidding, he's now doing good deeds." She chuckled. "Compulsion can be used for good, and in this case, it was used exceptionally well. The cartel thugs are now compelled to rebuild the communities they destroyed." The smile slid off her face. "Not that it will help all the people they murdered and their families, or that it will help all the females their henchmen violated."

The horrified expression on Ell-rom's face gave her pause.

"I shouldn't have told you all that. You are not ready for the ugly side of humanity yet."

He shook his head. "I know that I lived a sheltered life, but it wasn't a pretty life. I know that even without remembering much. You don't need to coddle me or show me just the pretty things."

Jasmine let out a breath. "True, but I haven't shown you anything pretty yet while hinting at a lot of ugliness. When we get back to your room, I'm going to put the television on and show you the nicer things about living on Earth. Do you know what a television is?"

"It's a device that broadcasts programs. Entertainment and news." Ell-rom looked at the teardrop hanging from her neck and then looked up at her. "Will your translating device work together with the broadcasting device?"

Jasmine's excitement dimmed as she realized the complication. "You're right. You'd need the translating earpieces." She tapped her ear. "I'm not sure if they have a pair for you yet."

She would need to ask Bridget about that, or maybe William. She was quite certain that they wouldn't give Ell-rom the compulsion filtering earpieces, but maybe William had a pair that did the translating part without the filtering.

By the time they reached Ell-rom's room, his steps had grown more labored, and there was a sheen of sweat on his forehead.

"You did wonderfully," she praised. "I just need you to make it to the bathroom so we can wash your feet."

He looked at the door with a pained expression on his face. "I don't have the energy to do that."

"You just need to get in there." She held the door open for him. "I'll do the rest."

Somehow, he managed to walk up to the shower, and she helped him sit on the stool.

"If you turn the water on, I can do it myself," he said.

"Don't be silly." She kicked off her flip-flops and got inside the shower with him.

Holding the handheld spout, she turned on the water and checked the temperature. When it was just right, she grabbed the soap, crouched at Ell-rom's feet, and washed them until they were perfectly clean.

When she looked up, she was struck by the glow in Ell-rom's eyes, and to her surprise, she felt her cheeks heating up.

It hadn't occurred to her that he might find the experience arousing.

"I'll bring a towel." She pushed to her feet, grabbed a towel from the vanity, and returned to her spot. "Now you can get in bed and rest." She dried his feet as best she could, given that the shower floor was wet.

Tossing the towel back on the counter, she stood up and offered Ell-rom a hand up. "Careful now. The floor is slippery."

When she got him in bed, he sank onto the pillows with a grateful sigh. "I'm beyond exhausted," he admitted. "But it felt good to move. I just wish I had enough energy left over to go see my sister."

Jasmine smiled. "The day is still young. Rest a little, and when you wake up, you'll have lunch, and then we will go see your sister." She leaned over him and kissed his forehead. "I'm so proud of you. You're making incredible progress."

Ell-rom's eyes were already drifting closed, but a small smile played at the corners of his mouth. "Thank you," he murmured.

14

PETER

"Thank you for allowing me in here." Kagra sat down on the sole chair in the security office.

The room was small, with one wall covered entirely with screens that displayed various areas of the village, one desk, one chair, and a small fridge in the corner with bottles of water and snacks for the Guardian on duty.

Peter leaned against the edge of the desk and crossed his arms over his chest. "This is the most boring job there is, and both Jason and I are very happy to have you do it."

She smiled. "Yeah, I saw the big grin on Jason's face when you told him that we would be taking over for the next hour. He couldn't wait to run out of here."

Peter studied her profile, noting the changes in her since their time together. She seemed harder now, but the playful spark that had initially drawn him to her was still there.

Unlike most of the pureblooded Kra-ell, Kagra smiled often, which had been the reason he'd assumed she was different than the other females. She'd seemed more approachable, which was still true, but at her core she was a Kra-ell predatory female through and through, and she was not built for monogamous relationships. Or maybe she just hadn't clicked with him. After all, Jade was the apex predator of her community, and she seemed very happy in her exclusive relationship with Phinas.

Not that it mattered anymore. Peter was over Kagra, and he was in love with Marina.

"Can you blame Jason?" He waved a hand over the small space and the array of monitors covering one entire wall. "Can you imagine spending eight hours staring at these screens?"

She grimaced. "I would go crazy. Did you ever have to do this?"

He nodded. "Sure. Thankfully, I got promoted, so I no longer need to watch paint dry in here."

She frowned. "How often do they paint this office?"

Peter laughed. "It's an expression. It means doing something extremely boring and unproductive like watching paint dry." He waved at the monitors again. "Nothing ever happens, and it's difficult to stay alert when the expectation is that nothing will happen during the shift. It's all too easy to pull out a phone and start scrolling through social media and watching funny cat videos."

She arched a brow. "Are you speaking from experience?"

He affected a mock, innocent face. "Maybe."

Kagra shook her head. "I would have never guessed you were a cat lover."

"Cats are entertaining, and they keep the mice away, so they are also useful."

"I'll take your word for it." She lifted the tablet that served as a controller for surveillance footage of the array of monitors. "Show me how to use it."

As he leaned over, the familiar scent of Kagra's shampoo was like a whiplash of déjà vu, and a wave of nostalgia washed over him. All the good times they had together, the wild sex, trying out the part of the submissive to her dominance…

Peter shook his head and leaned away to dispel the effect of the memories.

Was Kagra as affected by his scent? His proximity?

If she was, she was hiding it much better than he did, maintaining a professional demeanor while still being friendly.

He grabbed the tablet. "The best way is to show you. This screen is the miniature representation of the large array. We want to start with the mailroom, so I will touch that square. When it fills the screen, the controls pop up, and you can go back in time, speed up the recording, slow it down, and zoom in and out. You can also take screenshots of whatever." He handed her the tablet. "Got it?"

"It's easy enough." She started playing with the controls.

He peered at the screen over her shoulder. "Nothing has been stolen since the cameras were installed, so I don't know what you hope to see."

"Someone acting suspiciously." She narrowed her gaze on the monitor. "But that's hard to do at ten times the speed. I will have to slow down when I see something suspicious. I'm looking for someone who seems to be checking for cameras."

"They were only installed Sunday night, so there isn't that much footage to go over."

Kagra paused the replay and turned to face him. "How many people know about the cameras in the mailroom?"

Peter made the mental tally. "All the Guardians have been briefed, plus William's crew who installed them. You and Jade know, of course, and probably Phinas, too. And if Phinas knows, Kalugal knows as well, and so does Rufsur. I don't know if Kian informed the council, although I doubt he would have bothered them with such a little thing."

"That's a lot of people. Do you think the rest of Kalugal's men know about the cameras as well?"

Peter shrugged. "I don't think Kalugal would make a big deal out of petty thefts that most likely have nothing to do with his men. They've been living in the village for a while now and haven't caused any problems. Besides, they live in their own secluded section, and they are not as affected by the Kra-ell newcomers as much as the rest of the villagers."

Nodding, Kagra resumed the replay at only six times the speed. "Frankly, I don't think it's one of your clan members. I suspect my people. Especially the teenagers."

"I don't think we should exclude anyone. We know that some of the clan members are not happy about the way things are in the village. The integration everyone was hoping for is not happening. Except for a few notable exceptions, there's very little contact between the three groups."

Kagra's lips quirked into a wry smile. "Oh, I wouldn't say that. There's plenty of contact happening at night between Kalugal's males and the clan's females."

Peter was aware of the hookups. Living in such a close-knit community, it was hard to be ignorant of that, but there was a big difference between hookups and relationships, which for some reason failed to arise despite the robust activities.

The Kra-ell were too different, so he could understand that, but Kalugal's men were perfectly compatible, at least physically, and there should have been more couples than just Ingrid and Atzil, and Edna and Rufsur. Evidently, though, the clan ladies found it hard to forget that the males were former Doomers.

It was also possible that the Fates had different plans for all of them.

"True, but so far, there have been only two integrated couples between the clan and Kalugal's group, and only Edna and Rufsur are bonded mates. Atzil and Ingrid treat each other as placeholders until their one and only appears."

Kagra nodded. "Speaking of Atzil, have you been to his bar yet?"

Peter shook his head. "No. Why?"

"You should check it out. Take Marina there for a drink," Kagra murmured while intently watching the screen. "It's only open on weekends for now, but it's a good place for Kalugal's men to meet clan people. I mean, aside from the ladies they're already acquainted with."

"I might do that. Thank you for the suggestion. Marina would love it there."

His voice must have changed cadence when he spoke about Marina because Kagra slowed down the recording again and turned to him. "You really care for her, don't you?"

Peter ran his fingers through his hair. "I love her, and as impossible as it seems, I think she is my one and only."

As he'd expected, Kagra's lips twitched with a smile, but she didn't say anything. Instead, she turned back to the monitors, all business once more.

He knew that she thought that he was in love with the notion of love and was imagining the bond he felt with Marina, but Peter also knew that Kagra was wrong, and he was right.

Marina was his truelove mate, which meant that the Fates would find a way to make her immortal.

15

MARINA

As the doorbell rang, Marina wiped her hands on the dish towel and walked over to open it.

"Good evening." Lusha entered with a small bouquet of roses in hand. "These are for you."

Marina took the small bundle and brought the flowers to her nose for a sniff. "These are lovely. Where did you get them?"

"Mo-red trimmed the rose bushes in front of the clinic today and brought these home, so I commandeered some. I'm staying with him and Vanessa."

That was news to Marina. "I didn't know that. Why are you staying with them?" She motioned for Lusha to follow her to the kitchen.

"Vanessa invited me to stay with her during the trial, and when I decided to move to the village permanently, she offered me the guest room, and I happily accepted. I'm barely there, so it's not like I'm in the way, but I like having a place I can escape to when Pavel is having his Kra-ell friends over."

"That doesn't sound like a committed relationship, " Marina said.

Lusha shrugged. "It's not. Most of my things are at Vanessa's place. I only keep a few items at Pavel's. I think that says it all."

"Indeed." Marina put the roses in a vase and filled it with water. "How are you getting along with Mored?"

"Splendidly." Lusha leaned on the counter and crossed her arms over her chest. "First of all, I'm dating his son, so he needs to be nice to me. And secondly, he owes me a life debt, as do the others whose necks I saved from Jade's sword."

Marina winced. "Yeah, I bet. That female scares me, but I hear good things about her. She's trying not to be as totalitarian in her approach to ruling as she used to be."

Lusha sighed. "It's not going to work with the Kra-ell, but who am I to give Jade advice?"

"Why not?" Marina took out the chopping board.

"Because they are not ready for that. They need a totalitarian leader who rules mercilessly over them because that's the only thing they respect. They need time to absorb the ideas of democracy and equality and all those nice concepts the clan believes in. The problem is that they are long-lived people, so waiting for the current generation to die out along with their traditions and ways of thinking will take a long time, and in the meantime, they are indoctrinating the younger Kra-ell. I'm trying to think of a solution to this predicament, but most of what I come up with has already been tried in the human world and failed."

Marina took out four tomatoes and started chopping them into small pieces. "That doesn't sound encouraging."

"It is what it is." Lusha pushed away from the counter. "Can I do the chopping? I came early with the intention to help make dinner."

Given Lusha's own admission that she wasn't much of a cook, Marina didn't trust her with the sharp chopping knife.

She smiled. "You are my guest, and I want you to relax and enjoy. Can I offer you something to drink?"

"What do you have?" Lusha seemed relieved.

"Take a look in the fridge."

Lusha did as instructed and pulled out two Coronas. "I bet these are not Peter's or Alfie's. The immortals only drink that super potent Snake Venom beer that they import from Scotland."

"Good guess." Marina paused her chopping to take one of the beers. "Peter got them for me. You'll find an opener in that drawer on the right." Once they had both opened their beers, Marina clicked her bottle with Lusha's. "Cheers."

"Cheers." Lusha took a long swig. "This is good." She leaned against the counter again. "So, any advice about seducing an immortal?"

"Don't be shy." Marina grinned. "Which doesn't seem to be a problem for you. Just walk up to someone who catches your eye and start a conversation."

Lusha arched a brow. "Is that what you did?"

"Yep. Peter was having a drink on the lido deck, and so was I, and I asked him if I could join him. We started talking, and one thing led to another, and here we are."

"And here you are." Lusha lifted her bottle for another salute. "Planning a wedding."

Marina laughed. "Not yet."

"When you are ready, let me know. I'll help you organize."

Marina slanted her a look while dicing an onion. "Aren't you busy with that mysterious new job you got?"

"It's not mysterious. I'm working for Edna, the clan's judge and attorney. It's mostly paralegal-type stuff for now, but it's not like I can do anything else while residing in the village or in Safe Haven, and I don't think I will be allowed to venture out on my own anytime soon." She sighed. "When I do, I hope Edna will hire me for her office in the city, but to do actual legal work, I will need to pass the California bar exam."

"What's that?"

"It is necessary to pass that test to practice law in the state. It's proof that I've met all the educational requirements and I know the California law as well as general legal principles. Each place has its own legal system, and that's why attorneys need to study local law and pass exams to prove that they know it."

Marina nodded. "You studied in Finland. They probably have different laws, right?"

"Many of the principles are the same, but there are differences and nuances, of course. I'm studying when I have the time. Edna says that the test is a bitch. It is spread over two days, and many students take it several times before they pass."

"That sounds intense."

"It is," Lusha agreed, "but it's necessary to ensure that only those who are truly prepared and knowledgeable can become licensed attorneys. Once I pass the exam, they are also going to check my background, which I will need the clan to fabricate for me, and if I pass all that and a test on professional responsibility, I will be eligible to be admitted to the bar."

"Good luck. That sounds like one hell of an undertaking."

Lusha shrugged and took another swig of her beer. "I know how to study, and my English has gotten much better since I got here and was forced to speak it exclusively. If the clan will help with fabricating a background for me, I can do it."

"I admire your tenacity." Marina squeezed a lime into the salsa and added salt. "Do you really think that you'll ever be able to practice law here?"

Lusha sighed. "It will probably take years before Kian will be comfortable letting us come and go as we please."

The mention of years brought Marina's thoughts crashing back to the elephant in the room—the vast lifespan difference between her and Peter. She felt the familiar weight of that reality settling in her chest.

"You should reconsider seducing an immortal. It's not really fair to them if they fall in love with a human. The children I will bear to Peter, if we get so lucky, will be human, and he will have to watch not only me die but our children as well."

"What about you? What's the downside for you, if there is any? From here, it seems that you can only benefit from being with him."

And here she thought that Lusha was a smart woman. "The downside for me is that I will get old while Peter will stay young. Do you really think that he will want to stay with an old woman when in fifty years' time he'll look exactly like he does now, and I'll look like a prune?"

"You might age slower than you would otherwise."

Marina rolled her eyes. "Fine, so in a hundred years, I will look like a prune, and he will still look exactly like he does now. It will still happen."

"Have you talked to Peter about this?" Lusha asked.

Marina nodded. "He says that he will take whatever years I can give him. He wants to be with me for as long as we have. He wants us to take it one day at a time and not think about the future. Sometimes I manage to do that, and sometimes I can't."

Lusha's eyes sparked with determination. "Peter is right, Marina. We are living in a world of gods and immortals, and their doctors are working on unraveling the secret to their immortality. One day, they will figure it out, and we will be the first ones they will test it on because we are here, and we are willing to be their test bunnies."

16

PETER

The mailroom was a bustling place, with clan members, Kra-ell, and Kalugal's people all coming and going throughout the day. Seeing the three groups interacting in such a mundane setting was actually reassuring. They might not be one cohesive community, but they were cordial to each other as they collected their packages.

Kian was convinced that the theft and sabotage were symptoms of a deeper problem and that the lack of meaningful integration between the groups was a ticking bomb that, if not addressed, could trigger a real conflict. But what if they were not dealing with a global issue afflicting the community? What if this was all the doings of one troubled individual?

"You know." Peter shifted his gaze to Kagra. "Maybe we're looking at this all wrong. All of that malicious mischief might be the actions of one unhappy individual. Maybe it's an attempt to get attention or vent frustration."

Kagra turned to him, her eyebrows raised. "That's an interesting theory. What makes you say that?"

Peter shrugged. "Look at what was taken—small items mostly, nothing of real value. It's like whoever's doing this wants to shake things up."

"If it were only the thefts, I might have agreed with you, but the sabotage is dangerous. Light seen at night might draw attention to the village, and none of the three groups wants that to happen."

"None of the sane people want that, but teenagers often don't think rationally, and sometimes adults don't use their brains properly either. Still, I agree with you that it's most likely the teenagers."

Kagra stopped the replay and leaned back in the chair. "So, we both think it's the teenagers, and you think it is a cry for attention?"

"People do crazy shit to be noticed, and many times it's not positive."

Kagra was silent for a long moment, considering his words. "It's a dangerous game to play just to get attention. If it's one of ours, they will be flogged."

Peter winced. "Yeah, we have the same brutal way of dealing with unruly immortal teenagers, but the difference is that ours heal in hours while yours heal in days. So, yours is a more severe punishment in a sense."

"We are tougher people, and our tempers run hotter. We need to be stricter to control our youth." Kagra smiled coldly. "I've gotten flogged and beaten by Jade even before we were captured by Igor, and I was her favorite, the one she chose as her second." Kagra took a long breath. "She's not nearly as strict with Drova, and she's doing the girl a disservice. She's much too strong-willed, and given who her father was, letting her run wild is dangerous."

Drova was Igor's daughter, and Igor was an incredibly strong compeller. If Drova had inherited his power, she could cause much more trouble than stealing from the mailroom or sabotaging window shutters.

Peter frowned. "Do you think it's her?"

Kagra nodded and turned back to the tablet. "Let me show you something." She rewound the replay and then ran it forward until she found the timestamp she'd been looking for and slowed it down to half speed. "Watch her."

Drova was in the mailroom, checking the labels on the stacks of packages like everyone else. The Guardians who brought the mail from the keep just dumped the packages on the tables, so there was no discernible order to them, and the only way to find what you were looking for was to estimate the size of your package and then check the labels on each one that matched more or less. Sometimes, though, shippers put small items in large boxes, so eliminating by size didn't always work.

"She's just looking for her stuff," Peter said.

"She's doing more than that." Kagra rewound the recording a few minutes back, let it play again, and then stopped and zoomed in. "Do you see that expression?"

Drova was slanting a glance straight at the hidden camera as if she knew it was there, a conceited little smile playing on her lips.

"I see that, but it's not proof that she's the culprit."

Kagra put the tablet on the desk and turned toward him. "It's not proof enough, but it's a hint. Just think about it. She could have heard Jade and Phinas talking about the mailroom and the need to install cameras there. After that, she knew not to take anything that didn't belong to her, but she was curious to find the hidden camera, so she pretended to be looking for a package and reading all the labels while inconspicuously searching for the camera's location. When she spotted it, she couldn't help the satisfied look on her face."

Peter shook his head. "So, this is all about getting her mother's attention?"

"I didn't say that." Kagra crossed her arms over her chest. "Drova and Pavel hang out together a lot, and it doesn't seem to be a romantic thing. Pavel is much older than her. Maybe they are working together on this. Pavel is just the guy who does the small sabotages, and Drova steals small packages."

Peter nodded. "Perhaps, but to what end?"

"I don't know." Kagra sighed, running a hand over her long ponytail. "They might have more accomplices. We need to keep investigating and assign watchers to them."

They'd already had Borga followed, but so far, she hadn't done anything suspicious. Assigning two more Guardians to Pavel and Drova was a waste of resources.

"Do you have people you trust?" he asked.

"There are many, but none that I would trust to follow Drova and Pavel. No one will want to be the betrayer of our people."

"What if Jade's commanding them to do this?"

Kagra shook her head. "I don't want to tell Jade my suspicions yet. If I'm wrong, she will never forgive me for accusing her daughter."

"Good point." Peter smoothed his hand over his goatee. "I'll talk to Onegus and see who we can spare."

'You do that." Kagra picked up the tablet. "Let's watch the rest of the recording. Perhaps someone else will start acting suspiciously."

As she brought the replay to where she had stopped it before they had discussed Drova, the two of them lapsed into silence again, their eyes scanning the screen for signs of suspect activity.

A few minutes into the replay, Peter's mind started to wander, and he thought about his date night with Marina at Atzil's bar. Perhaps he should also make reservations at Callie's, but the waiting list was so long that it was harder to get a table at her restaurant than at *By Invitation Only.*

Perhaps he could cook dinner for Marina for a change. She insisted on cooking and was great at it, but after long days working at the café, she could barely stand.

"What are you thinking about?" Kagra asked.

"Cooking dinner for Marina."

She chuckled. "You never cooked for me."

"That's not true. I made you breakfast plenty of times."

"And I baked you muffins."

Kagra sounded like she missed those days, but Peter knew she didn't.

"We had fun, but it wasn't meant to be," he said without looking at her.

"No, it was not." Her eyes remained glued to the screen.

17

JASMINE

Jasmine scrolled through the shoe selection on her favorite shopping app and wondered what kind of footwear Ell-rom would like. Jade wore combat-style boots, the gods had worn hiking and running shoes, and Kian wore dress shoes with slacks and a button-down dress shirt, sometimes with a suit jacket over it and sometimes without. Even on the cruise, she hadn't seen him in jeans.

She lifted her gaze to the peacefully sleeping Ell-rom and tried to imagine him in a pair of jeans and a T-shirt, but the only thing popping into her mind was a medieval-inspired princely outfit in the style she'd seen in the *Game of Thrones*.

A mid-thigh velvet tunic in deep burgundy that was adorned with intricate gold embroidery and tailored to fit his slim frame. The leather trousers were black and snug and tucked into knee-high boots made of the finest hide with their glossy finish. She wanted to add a sleeveless coat made of some exotic fur, but since the Kra-ell did not kill the animals that they fed from, they would not have used fur or leather, for that matter.

Still, it didn't make sense for a nomadic, violent culture to make clothes from plant fibers. They might not have killed animals to eat them, but they did so for their hides. She was pretty sure of that, but perhaps she should ask before ordering Ell-rom leather shoes.

He'd fallen asleep before she could introduce him to the wonders of internet shopping, and if she waited for him to wake up before ordering, the shoes wouldn't arrive by tomorrow.

Perhaps Bridget knew whether the Kra-ell had a problem with leather goods.

Getting to her feet, Jasmine cast another glance at Ell-rom's rising and falling chest and walked out of the room.

She found Bridget in her office, looking at her computer screen with a deep frown on her face.

She knocked on the open door. "Are you busy?"

Bridget shifted her gaze away from the screen and smiled. "I'm just reading an article in *Nature* about the latest breakthrough in computational neuroscience. The math is too complicated for me to grasp, though. I should forward it to Kaia."

Jasmine had no clue what the physician was talking about, but she smiled and nodded as if she understood. "Yeah, that's a good idea."

Bridget smiled. "What can I help you with?"

"I have a silly question. Do the Kra-ell wear leather shoes? I want to order some for Ell-rom and I thought about his aversion to animal products. I don't want to order him something that he might find offensive."

Bridget frowned. "I'm not aware of them having a problem with that, but maybe their priests are not supposed to wear leather. I'll ask Jade for you." She pulled out her phone and typed a message so fast that her fingers were a blur over the screen.

As they waited for the return text, Jasmine remembered the other thing she needed from Bridget. "Do you have a measuring tape I can borrow? I want to get Ell-rom's shoe size."

"No need for that. I've got all his measurements right here." She tapped on her tablet. "I'm sending them to you."

A moment later, Jasmine's phone pinged with an incoming message, and when she opened it, she saw that Bridget had sent her much more than Ell-rom's foot size. She had all of his measurements, which would make ordering clothing much easier.

"Thank you. This will make shopping for him a

breeze. I just need to find a calculator that translates measurement into apparel sizes."

The doctor nodded. "While you're at it, order him some swimming trunks. I want to start him on pool therapy tomorrow."

Jasmine's eyes widened. "Does that mean that you will allow me to take him up to the penthouse? There is a lap pool on the terrace."

Bridget chuckled. "Soon, but not yet. We have an Olympic-sized pool right here in the underground complex. The lap pool in the penthouse is a good idea for later when he gets stronger. I'm not expecting him to swim laps yet. I'm expecting him to do a few exercises in the water and waddle a little. That's all. It's an excellent way to build strength without putting too much stress on his muscles and joints."

"I see."

Jasmine was disappointed.

Ell-rom would have loved to see the sun and breathe some fresh air, even if it was the smog of downtown Los Angeles.

When Bridget's phone pinged with an incoming message, the doctor read it silently and then put her phone down. "There is no prohibition on leather. Hides and furs were common on Anumati when she was there, which was seven thousand years ago, so things might have changed since then, but the prince is from the same era."

Jasmine gave herself the proverbial pat on the back for guessing correctly. "I thought so, but I wasn't sure. Since they don't eat animal meat, killing just for the hides seemed less likely, but then I couldn't imagine nomadic tribes using plant fibers to weave fabrics."

"Evidently, they do, or at least did. Things might have changed."

She wanted to ask Bridget's advice about what to get for Ell-rom, but she had already taken up enough of the doctor's time, so she rose to her feet. "Thank you for the help. I appreciate it."

"Don't go overboard with the clothing," Bridget cautioned. "Ell-rom is going to bulk up once we get more food in him, and then everything other than the shoes will be too small for him."

"I don't know what to get him." Jasmine sighed. "What he will like."

"Simple leisure clothing that is loose and comfortable. He's still spending most of his time in bed."

"You are right. He was so exhausted after the little walk this morning that he's still sleeping."

Bridget nodded. "He's also a finicky eater. I found a vegan delivery service of healthy, protein-rich meals."

She chuckled. "Kian must have taken after his uncle, being a vegan, I mean."

Jasmine's eyebrows shot up. "Really?"

Bridget laughed. "No, not really. Kian wasn't always vegan. He decided to become one later in life for moral reasons." Her expression turned thoughtful. "Ell-rom's digestive system might be close to that of a human, but he might lack the enzymes necessary to process animal products. It is also possible that he's repulsed by them because of how he was raised. They could probably sneak some fruits and vegetables into the temple for him and his sister, but they could not cook for them, especially not meat. The smells would have given them away."

The more Jasmine learned about the Kra-ell society, the stranger it seemed. "It must be so different." She leaned against the doorframe. "So much of human interaction happens around shared meals. What do Kra-ell families do? Go hunting together?"

"I guess so," Bridget said. "It fits with their overall way of life. It also explains why they are not happy in the village. They need to go hunting."

The visual of that sent shivers down Jasmine's spine.

A bunch of vampire-like people attacking a herd and sucking its blood was not a pretty picture, even if they didn't kill the animals.

She was so glad that Ell-rom wasn't like them.

Shaking off the unsettling thoughts, Jasmine pulled out her phone. "I also need the delivery address. Should I order things to the penthouse?"

"You sure can." Bridget's finger flew over her screen again. "I sent you the address."

"Thank you." Jasmine's phone pinged a moment later. "I apologize for taking up so much of your time."

Bridget waved a dismissive hand. "I'm here to take care of the twins, and you are welcome in my office anytime you have a question regarding either of them or just if you need to talk to someone. What you are doing for Ell-rom is not easy, and we all appreciate it."

Jasmine dipped her head. "Thank you."

18

MARINA

The aroma of sizzling meat and warm spices filled the dining room as Marina put the finishing touches to the Mexican-inspired feast. She had found the recipes online and adapted them to her taste—carne asada, fluffy Mexican rice, refried beans, a couple of homemade salsas, and a large bowl of guacamole.

As Marina set down the bowl of pico de gallo, Lusha smiled. "It all smells wonderful, and I can't wait to dig in."

"You and me both." Peter draped a napkin over his lap. "Marina is spoiling us. Alfie and I didn't eat so well even when we were boys and our mothers cooked for us."

"Men." Marina rolled her eyes as she sat down. "Cooking is simple and rewarding. What is so difficult about learning to make a few dishes and feeding yourself properly?"

Peter leaned over and took her hand. "We never could have reached your level of mastery, love. You imbue your creations with something special."

Alfie cleared his throat. "Can we please eat? I'm starving."

He wasn't comfortable with their displays of affection, and Marina tried to respect his boundaries and keep them to a minimum when he was around.

"Dig in." She waved a hand at the spread on the table.

For a few moments, everyone got busy piling their plates and sampling the dishes.

"This is amazing," Lusha said. "You really have a talent. When I try to make something, I always overdo it with too much oil or too much pepper or salt, and it comes out barely edible."

Marina tilted her head. "So, what do you do? Eat sandwiches for breakfast, lunch, and dinner?"

"More or less." Lusha took a warmed-up tortilla from the plate. "Pavel doesn't keep any food in his place other than frozen blood bags, but I got a few boxes of cereal that I munch on. Vanessa cooks from time to time, and she's good." Lusha sighed dramatically. "She's a lady of many talents, while I'm a one-trick pony."

Alfie snorted. "A very impressive pony who successfully defended a bunch of murderers and saved them from execution."

Lusha shrugged. "Thank you, but the truth was that they were not guilty. They were as much victims of Igor as everyone else in the compound. They had no choice but to do what he commanded. All I had to do was to convince everyone else that they would have been just as helpless against Igor's compulsion as these males were."

"It wasn't easy to do," Alfie said. "The Kra-ell who lost loved ones weren't willing to listen, but you turned the trial into a theatrical production, and they got swept away by your narrative. It was brilliant."

Lusha dipped her head. "Thank you."

"And now you're working for Edna," Marina said.

Alfie's eyes widened. "I didn't know that. How are you getting along with the Alien Probe?"

Marina's eyebrows shot up. "The Alien Probe? What does that mean?"

Lusha finished assembling her taco. "Edna has a unique ability. She can reach into a person's soul, so to speak, and see their true intentions. When she judges people, she relies on more than just the evidence. She says that those who are guilty would rather confess than succumb to her probe. She also probes newcomers to the village, so don't be surprised if you get an invitation."

Marina didn't like the sound of that.

"Did Edna probe you?" she asked.

"Of course." Lusha lifted her taco and then put it down again. "Edna wouldn't let me work for her without the probe."

Marina leaned forward. "What was it like? It sounds invasive."

"It was strange," Lusha admitted. "But I didn't fight her. I just opened my mind to the probe, so it was relatively quick and painless."

Peter piled his plate with a second helping of carne asada and rice and then turned to Lusha. "I hear that you and Pavel are close."

Lusha cast a quick glance at Alfie before answering. "It's not serious."

"I see." Peter nodded. "Did you notice any unusual activity while you were at his place?"

"Like what?"

Peter pretended nonchalance. "You speak Kra-ell, right?"

"Of course."

"And you were at his house when his friends came over."

"Sometimes. I usually leave when he has his meetings. They get rowdy."

Marina tensed. Meetings sounded much more formal than friends coming over to drink vodka and play cards.

Peter arched a brow. "Why is that? Do they argue about things?"

Lusha snorted. "Since the liberation, they always argue. Under Igor, they couldn't speak freely, and now that they can, they get into heated discussions about every little thing."

Seemingly satisfied with the answer, Peter nodded. "Does Drova attend these gatherings?"

A flicker of something crossed Lusha's face before it was quickly masked. "She does, but despite what her mother thinks, there is nothing going on between her and Pavel or any of the other young Kra-ell. Drova is off-limits, and not just because she's too young."

"Because she's Igor's daughter?" Peter asked.

To Marina's surprise, Lusha laughed. "Igor is in stasis, so he's hardly a threat to anyone right now. Drova is off-limits because she's Jade's daughter. And everyone is afraid of Jade."

19

JASMINE

Back in Ell-rom's room, Jasmine settled into the chair and watched him for a long moment. Sleeping soundly, his chest rising and falling in a steady rhythm, he looked so peaceful, even serene.

He was truly beautiful, and she couldn't help but feel angry at the injustice of him having to hide all this beauty behind a veil. It must have been difficult to breathe; his sight had been obscured, and he must have constantly feared an attack.

What a miserable way to spend one's life. Hopefully, he was dreaming about a different reality than the one he had lived through.

Getting him new clothing would symbolize the start of a new life for him, a life that was free of oppression, free of fear.

With a sigh, Jasmine lifted the phone she'd been clutching in her hand and started scrolling through her favorite shopping app. She'd already calculated all of Ell-rom sizes with the help of another app she'd found, and now it was time to start putting things in the cart.

It was a little strange to shop for a guy, and Jasmine had never done it before, but it wasn't that complicated. Ell-rom needed everything, starting with underwear and socks. He wouldn't grow out of those, so she put in the cart a week's supply of each. Next were two pairs of comfortable pants, some soft T-shirts, and a light hoodie. It was summer, but the underground was kept pretty cool.

On a whim, she added a white button-down shirt and a pair of slacks, imagining how handsome Ell-rom would look in them. Pajamas were next, followed by a warm, fluffy robe.

Then it was time for shoes.

As she scrolled through options, Jasmine smiled, happy to be the one who would supply Ell-rom's first possessions in this new world, the beginning of his new life.

She selected a pair of comfortable slip-on shoes with rubber soles, perfect for his physical therapy sessions, a pair of athletic shoes for when he was ready for more rigorous activity, a pair of flip-flops for the pool, and a pair of dress shoes to go with the slacks and the button-down. After all, Ell-rom was a prince, and once he felt a little better, he would no doubt want to look more elegant during his sister's visits.

The goddess hadn't come today, and since it was getting late, Jasmine didn't think she would. Perhaps Bridget had told the Clan Mother that Ell-rom was tired after his physical therapy session, or maybe the goddess had something more important to do and couldn't spare the time to visit her brother.

Whatever the reason, he would be disappointed.

With a sigh, she moved to the next item on her list, which was the swimming trunks. There were so many options and different styles, but she knew that it wouldn't matter to Ell-rom. What mattered to him was his still too-thin body.

He would probably be embarrassed to be seen by her without clothing, but she hoped he would get over it because she planned on getting in the pool with him and helping him with his exercises.

In the end, Jasmine chose a simple, classic design in a deep blue that she thought would complement his eyes.

He didn't need the basic toiletries like a toothbrush and toothpaste because those had been supplied by the clinic, but he would need a deodorant and a cologne. What about a shaver, though?

Should she get him one of those electric models?

The shadow on his cheeks and jaw indicated that he was starting to grow facial hair, but it might never develop into more than that. The shaver could wait for later.

Finalizing her order, she selected express delivery to ensure that everything would arrive by the next morning. Hopefully, Ell-rom would like what she'd gotten for him, and she wouldn't have to replace too many items.

It occurred to her that it was strange that she cared so deeply for a male she knew so little about. She didn't even know what colors he favored and had gotten everything in gray, dark blue, and white.

Jasmine's gaze drifted back to Ell-rom's sleeping form. He hadn't stirred in hours, and even though she could see his chest rising and falling, a flicker of worry ignited in her chest.

Setting her phone aside, she approached the bed. Ell-rom's face was relaxed in sleep, his long lashes casting shadows on his cheeks. As she was struck again by how handsome he was and how vulnerable, the worry in her chest morphed into a wave of protectiveness.

Careful not to wake him, Jasmine brushed a kiss across his temple and was reassured that he was okay when her lips felt the warmth of his skin. She lingered for a moment, breathing in the clean scent of him, and contemplated crawling into the bed beside him and holding him close.

She had done it the night before, and no one had reprimanded her, but it was still relatively early, and Bridget would no doubt appear to check on Ell-rom at least once before she called it a night.

Sitting back down, Jasmine thought about Margo and the promise she'd made to see her the day before. She had apologized for it this morning, but maybe she should call her friend and schedule something for tomorrow.

Maybe Margo could come to the clinic?

She hadn't seen Ell-rom awake, and she must be curious. Would he agree to meet her?

A soft sound from the bed caught Jasmine's attention, and as she looked up, she saw Ell-rom looking at her with those incredibly blue eyes of his.

"Good morning." She rose to her feet. "Did I wake you up?"

20

ELL-ROM

Ell-rom wasn't sure what had woken him up. He had dreamt about Jasmine kissing his forehead, and it had felt incredibly real.

"Good morning? Did I sleep through the night?"

She laughed. "I should have said good evening, but it sounds off as something to say to someone who has just woken up."

With her face hovering so close, he could just lift his head and capture her lips in a kiss, but what if that was unacceptable?

He didn't know enough about Earth's customs, or any other customs for that matter, and he couldn't use common sense because that needed to be based on something, and he had next to nothing to go on.

"How are you feeling?" she asked.

"Good. Refreshed." He also felt an urgent need to empty his bladder, but he wasn't going to mention it.

Some things were instinctive, and Ell-rom knew that asking Jasmine to help him in the bathroom was not advisable. Perhaps it was Bridget's comment about males needing to appear strong and capable in front of the females they were interested in.

Glancing at the walker standing by his bed, he considered braving the bathroom by himself instead of calling Julian to help him. If he could manage that, it would be a huge improvement in the quality of his life.

It was such a simple thing, just to be able to use the bathroom in privacy so he could preserve his dignity, and it would be a big step.

Ell-rom lifted his hand and cupped Jasmine's cheek. "I have a favor I need to ask of you."

"Anything," she breathed.

"Could you help me to the walker? I'd like to try using the bathroom on my own."

For a moment, she looked disappointed, but then her eyes widened. "I'll gladly help you to the bathroom."

"Just with the walker, please. I want to do the rest by myself."

"Are you sure? Maybe we should call Julian..."

Ell-rom shook his head, determination setting in. "No, I know that I can do this. If I managed to walk up and down the corridor with the walker, I can get to the bathroom. I just need a little help getting started."

Jasmine nodded and turned to get the walking device. She positioned it next to the bed and then helped Ell-rom swing his legs over the side.

With her support, he managed to stand, gripping the handles of the walker with all of his meager strength.

"Thank you," he said, offering her a reassuring smile. "I've got it from here."

She followed him to the door, but as he opened it, he turned and shook his head. "I'm going in by myself."

Jasmine didn't look happy. "I'll be right here. If you need me, call out."

"I'll be fine." Ell-rom gave her one last reassuring smile before closing the door behind him.

Once inside, he was grateful for the special holding bars installed throughout the space. They provided much-needed support as he lowered himself onto the toilet and, when he was done, to hoist himself back up.

Feeling emboldened by his success, Ell-rom decided to push himself a little more. He had been a little sweaty after his walk, and washing his feet had not really addressed the rest of his body.

Besides, he longed for the experience of taking a shower by himself.

Carefully maneuvering so he could undress while leaning against the counter and holding one of the bars, he got rid of the blue matching set of pants and shirt, stepped into the shower, grabbed hold of another bar, and sat down on the stool.

For a moment, he just sat there to catch his breath, and then he reached for the handheld spout and turned the water on.

It was a strain to hold the spray nozzle over his head and then move it around his body to reach all the places he needed to be cleaned. The soap dispenser was thankfully within reach, and Ell-rom took care to soap every part of his body and then wash the soap off.

"Ell-rom?" Jasmine called from behind the closed door. "Are you okay in there?"

"I'm perfect. I'm just finishing my first independent shower."

"Be careful, will you? Don't you dare slip on the wet floor and break something."

"I'm being very careful, and I am holding onto the bars all over this bathroom. Can you do me a favor, though? I need a fresh set of clothes. Julian said that there are plenty of them in the supply closet."

"I'm on it. Just don't move until I'm back."

He had no intention of staying seated on the stool and air drying. There was a big, fluffy towel hanging outside the stall that called to him.

"I'm just going to brush my teeth," he called out.

"Be careful. Please."

Wrapping himself in the towel, Ell-rom stood in front of the mirror and leaned against the vanity for support. He reached for the toothbrush and the toothpaste and squeezed out a little of it on the brush like he had seen Julian do.

As he brushed, Ell-rom studied his reflection. The face staring back at him was still unfamiliar, but he was starting to acknowledge it as his own. His head was nearly bald, with a fuzzy growth of dark hair, but he didn't mind the look. Perhaps he would keep it that way.

A knock on the door interrupted his musings. "Ell-rom?" Julian's voice came through. "I've got clothes for you."

"Come in," he called, making sure his towel was secure around him.

Julian entered with a bundle of folded clothing in his arms.

"Well, look at you." He grinned. "Congratulations on your first independent shower." He put the bundle on the counter next to Ell-rom. "Just don't get too confident. Falls can be dangerous in your condition.

Your bones are still regenerating, and they are still brittle."

Ell-rom blinked in surprise. He hadn't realized his bones had been affected by the stasis. "I didn't know that," he admitted.

"Do you need help getting dressed?" Julian asked.

Ell-rom shook his head, determined to complete this task on his own as well. "No, thank you. I want to do everything myself from start to finish. I need this small victory."

"I get it." Julian nodded. "But don't hesitate to call if you need assistance. I'll stay outside the door until you are out."

It was a reasonable compromise. "Thank you. I appreciate it."

When the door closed behind Julian, Ell-rom turned his attention to the clothes. They were the same as the ones he wore before. Julian explained that medics wore those when they were on duty, and that was why he had a bunch of them on hand. They were made to fit different body types and were loose and comfortable. The pants could be cinched at the waist by pulling a drawstring, and he managed to tie it after a few fumbling attempts. The shirt was a simple, square-cut design that he pulled over his head. The fabric was soft against his skin, and the garments had a faint smell of cleaning detergent that was quite pleasant.

Ell-rom felt a nearly euphoric sense of accomplishment at what he had managed.

Taking hold of the walker, he moved across to the bathroom door, opened it, and walked out.

Jasmine's face lit up as she saw him. "Look at you!" She clapped her hands. "You did it!"

He smiled. "It feels good to be a little more self-sufficient."

21

JASMINE

Ell-rom's nostrils flared as he smelled the food that had been delivered while he was in the bathroom, and as he shifted his gaze to the two trays on the bedside table, his eyes widened.

"Are you eating with me?"

"Yes. Bridget ordered two meals to be delivered each time so you could choose what you like. It's important that you eat enough to get stronger. Whatever you don't want, I'll eat."

He frowned. "That's not how it should be. I'll eat whatever you don't like."

"That's so sweet." She motioned for him to return to his bed. "But I'm not the one who almost died and is recuperating from a seven-thousand-year stasis. When the roles are reversed, I'll get to choose."

He didn't look happy. "I love it that we get to eat

together, but I wish we had a proper table and another chair."

"I can help with that," Julian said. "The height of the bedside table can be adjusted so it can serve as a dining table, and I'll get another chair in here."

The expression on Ell-rom's face was heartwarming. He looked as if Julian had offered him a great gift or delivered very good news. "Thank you."

Jasmine waved at her chair. "Sit down. And I don't want to hear arguments about waiting for Julian to get the other chair in here."

He looked at the chair with an embarrassed smile, tugging at his lips. "There are no grab bars in here, so I will need a little help."

"Of course." She offered him her arm. "Grab on to me. I will be your grab bar."

He hesitated for a moment but then gently gripped her hand to move from the walker to the chair. He barely put any pressure on it, using it mostly for stability.

"There are no animal products in any of the dishes." Jasmine rolled the bedside table to the chair and adjusted the height. "Bridget found a service that delivers healthy and well-balanced vegan meals."

Julian entered with a chair that was identical to the one that was already in the room and positioned it on the other side of the table. "Enjoy your meal." He turned to leave.

"Wait," she called after him. "Did you take the chair from Morelle's room?"

"Yes, why?"

"We want to sit by her side after we are done eating, but don't worry about it. I will carry the chairs over."

He shook his head. "I'll get two other chairs in there."

"Are you sure? It's really no bother."

"I'm sure." He closed the door behind him.

"He's a good male," Ell-rom said.

"They are all nice people." Jasmine removed the covers from the two trays. "Go ahead and taste each of the dishes. See which ones you like."

He regarded the two trays. "It smells delicious and looks appetizing, but can you tell me what is what?"

"Sure. That looks like lentil and vegetable stew. Lentils are rich in protein, which is important for your muscles. The vegetables are carrots, potatoes, and parsnips, and I can smell thyme and rosemary with a hint of smoky paprika." She looked up at him. "Did the translation make sense? I bet you don't have Kra-ell names for earthly vegetables."

He smiled. "Now I know why it repeated the word vegetable twice. Whoever provided the Kra-ell vocabulary for the translator probably didn't know the names of similar fruits and vegetables that grow on Anumati because that's not what they eat."

That made a lot of sense. The Kra-ell, who Ell-rom and Morelle grew up among, consumed blood, but the gods, who were their neighbors on the same planet, ate everything.

Jasmine wondered if the gods had brought seeds with them to Earth to plant so they would have a taste of home. Still, even if the gods knew the names of those vegetables, their language was not the same as the Kra-ell's, and the translator only knew the latter.

"You will have to learn English at some point, but for now, we will call them the orange and white vegetables."

She pointed to the quinoa, which looked delicious. "This is a grain with vegetables and mushrooms." In addition to the sautéed mushrooms, there were onions, bell peppers, and parsley, and her mouth watered to try it all.

"You seem to like this dish." Ell-rom removed the container from his tray and placed it next to hers. "Eat and tell me if it's as good as it looks."

"With pleasure, and we can share." She unfolded the napkin, draped it over her lap, and lifted a forkful of the quinoa to her mouth. "It's delicious," she said after she was done chewing. "You have to try it." She pushed it toward him.

He dipped his fork inside the dish and lifted a small quantity to his mouth.

His eyes widened. "It really is delicious."

"Let's try the other stuff." She reached for the roasted vegetable medley on her tray and put it between them. "All I can say about this is that it is made from roasted vegetables." She stabbed a chunk of sweet potato.

In addition to the potatoes, the medley included zucchini, red onions, and Brussels sprouts, all roasted to caramelized perfection and lightly seasoned with olive oil, garlic, and a little salt.

"This service is a great find. I need to tell Margo and the girls about it. They keep ordering food from the Golden Dragon, and it's delicious, but this is healthy stuff. Not that they care about that. They are all immortals."

Ell-rom canted his head. "Do dragons make good food? And why is this one called golden?"

Jasmine laughed. "It's just a fancy name for a restaurant. We don't have dragons on Earth. Do you have them on Anumati?"

"I don't know, but I know what a dragon is, so maybe we do."

Next, they ate the chickpea and spinach curry and crispy tofu bites that were marinated in a soy-ginger glaze and garnished with sesame seeds and thinly sliced green onions.

The trays were a symphony of flavors and textures, each dish complementing the others to create a satisfying and nourishing meal.

They ate in companionable silence for a few minutes, with only the sounds of chewing and her occasional moans of pleasure disturbing the silence.

When Jasmine was so full that she needed a break, she wiped her mouth with a napkin and leaned back. "So, any favorites so far?"

"Yes." He looked at her mouth. "I'm not sure which one I like better, though. The sounds that you make when you taste something you like and the way your lips move when you chew are both arousing."

Jasmine laughed. "It's amazing how all males think alike. I thought that it was a cultural thing and that they learned from one another, but it looks like it's innate."

He looked confused. "I don't know how to react. Is it a good thing or a bad thing that I find everything about you so attractive?"

She leaned forward. "It's a good thing. And the best part is that there is no artifice in it. You mean every word."

22

ELL-ROM

"All done." Jasmine returned to the room after disposing of the remnants of their meal. "I told Bridget that this service is a winner and that you ate your entire tray and a third of mine."

He frowned. "I'm sorry. We were sharing all the dishes, and I didn't realize that I ate more than my share."

"That's okay. You are bigger than me, and you need more food. The only reason I was even paying attention was to let Bridget know how much you ate. She was worried about you not eating enough."

Next time, he would be more mindful and make sure that he didn't eat more than his share.

Gripping the handles of his walker, he pulled himself up. "Are you ready to see Morelle?" He pushed one leg in front of the other, hating how weak his muscles still were.

He had accomplished many things today, so he should feel encouraged, but the road to recovery was still long.

"Are you sure you're up for this?" Jasmine asked. "We can always visit Morelle tomorrow. Instead of going over to her room, we can lie together in your bed, and I can show you the wonders of television. Perhaps I can angle the teardrop in a way that it will translate for you."

The prospect of having Jasmine pressed against him was much more enticing than anything she could show him on the small screen hanging on the wall across from his bed, but they could do that after visiting Morelle. Hopefully, he would be able to keep awake long enough to enjoy it.

"As tempting as your offer sounds, I want to see my sister first."

Ell-rom wondered why Annani hadn't come to visit today, but when he tried to remember whether she had promised to return today or tomorrow, he couldn't. Was he having trouble retaining even his new memories?

There was another thing he had trouble with. He was almost sure that Jasmine had said something about shopping for clothing together, but she hadn't mentioned it, so maybe they had done it already, and he didn't remember. Or maybe he had dreamt it?

Was his brain damaged?

"What's the matter?" Jasmine put a hand on his arm. "Your face has suddenly lost color. Is the food not agreeing with you?"

Ell-rom paused, confused by the question. Given the context, he realized that, once again, this was a figure of speech like so many that Jasmine used to his great confusion. "It's not the food. I'm trying to remember if Annani promised to visit me today or some other time."

"I thought about it before you woke up. When the Clan Mother was about to leave, she said that she would come back tomorrow, which is today, but Bridget might have told her that you were starting the physical rehabilitation and that you needed time to rest."

"We can ask her on the way." Ell-rom shuffled toward the open door.

Bridget wasn't in her office as they passed by it on the way to Morelle's room, and she wasn't with his sister either.

"I wonder where she went," Jasmine murmured. "She was here only a moment ago."

Ell-rom walked over to Morelle, leaned on his walker, and clasped her hand. "Hello, sister of mine," he said quietly. "Don't you think it is time to wake up? I need you by my side." He lifted her warm, delicate hand to his lips. "They cut your hair off, and now we have identical haircuts. I wonder if you would find it funny that we are both bald. You are beautiful even without the hair, so you shouldn't worry about it."

Behind him, Jasmine slid into one of the chairs and sat quietly, listening to his ramblings.

Morelle looked so fragile. Her skin was pale, almost translucent, and she looked a lot like him, and not just because of their matching bald heads. They weren't identical, and she was much better looking than he and softer, but the resemblance was obvious.

Turning around, he shuffled to the chair next to Jasmine and sat down using the chair's armrest for support. "I don't know what else to say to her." The room was so small that he could lean forward and reach his sister's hand.

"You can tell her about all the new experiences you've had since waking up. Tell her about the Clan Mother and Kian and the clan." She shifted her gaze to Morelle's face. "She looks peaceful. Like she's just sleeping."

Ell-rom nodded. "She always slept more soundly than I did. Even when we were children..." He trailed off, surprised by the sudden rush of memory.

"You remember that?" Jasmine asked.

"Just flashes." Ell-rom frowned as he tried to grasp the fleeting images. "We shared a room in the temple. Morelle would fall asleep as soon as her head hit the pillow, but I'd lie awake for hours, listening to the night sounds and worrying about... something. I can't quite remember what."

Jasmine smiled encouragingly. "That's good progress. Your memories are coming back, bit by bit."

Ell-rom squeezed Morelle's hand gently. "You need to wake up so we can piece it all together."

"Tell me about her," Jasmine said. "What else do you remember?"

Ell-rom closed his eyes, focusing on the warmth of Morelle's hand in his and using it as an anchor to draw out more memories.

A smile tugged at his lips. "She was protective of me. I remember her standing up to someone. I assume it was the head priestess, but I can't quite see who. I just remember feeling more secure with Morelle at my side. We were a team."

As he spoke, more memory fragments surfaced. "I don't know if I remember us training together or whether it is something I dreamt up. Swords, javelins, sticks, hand-to-hand. She wasn't as strong as I was, but she was fast and agile."

The memories were so elusive that he hoped he wasn't making them up, creating in his mind the perfect sister he wanted Morelle to be.

"She sounds wonderful," Jasmine said. "I can't wait to get to know her."

"She'll like you," Ell-rom smiled. "We are twins, so she must have the same preferences as I do."

Jasmine laughed. "You are not identical twins. You might have very different personalities and likes and dislikes. I hope she likes me, and I will do everything I can so she does, but it's not guaranteed."

Ell-rom turned his attention back to Morelle. "You'd better like my…" What was he supposed to call Jasmine? His friend? His mate? His love interest?

"Girlfriend," Jasmine said. "You can call me your girlfriend."

He frowned. "You are my friend, but you are more than that."

"That's what a girlfriend means. It means a romantic friend."

"But Morelle won't understand that. Can I call you my mate?"

Jasmine chewed on her lower lip. "I think that the term mate implies a permanent relationship. I would like to think that we might have that one day, but it's too early for that. Right now, we are just getting to know each other."

He had no idea how things like that worked, so he had to rely on Jasmine's experience and knowledge of the subject. "A romantic friend, then. That's what I will call you."

Her lips twitched as if she was trying to stifle a laugh. "It sounds a little awkward, but it will do for now." Her eyes suddenly widened. "What about a paramour? How does that translate to Kra-ell?"

"A concubine?"

Jasmine grimaced. "Let's stick with the romantic friend when you tell Morelle about me, and a girlfriend when you talk about me with everyone else."

He nodded. "That's a good compromise."

For a long moment, they sat in silence, but then he remembered Jasmine's advice to tell Morelle about his experiences since awakening.

"I wonder what she'll think of this new world," he said. "Will she be as happy as I am at finding that we have a sister on Earth and a community we can belong to?"

"I'm sure she will. Who wouldn't? If she remembers more than you do when she wakes up, she will know how lonely the two of you were, and she will be just as happy as you are for having been found, accepted, and loved."

23

JASMINE

By the time Jasmine and Ell-rom left Morelle's room, he could barely put one foot in front of the other, but he looked contented. Talking to his sister and sharing with her all that he had learned so far seemed to have been cathartic for him.

"It's been a long day," Jasmine said as she struggled to walk as slowly as Ell-rom.

She imagined just scooping him into her arms and carrying him to bed, but that was a silly thought.

He was skinny, but he was very tall, and he probably was heavier than he looked. Besides, even if she were strong enough to lift him, she wouldn't humiliate him like that.

"It has." Ell-rom smiled. "Thank you for being here and supporting me every step of the way. I can't imagine how much more difficult this would have been without you by my side. I feel so lucky to have you."

"Oh, Ell-rom." Jasmine put her hand over his on the handle. "I'm so glad that I could be here for you, but the credit is not mine alone. Kian and his clan made it possible for me to quit my job and dedicate my time to you. Then there are Bridget, Julian and Gertrude. They moved here from the village so they could take care of you and Morelle."

Jasmine pushed the door open so Ell-rom could get in.

"I'm grateful to all of you." He leaned over his walker. "Would it be too presumptuous of me to invite you to lie down beside me on my bed?"

She wished it meant what it sounded like, but she knew what Ell-rom had in mind, and it wasn't sex. At best, she could hope for another kiss.

"Just for a little bit. The bed is too narrow to accommodate the both of us comfortably, and you need a good night's rest for tomorrow's physical therapy."

Ell-rom sighed. "I hate seeing you sleep in that chair, all contorted and uncomfortable."

The poor guy had been so out of it that he hadn't noticed that she had a sleeping bag stashed under his bed and that she took naps on the floor from time to time to stretch out her aching muscles.

"I have a secret." She leaned down and pulled out the big bag she'd put under his hospital bed. "I don't spend all of my time in the chair. Sometimes I use this to sleep on the floor." She pulled out the compact sleeping bag that had been her companion in Tibet. "It looks small, but it's very warm." She pulled out her rolled-up thin mattress. "And I use this to cushion the floor. I got these things for the trip to Tibet and snuck them in here. Gertrude and Julian know, and I'm pretty sure that Bridget knows as well, but she pretends that she doesn't."

He looked at the camera mounted near the ceiling. "Doesn't she see what's going on in this room whenever she wants?"

"She does, but I put down my sleeping apparatus on the other side of the bed, where the camera can't see me."

"Smart." Ell-rom's expression was part admiration and part guilt. "You don't have to do this. I'm getting better, and I'm not on the verge of death anymore. You don't have to watch me every minute of the day and night. You should sleep somewhere comfortable."

Jasmine felt a lump form in her throat. "I know. But I want to be here."

"Do you have somewhere else you can sleep?"

"I do, but I'll tell you about it when we're in bed. You are tired, and I need to freshen up. Do you need help getting in?"

"I need to use the bathroom first. Are you in a rush, or can I go in? I just need a couple of minutes."

"You can go in."

As she opened the door for Ell-rom and watched him struggle to cross the few feet, Jasmine was tempted to wrap her arm around his middle and help him, but he wouldn't want that, so she forced herself to stand aside and close the door behind him. "I'm right here if you need me."

"Thank you," he called.

While she waited, Jasmine pulled a change of clothes and a toiletry bag out of her oversized bag.

As he had promised, Ell-rom took only a few minutes, and when the door opened and he stepped out, she could smell the fresh, minty scent of the toothpaste he had used.

"Let me help you get in bed." She put her bundle on the bedside table.

He didn't argue and let her help him, which was proof of how tired he was. Or maybe he'd just wanted to feel her arms around him as she helped hoist him up.

"Thank you," he said as he lifted his legs and sprawled on the bed. "It feels so good to lie down."

"I bet." She brushed a soft kiss against his temple. "I'll be right back."

24

ELL-ROM

Exhaustion weighed heavily on Ell-rom, but he refused to succumb and close his eyes. If he did, he would be asleep in seconds, and he would miss out on holding Jasmine in his arms.

He heard the shower go on, but thankfully, she didn't take long. A few minutes later, the door opened, and she walked out wearing clothing that left very little to the imagination. The pants clung to her curvy legs almost indecently, and the oversized shirt had such a broad neckline that one soft shoulder was exposed. But that wasn't the best part. Her breasts were perfectly outlined under the thin fabric, and he could even see the darker shade of her nipples through the light color of the shirt.

She was killing him.

Was his heart muscle recuperated enough to withstand the pressure of all of his blood pooling in his groin?

"You look..." He trailed off. "The clothes you are wearing. They are...they make you look so...desirable."

Jasmine laughed. "It's just comfy clothes. Nothing special." She climbed into the bed and lay on her side, looking at him. "You look beat."

He frowned. "Do I have bruises?"

A smile tugged on her lush lips. "It's an expression. It means that you look tired. We really need to start teaching you English." She lifted the translation device hanging from her neck. "This thing is great, but it has its limitations."

"How about these?" He reached with his finger to touch one of her earpieces. "Are they doing a good job?"

"They are programmed with the same input as the teardrop, so I guess that they are doing just as good a job. I find it curious that Kra-ell is such a straight-up language. You don't have idioms or phrases that say one thing and mean another."

"I wouldn't know," he admitted. "I'm thankful for having retained the memory of spoken language at all, but if there are intricacies of using it, I don't remember them." He wound a long lock of her hair around his finger. "So, tell me. Where do you usually sleep?"

Jasmine sighed, snuggling closer to him. "Usually is a transitory term for me lately. Before I went on that ill-fated vacation I told you about, I had an apartment and a job. I was lucky to have secured an apartment many years ago in an area that was rent-controlled, which means that my rent couldn't get significantly more costly and remained reasonable." She paused and looked at him to make sure that he understood everything she'd told him.

"It's okay. So far, I'm not confused."

"Good. So, then everything I told you about happened, and Kian offered me a job." She scrunched her pert nose. "Sort of. He said that I couldn't return to my place and my job because the bad guys could find me there, and he said that he would find me a better-paying position and offered me a room in a very luxurious apartment at the top of the building we are under. So, that's where I go when I'm not here."

"Does your room have a comfortable bed?"

She nodded. "It's heavenly. When you get stronger, I'm going to try to convince Bridget to let you come up there. That bed is definitely big enough for two."

Ell-rom stiffened and felt his ears getting warm. "I would like that."

Jasmine had just invited him to her bed, and even though he didn't know much about those kinds of things, he knew it was a significant development.

She chuckled throatily, which made his situation even more dire. "I mean actually sleep, Ell-rom. You are not ready for anything else."

"Oh." His ears were on fire.

Jasmine laughed. "You've got a dirty mind, my prince."

Was that one more of the confusing expressions?

"What does that mean?" he asked.

"That you are thinking naughty carnal thoughts." She leaned closer to him and pressed her lips to his.

He was so aroused that if she moved just a little closer to him, she would feel the evidence of it.

Would she be offended by it?

Shifting so his bottom was nearly hanging over the other side of the bed, he put his arm around her and concentrated on the kiss, which was becoming more heated and passionate. He was lost in the sensation, the warmth of her lips, her small tongue that darted out and licked at the seam of his lips.

He opened up for her, surrendering to the kiss instead of taking over like he craved. He was a novice and wasn't ready to take over. He had to follow her lead.

When they broke apart, Jasmine rested her forehead against his. "You are a very good kisser, Ell-rom."

That was a surprise. "I am?"

"Yes." She leaned away. "You're a natural."

Well, in that case, maybe he could become a little more daring.

"Will it be okay if I kiss you?" he asked.

"You just did."

"I mean, if I took over the kiss. Will that be okay with you?"

Instead of answering, she nodded, and he wondered if that was because she'd become breathless.

"I need you to tell me what I can and cannot do."

The smile that spread over her face was temptation personified. "You can do whatever you want to me, and I promise to like it." Mischief dancing in her golden eyes, she took his hand and put it over her breast.

Ell-rom nearly choked on his own saliva, and his erection got so hard that it was painful.

For a long moment, he didn't move, his hand resting on Jasmine's full breast, her erect nipple tickling his palm. He didn't know what to do next.

"Kiss me," she whispered.

He swallowed. "What about the camera?"

"They can't see what we are doing under the blanket," she whispered. "And if they do, I don't care. We are both consenting adults."

She removed his hand from her breast, and before he had a chance to mourn the loss of contact, she pulled her shirt up and returned his hand to her naked flesh. "Better?"

He was going to climax.

Jasmine chuckled. "I guess that your stunned silence is answer enough." She closed the distance between their mouths and kissed him again.

25

JASMINE

A groan ripped from Ell-rom's throat, and he seemed afraid to move his hand from Jasmine's breast, just leaving it where it was. He got a little bolder, though, pushing his tongue past her lips.

She moaned in encouragement and kissed him harder while moving her body closer to his and throwing a leg over his hips. He was still so painfully bony that it wasn't a comfortable perch for her leg, but the hard length she discovered was worth it.

Another groan ripped from his throat, and he dragged a hand down her back to clamp over her ass.

If she hadn't been kissing him so passionately at that moment, she would have smiled and pumped her fist in the air in triumph. Ell-rom was losing his shyness and letting his male instincts take over. Instead of trying to hide his erection, he was now pressing it into her soft belly. If she didn't stop him, he would come in his pants, which she was totally on board for, but on second thought, she realized that it might be a blow to his ego.

He might be an innocent who didn't know the first thing about sex, but he was smart, and he would know that it indicated a loss of control.

The problem was resisting the need to continue what she had started.

Jasmine could no more let go of Ell-rom than he could let go of her, but since she was the one with sexual maturity, she should be the one to act responsibly.

With a sigh, she removed her leg from his hip, pulled his hand from under her shirt, and ended the kiss. "We can't continue," she whispered.

Swallowing, he nodded. "The camera."

"Yes," she agreed, even though she had forgotten all about it.

"I'm sorry," he murmured.

"For what?"

"For getting so excited."

"I got excited, too." She cupped his cheek. "You can probably smell my arousal, and that fuels yours."

His eyes widened. "Yes. I didn't realize what that intoxicating smell was."

She chuckled. "I'm not really qualified to deliver an intro to immortal physiology, but I know a thing or two."

Perhaps hooking up with Edgar had been part of the Fates' plan. Thanks to him, she knew some basic things about immortal males.

Ell-rom frowned. "Introduction to immortal physiology? What do you mean by that?"

It really wasn't the right time to tell him about Edgar.

Jasmine waved a dismissive hand. "Intro is the name of the first class on something. What I was saying was that I don't know enough to deliver that first class."

He turned on his back. "I will ask Julian. It's worth the embarrassment to learn what I need to know." He sighed. "Even if I recover my memories, I doubt that I knew those sorts of things after being raised without any males around."

He must have at least masturbated, but she didn't want to embarrass him by pointing that out. Hopefully, Julian would be open with Ell-rom. If he wouldn't, she would have to take matters into her own hands, so to speak, and teach Ell-rom everything about his male anatomy and physiology.

"Talking with Julian is a very good idea." She pressed a kiss to his cheek. "You should sleep now. You've had a big day today, and tomorrow, you start anew."

Ell-rom turned toward her and put his arm around her. "I don't want to sleep," he murmured. "I'm afraid I'll wake up and find this was all a dream."

Jasmine's heart melted a little. "It's not a dream. I'll be right here when you wake up. I promise."

"In bed with me?"

She smiled. "I can't promise that, but I will be here in the room with you."

"Stay in bed with me."

He was fighting against his exhaustion, his eyelids growing heavier by the second, but she had a feeling that he wouldn't let himself fall asleep if she didn't promise to stay.

"Okay."

A soft smile lifted his lips, and then he let out a sigh. "Thank you."

"Sleep, my sweet prince," she whispered, running her fingers gently over his brow. "I've got you."

When Ell-rom finally succumbed to sleep, his breathing evening out, Jasmine lay awake a while longer, watching the rise and fall of his chest and marveling at how quickly and deeply she had fallen for this male from another world.

She knew she should move to her makeshift bed on the floor and give Ell-rom space to rest properly, but she had promised him to stay, and she didn't want to break her promise.

Besides, the truth was that she didn't want to leave the warmth of his embrace. She wanted to stay and listen to the steady rhythm of his heartbeat, the soft whoosh of his breath, and look upon his achingly beautiful face.

He was still too gaunt, his cheeks too hollow, and his color pallid, but he was getting better by the hour, not just by the day.

The best indicator of his improving health was the erection that he had sported minutes before. She might not know much about health, but she imagined that virility was closely connected to that.

It had been an eventful day, and Ell-rom had forgotten about her promise to take him on a virtual shopping trip, which was great because she could surprise him tomorrow with all the stuff she'd ordered for him.

He'd also forgotten about the tarot, but there was no rush, and she could do the reading tomorrow as well.

26

KALUGAL

Kalugal leaned back in his chair with a contented smile playing on his lips as he watched Jacki feed their son. The morning sunlight streamed through the large windows of their breakfast nook, casting a warm glow over the scene.

Moments like these made Kalugal truly appreciate the life he'd built for himself and his family.

"Come on, precious," Jacki cooed, offering Darius another spoonful of pureed sweet potato. Their son eyed the spoon warily for a moment before opening his adorable little mouth and accepting the offering with his overly serious demeanor, which sometimes seemed judgmental to Kalugal.

Darius was still a very young child, but his character had been evident early on. He wasn't the cheerful sort. He was more of a cautious observer.

"He likes this," Jacki said. "He didn't like the mashed peas. Just refused to open his mouth."

"Can you blame him? Mashed peas look and smell gross. Sweet potatoes are much more flavorful."

Jacki chuckled, wiping a bit of orange mush from Darius's chin. "He still prefers to wear his food rather than eat it."

As if to prove his mother's point, Darius reached out, his tiny hand knocking the spoon out of Jacki's hand and sending a splatter of sweet potato across the high chair tray. The action was followed by a delighted giggle, which was so adorable that Kalugal felt like kissing Darius on his mush-covered cheeks instead of getting up and cleaning the mess.

But someone had to do that, and Shamash was busy cleaning the office.

As he stood up and moved to grab a cloth to wipe up the splatter, his phone buzzed in his pocket. Glancing at the screen, he was surprised to see the displayed name.

"It's Kian," he told Jacki.

She rose to her feet. "Talk to your cousin." She waved him off. "I'll clean up."

"Thanks," he mouthed as he accepted the call. "Morning, Kian. What an unexpected pleasure to receive your call first thing today."

"I hope I'm not interrupting anything."

"You are not. Your call saved me from having to clean up the mess my son has just made with his mashed sweet potatoes."

Kian chuckled. "I remember those days, and I'm glad they are behind us, but each stage has its challenges. Allegra is no longer a messy eater, but she turned into a very picky fashionista. It takes her forever to choose her outfits."

"She takes after her aunt." Kalugal smiled as he imagined his short-tempered cousin dealing with his little princess fussing over her outfits in the mornings. "Amanda must be thrilled."

"She is." Kian sighed. "I should ask her to stop by every morning and help with Allegra's wardrobe choices."

Kalugal walked out of the kitchen and stepped into the living room. "As lovely as it is discussing our dear children, I'm sure that is not the reason for your call."

"Naturally. Brandon wants a meeting with you to discuss InstaTock and how it can be used to promote the clan's agenda."

Kalugal frowned. "Why the sudden interest?"

"He will explain when we meet. Can you stop by my office today?"

It was so like Kian to assume that everyone was free to jump to do his bidding at a moment's notice. As it happened, Kalugal had planned to work from home, but his schedule was already full. He had several conference calls that he needed to make, which would be a pain to reschedule.

"My day is already full, but I've blocked off time for lunch. How about you and Brandon come over to my house, and we can have lunch together?"

There was a long silence, and Kalugal could imagine Kian trying to come up with excuses as to why it was better to meet at his office.

"I can order lunch at my office," he said.

"Oh, come on. What are you going to order, sandwiches from the café? At my place, you will be treated to a proper meal cooked by a chef. Atzil will whip up something special for lunch. Besides, Brandon hasn't seen the place yet, and it's about time that he did."

"You remember that I'm vegan, right? I'm the scourge of every self-respecting chef."

"That is true." Kalugal laughed. "But I have no doubt that Atzil will rise to the challenge and prepare a delicious vegan meal for you."

Kian sighed. "Let me check with Brandon. If he's free for lunch, I'll text you to confirm."

"Good deal. I'll wait before informing Atzil about the change in the menu for today." He ended the call and walked back into the kitchen.

While he'd been gone, Jacki had cleaned up the mess on the floor and their son.

"What did Kian want?" she asked.

When he told her, she snorted. "Atzil's going to throw a tantrum. The only vegan dishes he makes are steamed beans and roasted carrots or Brussels sprouts."

Kalugal shrugged. "That counts, right? What else are you supposed to serve a vegan?"

"I don't know. Something made from tofu?"

Kalugal grimaced. "It's so like Kian to suck the joy out of his own life. It's not like he needs to deprive himself for health reasons."

"He feels it's morally right," Jacki said. "But it takes willpower that I don't have."

"Save your willpower for more important things." Kalugal turned his attention to Darius, who was attempting to grab his own feet, fascinated by discovering them once again. "Now, what do you say we have some father-son bonding time before Daddy needs to go to his office?"

He scooped Darius out of the high chair and spun him around, earning a delighted squeal. He laid him down on his play blanket in the family room and sat beside him on the floor. "Alright, my little fighter. Show Daddy how well you can roll over."

Darius gurgled, his eyes fixed on Kalugal's face, and stuck a finger in his mouth, sucking greedily as if there was milk in it.

Kalugal lay down on his side next to the baby. "Watch Daddy. I'll show you how to do it, alright?"

"Like this, see?" He rolled onto his back and then his other side. "Easy."

Darius watched with rapt attention but didn't show the slightest interest in moving.

"He's too young to understand," Jacki said. "Put him on his belly, and he will roll onto his back."

The moment Kalugal did as Jacki had instructed, Darius rolled onto his back and gave Kalugal a look that seemed to say, *you doubted me?*

"Very good." Kalugal leaned down and peppered his son's wet cheek with kisses. "You've got this."

Kalugal looked up to see his wife leaning against the doorframe and watching them with a soft smile. "Our little guy is growing so fast."

Jacki moved to join them on the floor, running a gentle hand over Darius's head. "It seems like he was born just yesterday."

Sensing he was the topic of conversation, Darius babbled a string of "ba" and "da" sounds.

"Is that so?" Kalugal asked seriously, nodding as if he

understood every word. "Tell me more about your thoughts on the current political climate, son."

"The world is on fire," Jacki said in a near whisper. "I hope things will calm down by the time Darius is old enough to understand what is going on."

Kalugal nodded. "I bet that's what Brandon wants to talk to me about."

"Are you going to help?"

He sighed. "Do I have a choice?"

Kalugal hated politics and wasn't overly fond of humans, but he had created InstaTock with a specific vision in mind, and even though things hadn't worked out as he had planned, it was still a powerful tool.

"Not really." Jacki cast him a stern look. "If you have the means to stop the inferno, you cannot stand idly by and let it consume the world. You have to save them."

He arched a brow. "Even the idiots?"

"Yes, Kalugal. Even the idiots."

27

ELL-ROM

As Ell-rom stirred awake, the first thing he noticed was the comforting weight against his side. Jasmine was still nestled close to him, her breath soft and even against his neck, her breast pressed against his chest, and her leg resting over his hip.

The previous night's events came flooding back, bringing a mix of emotions: joy, discovery, embarrassment, and a lingering sense of inadequacy.

He remembered the heat of their kisses and the way Jasmine's bare breast had felt pressed against his palm, but he also recalled his fumbling responses, his uncertainty about where to put his hands, how to move, what to do next…

Jasmine had been patient and kind, but Ell-rom knew he had disappointed her, even if she would never admit it because she was just too nice.

He draped his arm over her narrow waist and caressed her back, tracing her delicate vertebrae through her shirt.

She stirred, her eyes fluttering open to meet his, and a soft smile spread across her face. "Good morning," she murmured, kissing his lips.

"Good morning. Have you been awake long?"

Jasmine stretched languidly. "Yeah, but I knew that you would be disappointed if you woke up and I wasn't in bed, so I got back in. Besides, I enjoy being close to you."

"I love having you close." He pressed a kiss to her forehead.

It felt so good, and what she had said felt even better. She enjoyed his closeness as much as he enjoyed hers.

Except, she deserved an adult male, someone who knew what they were doing, not a boy.

Jasmine yawned and turned on her back, nearly falling off the bed. "I need to go up to the apartment to get fresh clothing. I was just waiting for you to wake up." She slid out of his arms and out of the bed. "Gertrude peeked in about an hour ago, asking if you were ready for breakfast. I told her you needed more sleep, but now that you are awake, I suggest that you get out of bed and ready yourself for the day."

"'Yeah, good idea," he managed to murmur as panic gripped him.

What if she wasn't going to her apartment for clothes but using it as an excuse to get away from him?

What if she didn't return because he was such a great disappointment?

"Jasmine. About last night…" he said hesitantly.

"It was awesome." She leaned and kissed him on the lips. "Baby steps, lover boy."

Oh, no! She'd called him a boy!

Ell-rom was mortified.

Jasmine frowned. "What's wrong? You suddenly look like you are going to vomit."

"I'm so ashamed." He turned on his back and covered his face with his hands.

"Why?" She tugged at them, and he was too weak to prevent her from prying them away from his face. "Don't hide from me. Tell me what's gotten into you."

"I don't know what I'm doing. I'm like a boy, like a baby."

As understanding dawned, Jasmine burst out laughing. "Talk about lost in translation."

She was ridiculing him.

No, she wasn't.

Jasmine was kind and compassionate. She wouldn't do that. There must be some misunderstanding.

"What did I get wrong?"

She put a hand over her chest and sighed but then burst out laughing again. "I'm so sorry." She took in a deep breath. "Here. I'm fine now." She took another deep breath. "So, you know how many of the expressions in my language lose meaning when translated to Kra-ell?"

He nodded.

"Lover boy is a compliment. It means that I find you attractive, desirable, and very eager. Baby steps mean small steps, taking it slow and not rushing."

The lump in his throat dissolved. "You find me attractive?"

"Very much so." She leaned and kissed the tip of his nose. "And I love being your teacher. There is something very sexy and wicked about seducing an innocent cleric. It feels positively devilish." She waggled her dark brows.

It was on the tip of his tongue to declare his love for her, but he knew what her response would be, so he remained quiet and only smiled.

"I need to go. Margo is waiting for me. I promised to have a cup of coffee with her before she leaves for the day."

He nodded. "Come back as soon as you can."

"I will. But first, let me help you get down from the bed and into the bathroom."

"I think I can do it without help."

She nodded. "Go ahead. I'll stay to make sure that you don't fall."

"That makes sense. Thank you."

As he pushed to a sitting position and then moved his legs over the side of the bed, Jasmine brought the walker over so that it was within reach. The bed was elevated, and his feet hung in the air, but the distance wasn't great, and as he slid his bottom to the edge of the bed, his feet touched the floor.

The next step was a little scary, and as he shifted his weight to his feet and pushed away from the bed, Jasmine hovered nearby to catch him.

There was no need. He was steady even before gripping the handles of the walker.

"Bravo!" Jasmine clapped her hands. "You did it!"

He grinned. "I did."

"I'll wait for you to be done in the bathroom and then leave."

"It's okay." He leaned on the walker and released one of the handles to free his hand to cup Jasmine's cheek. "Your friend is waiting for you. Just inform Gertrude or Julian on your way out that I'm in the bathroom."

"Okay." She leaned her cheek into his hand for a

moment and sighed. "Why is it so hard to leave you even for a few minutes?"

"I don't know, but I feel the same."

28

JASMINE

Jasmine hated leaving Ell-rom in the bathroom without anyone to help him if he fell or did something else to hurt himself.

Thankfully, she saw Julian sitting behind the desk in the office, and as she walked over, she knocked on the open door.

"Hi, do you have a moment?"

"Sure." He beckoned to her. "Come on in."

Even after all the time she had spent with Julian and Bridget, Jasmine had a hard time reconciling that they were mother and son. They looked more like siblings, but the illusion disappeared when they talked. Bridget spoke with the confidence and authority of someone with decades of experience, while Julian was less sure of himself, and his speech patterns matched the age he looked.

Still, Bridget's youthful looks were easier to accept than the Clan Mother's. The goddess presented the most striking dichotomy between appearance and age—an ancient soul housed in the body of a teenage girl.

"What can I do for you?" Julian asked.

"I'm heading out for a little while, and I wanted to let you know that Ell-rom is in the bathroom. And also to report that he got there himself without my help."

"That's excellent progress." Julian rose to his feet. "I'll let Gertrude know that he is awake so she can warm up his breakfast."

"Awesome." She turned to leave but then turned back. "I'm worried about Ell-rom being alone in the bathroom, but the things I ordered for him yesterday were delivered, and I want to get them. He doesn't know, so don't tell him. I want to surprise him."

"No problem." Julian gave her a reassuring smile. "I'll keep an eye on him while you are gone, but I'm sure he'll be just fine. He did very well yesterday on his walk, and today, we will get him in the pool."

"He's looking forward to it."

"Will you be joining us in the pool?" Julian regarded her with amusement in his eyes.

She scrunched her nose. "It depends on whether Ell-rom wants me there. I also hope his swimming trunks arrived with the rest of the things; otherwise, the pool will not be happening today."

"Did you order him underwear?" the doctor asked.

"Of course."

"Then he can use that in the pool. It's not like there will be anyone else in there."

"Right." Jasmine pushed a lock of hair behind her ear. "Then I'm sure he will prefer to do the pool exercises without me watching him. The prince is a proud male, and it might be embarrassing for him to have me see him swimming in his tighty-whities."

Julian chuckled. "I doubt he would know the difference. He has never seen swimming trunks and has no idea that they look different from underwear."

"Good point. But I still hope the trunks are among the packages delivered to the penthouse. I won't be right back, though. I promised Margo to have a cup of coffee with her."

Julian waved a hand in dismissal. "Don't worry about it. I'll keep Ell-rom busy until you get back. Take your time and enjoy your break. You need it."

"Thank you." She cast him a smile and walked out of the clinic.

Jasmine didn't want to tell Julian that she didn't need a break from Ell-rom, and that being away from him was difficult for her. It would have made her seem clingy and desperate, like some pathetic groupie.

No one would believe that she was falling in love with a male who had just woken up from the equivalent of a seven-thousand-year coma five days ago and that it had nothing to do with his royal title.

As she stepped into the elevator, she looked in the mirror and finger-combed her hair. She didn't have any makeup on, hadn't bothered with it since the trip to Tibet, and the only thing she did with her hair after washing it was air dry it while twisting the ends so they wouldn't frizz all over the place.

She looked tired, with dark circles under her eyes from lack of proper sleep, but the contented expression on her face was in stark contrast to her usual one.

People always remarked on the intensity she exuded even when she appeared happy and relaxed, but she now realized that she had always been tense, always anxious, and covering it up with exuberance.

Realizing that she hadn't pressed the button for the penthouse level yet, she put her thumb on the scanner, and then the elevator lurched up.

Perhaps her momentary forgetfulness had been her subconscious not wanting to hear what Margo had learned about Lynda.

On the one hand, Jasmine felt a morbid curiosity to find out whether her tarot reading about Rob's fiancée had been correct, but on the other hand, she hoped that they had been wrong.

She didn't want to be responsible for breaking up an engagement, even indirectly.

Margo's brother and her parents would be devastated, or at least terribly embarrassed, if the wedding was canceled altogether after postponing the celebration twice. They probably couldn't get their money back at this point.

She couldn't imagine Rob's heartache at being cheated on by the woman he had been planning to spend the rest of his life with and then having to call his friends and extended family members to tell them that the wedding was off.

Perhaps it would be better for Rob and Lynda to go through with the wedding, even if it later ended in divorce. At least that way, the immediate pain and humiliation could be avoided.

No one made a big deal out of divorce anymore, and given what Jasmine had heard about Lynda so far, no one would be overly surprised either.

Still, Rob deserved to know the truth. The decision of whether to go through with the wedding or cancel it should be his.

29

ELL-ROM

Ell-rom stepped out of the bathroom and shuffled to one of the chairs while leaning heavily on his walker. Without Jasmine to observe him, he felt less pressured to perform.

He chuckled as he sat down. That's why he needed her around. Well, that and many other things. Like those sweet kisses earlier, her body pressed against his...

No, none of that.

At any moment, the door could open, and Gertrude would come in with his breakfast. He couldn't greet her with a tent forming in his loose blue pants.

Think of other things.

Like what?

His head was full of Jasmine, her smiling eyes, her soft lips, her alluring scent...

A knock at the door preceded its opening, and Julian entered carrying a tray.

"Good morning." The medic put the tray on the bedside table. "I hear that congratulations are in order. You managed the bathroom all by yourself today." He rolled the table to Ell-rom's chair and adjusted the height.

"Thank you. It felt good to regain some independence."

"I bet." Julian sat down on the other chair. "Do you mind if I join you for coffee?"

Ell-rom looked at the tray, confused by the question. "Am I allowed coffee?"

"Think of it as a reward for your bathroom achievement." Julian reached for a rounded container, and when he unscrewed the top, the rich aroma of coffee filled the small room.

"I love the smell," Ell-rom admitted. "I'm not sure about the taste, though. Jasmine let me take a sip from her cup, and I wasn't impressed. It smells better than it tastes."

Julian smiled knowingly. "Everyone takes their coffee differently. Jasmine likes cream and sugar in hers, or milk in the case of specialty coffees, but I have a feeling you will like it black." He poured a small quantity into a cup and handed it to Ell-rom. "Try it."

He took a small, experimental sip. "It's a little bitter, but I like the flavor." He took another sip and put the cup down. "Why is Bridget concerned about me drinking this beverage?"

"Coffee is a stimulant." Julian poured some into his own cup. "Some people are more sensitive to it than others, and coffee makes them jittery and affects their ability to fall asleep."

Ell-rom lifted the cup to his lips. "Then I should drink a lot of it. Maybe I'll be less sleepy."

"You need your sleep, and you need to eat. Both are important for your recovery."

It was a clear command to start eating, and Ell-rom obeyed, lifting the fork and spearing a lovely-looking piece of fruit with it. There was no name in Kra-ell for it, so if he asked Julian what it was, the translation device would just call it fruit.

He popped it into his mouth and nearly groaned with pleasure. It was sweet and tart at the same time, and the texture was soft but not too much so.

Julian smiled. "I'm glad you are enjoying the fruit."

"I really need to start learning Earth's language. There are many things that the teardrop can't translate."

The medic smiled again. "There is no such thing as an Earth language. There are many different ones. Even where you come from, there are at least two languages I know of. The gods and the Kra-ell don't speak the same language."

"I see." Ell-rom nodded. "I still don't remember much, but I should have realized that."

"It's not at all self-explanatory." Julian took another sip of his coffee. "If I found myself on an alien planet, I would probably assume that everyone spoke the same language even if my memory was intact. Your memory problem makes things even harder for you. You are like a child learning everything from scratch." He put his cup down. "But just so you know, you are lucky to have retained use of your language and basic skills like self-grooming, using utensils, and all the other things that we take for granted as adults. Some people who recover from a coma, especially after a brain trauma, have to relearn everything, like babies."

Ell-rom winced and put his fork down. "I feel like that in some respects." He swallowed. "Intimacy is the most difficult part for me. Jasmine is a grown woman, and I'm like a young boy who doesn't know what to do. I don't know what I am allowed to do and what I am not, and what is considered acceptable and what is not."

Julian canted his head. "I'm sure that Jasmine will tell you what she allows and what she doesn't. It's her responsibility to set limits."

That wasn't helpful.

"I don't want to be in a position where she needs to tell me that something I did was unacceptable. I need to know the rules."

Julian sighed. "The rules are very individual. What's okay for one person might not be okay for another."

"Can you give me general guidelines? Think back to when you were a boy just starting out. What were the rules that you were taught by your elders?"

Julian frowned. "I was taught that the most important rule was to seek consent, and that I shouldn't assume that consent for one thing translated to consent for other things. Sometimes, a female will be okay with a kiss, but she won't be okay with intimate touching. You need to make sure that your touch is welcome."

"That's obvious to me. My concerns are much more basic than that. How do I know what to do with my hands when she indicates her willingness to be touched? Is it normal to feel so overwhelmed by sensation? What if I get so excited that I empty my seed into my pants? Will Jasmine be mortified, offended, think badly of me?"

It was embarrassing to ask the medic these kinds of questions, but it was better than asking Jasmine or trying to guess.

Julian was quiet for a long moment. "I'll start with your last question, which is easier to answer. Jasmine won't think badly of you if you ejaculate in your pants, and she will probably feel flattered because she got you so excited. That being said, premature ejaculation is mostly a juvenile problem, but then, you are like a juvenile because you lack experience. Jasmine cares about you deeply, and she's a kind and easy-going female. She will understand and not judge you for it."

That was a big relief. "Thank you. That's very helpful."

"You are welcome." Julian took another sip of coffee, probably to buy himself time to think. "As for your specific concerns, I'll start with the basics. It's completely normal to feel overwhelmed at first. Your body is experiencing new sensations, and it can take time to adjust. The key is to take things slow and to communicate with your partner about what feels good and what doesn't."

He went on to explain various aspects of physical intimacy, from anatomy to techniques, while maintaining a professional, matter-of-fact tone that helped ease Ell-rom's embarrassment.

"Remember," Julian said, "intimacy is about connection, not perfection. It's okay to be nervous, to make mistakes, and to laugh together. In fact, those moments of vulnerability can bring you closer."

Ell-rom felt a weight lift from his shoulders. He still had much to learn, but making mistakes and fumbling around no longer scared him as much as it had before Julian explained that it was part of the fun.

"Thank you. I appreciate your no-nonsense, nonjudgmental explanation."

"You are most welcome." The medic leaned closer over the table. "My best advice to you is don't be shy, and share your concerns with Jasmine."

Ell-rom nodded and then rubbed the back of his neck. "I also need some information on using my fangs. Bridget explained the different kinds of venoms, the aggressive one and the aphrodisiac one, but I don't know how and when it is appropriate to use my fangs."

Julian smiled. "I will demystify it for you. By the way, did my mother explain what a Dormant is?"

Ell-rom shook his head. "Not that I remember. Maybe she did, and I forgot. I don't really trust my memory."

"That's okay," Julian said. "I'll explain it again."

30

JASMINE

As the elevator dinged, signaling Jasmine's arrival at the penthouse level, she steeled herself for Margo's news of the investigation.

It suddenly occurred to her that a tiny spy drone's filmed evidence was not admissible in court, but did that matter? Even if Rob and Lynda were married and the evidence of her infidelity was presented as cause for divorce, it wouldn't have changed anything. California was a no-fault state, which in the context of divorce meant that neither party needed to prove wrongdoing or fault by the other spouse in order to obtain a divorce.

When she opened the door to the penthouse, she found Margo in the living room, sprawled on her belly on the couch and looking at the screen of her phone.

"Hi. What are you doing?"

Margo lifted her head. "Shopping. I put all the packages that were delivered for you in your room. If you want to check whether everything arrived, I can brew coffee in the meantime."

"Sounds like a plan. I'll just make sure that the swimming trunks are here. Julian wants to start Ell-rom on exercising in the pool."

Margo sat up and then pushed to her feet. "When are the rest of us going to meet your prince?"

Jasmine hadn't thought of that. "I don't know. I'll have to check with Ell-rom to see if he is okay with that, and I also have to check with the doctors to see if they approve. It's also possible that Kian or Jade or both will visit, so I need to clear it with them."

The Clan Mother would no doubt show up later today, but Jasmine didn't know whether she was allowed to mention her.

"Busy guy, your prince." Margo walked into the kitchen. "How are things progressing with you two?"

"Nicely." Jasmine smiled. "Make the coffee. I'll check on the packages, and we will talk when I'm done."

Margo lifted the measuring cup she was using to spoon the coffee grounds. "I'll hold you to that."

The truth was that Jasmine preferred to talk about her budding relationship with Ell-rom to discussing Lynda's cheating. One was a happy subject, while the other was depressing.

With a sigh, she walked into the room she used to share with Edgar and looked at the pile of bags and boxes stacked on the floor.

After unpacking everything, she considered putting the clothing items in a wash before delivering them to Ell-rom, but that would take too long. Besides, he might not like some of them, and she would need to return them. It was better to show him what she'd gotten for him and then ask him if he wanted her to launder the items he decided to keep.

Jasmine loaded everything into two large shopping bags that she'd saved from before, put the boxes and delivery bags in the closet in case she needed to return anything and grabbed a fresh change of clothing for herself.

It was funny how little attention she gave her wardrobe these days.

Jasmine used to be so meticulous about her appearance. Most of her outfits were inexpensive, but she always wore one or two designer items to make everything else look classier. A pair of shoes, a handbag, or a pair of designer sunglasses—those things didn't show as much wear. Then there was hair and makeup, which she had never left her apartment without.

Now, she couldn't care less.

Ell-rom thought she was beautiful and sexy without

her having to put any effort into it, and it was so incredibly liberating.

When everything was stored inside the two large bags, Jasmine hefted them and returned to join Margo for coffee.

"So?" Margo arched a brow. "Did the swimming trunks arrive?"

"Everything did." Jasmine put the bags on the floor, walked around the counter, and sat next to Margo.

Margo put a mug full of coffee in front of her and placed cream and sugar next to it. "You and the prince. Talk."

"Each day, he's getting stronger, and each day, we are getting closer. I spent most of last night in bed with him. It was very enjoyable."

"Do tell." Margo lifted her mug and cradled it in her hands.

Jasmine shrugged. "Nothing much to tell. We kissed, we hugged, and things got a little heated, but he was in no condition to do anything yet. Besides, there is a camera in the room, so Bridget and Julian and even Gertrude can see what's going on if they want to take a peek."

Margo grimaced. "Yeah, that's not fun. You need to get that boy in a real bed and then have your wicked way with him."

Jasmine closed her eyes. "Don't say that word. I feel bad enough about seducing a celibate priest. He says that it wasn't a life he chose but one that was chosen for him, so he doesn't care about the restrictions of that position. But I'm worried that when his memories return, he might remember that he loved that lifestyle and that all he ever wanted to do was to serve others and lead them on their spiritual journey."

Margo shook her head. "If he felt that strongly about it, his subconscious would have remembered it." She smirked. "It's not like you had to do a lot of convincing to get him to transgress, right?"

There was something to what Margo had said, but it wasn't enough to completely assuage Jasmine's guilt.

She sighed. "I just hope he doesn't regret it later. I like him too much to lose him."

Margo arched a brow. "Just like?"

"The word love is not on the table yet." Jasmine sipped on her coffee and wished there was something to eat with it.

"What about in here?" Margo pointed at her heart.

"It might be growing in there, but I'm hiding it for now. It's too early to show it." She stood up and walked over to the fridge. "Is there anything to eat?"

"Cheese, cheese, and more cheese. The crackers are in the pantry."

"Perfect." Jasmine pulled out a tray of cheese and walked into the pantry to get the crackers.

When she returned, she put her loot on the counter and sat down. "I'm really dreading hearing your news about Lynda, but that's why I'm here, right?"

"It's a complicated story." Margo pulled a cracker out of the box. "Before meeting Rob, Lynda was engaged to a guy who broke off the engagement and joined the military. Rob knew that, and so did I, so that's not the big discovery. What we didn't know was that he had been discharged and was back in town, and Lynda had been meeting him in secret for months. So far, though, it doesn't seem like she's sleeping with him. Since we started spying on her, she's met him twice for lunch, and both times they kissed, not like friends, but like lovers."

"Then it's cheating," Jasmine said.

"Technically, it is not." Margo reached for a piece of cheese and put it on her cracker. "It looks like she still loves the guy, but she is not ready to leave Rob for him because of obvious reasons."

"What reasons?"

"Rob has a steady job and makes good money while her former fiancé is living off his partial military pension, which isn't much. He also left her once before, so she is not going to give up Rob for a guy that could disappear tomorrow."

Margo bit off a piece of the cracker.

"What are you going to do?" Jasmine asked.

"I don't know. That's what I wanted to talk to you about."

"Don't make me the bad girl who tells you that you need to tell Rob."

"Why the bad girl?"

"Because breaking up a couple is sad. And sad is bad." Jasmine took a slice of some kind of cheese she didn't recognize and put it on a cracker. "But if he were my brother, and by that I mean a real brother, not one of my evil stepbrothers, I would have to tell him even though it would break my heart."

Margo nodded, her eyes filling with tears. "It's going to destroy Rob."

Reaching over, Jasmine took Margo's hand in hers. "I know it's hard, but he needs to know the truth and decide for himself. There is also the small detail of him being a Dormant and deserving an immortal mate."

Margo's eyes widened. "I totally forgot about that, and it's the most important thing." She closed her eyes for a moment. "I wish I could get him to visit the village and see all the gorgeous single ladies that would fight over each other to get him."

"How do you know that? You've never been to the village."

"That's what Gabi and Ella say. I wish they could find a way for Negal, Aru, and Dagor to be in the village without endangering everyone."

Margo had explained something about that, but Jasmine didn't remember what it was. "Why do they endanger the village?"

"They have trackers in them, so their superiors know where they are and where they have been. If they stay in one place for too long, it will be suspicious. But that's not the main problem. The village and the existence of the immortals on Earth must stay hidden, and the people on Anumati, who might wish the clan ill, must never find out about it and them."

"You mean the evil Eternal King."

"Yeah. That dude."

"There must be a solution. I'll think of something."

Margo smiled condescendingly. "If there was, don't you think that all these smart people would have come up with it already?"

Jasmine shrugged. "Sometimes it takes someone who is removed from the problem to see the solution. They are also trying to figure out how to hide the twins' survival from the Eternal King, and I'm trying to come up with a good idea."

"Well, good luck." Margo lowered her head and rested her chin on her fist. "If you can find a solution for my predicament, I would be not only grateful but would also never doubt your genius mind again."

Jasmine laughed. "That's one hell of a challenge, and now I have to find a solution for you." She mulled over the problem for a long moment when, suddenly, the solution presented itself in a visual scene. "I know what you can do."

Margo lifted her head. "What?"

"You are monitoring Lynda in real time, right?"

"I'm not watching the feed twenty-four-seven, but I can rewind it to see what happened before."

"Can you find out when she's meeting her ex again?"

"Probably. Why?"

"Get Rob to meet you for lunch in the same place. Let him see Lynda with that guy for himself."

Margo grimaced. "She will just tell him that she's meeting her old friend for lunch. It's not like she's going to kiss her ex in front of Rob."

"She doesn't have to. Did she tell Rob that she was meeting the guy?"

"Of course not."

"Then that will be enough, and if it's not, well, then you will have to tell your brother that you were spying on his fiancée and saw her kissing the guy."

31

ELL-ROM

Ell-rom sat on the edge of his bed as Jasmine unpacked the bags she had brought. Soft shirts in various colors, comfortable pants, underwear, socks, shoes for various activities, and items for grooming in addition to what the clinic provided. There was also the swimming outfit, which turned out to be a pair of short pants with an inner liner.

The trunks were dark blue, with something written on the bottom of the right side. "What is that?" He smoothed his finger over the embossed lettering.

"It's the name of the manufacturer," Jasmine explained.

"Is it important to know who the manufacturer of a piece of clothing is?"

She nodded. "If the brand is well known, prominently featuring the name adds to the appeal and perceived value of the article. But don't worry, this one is not pricy. Athletic manufacturers also like to display their names on their products."

It seemed a strange practice to him, but perhaps something similar happened on Anumati. He needed to talk to Jade or one of the gods who had come from there more recently and find out more about the place he had come from.

It was strange that only Aru had visited him, and then only once. Weren't the others curious about him?

And what about Annani? Why hadn't she come yesterday?

Would she come today?

He should have asked Julian about it, but he had been too flustered after asking all those questions about intimacy and getting more answers than he had expected.

"Ell-rom?" Jasmine hooked a finger under his chin. "What were you thinking about just now?"

"Why?"

"You suddenly got red in the face. I don't know if I should call Bridget or Julian, or were you just thinking carnal thoughts about me, and then no medical intervention is needed?"

Before talking to Julian, Ell-rom might have tried to

avoid answering, but the medic's advice had been to be honest and open with Jasmine.

"I followed your advice and asked Julian about intimacy. He was very forthcoming with information. He wasn't sure about my venom and how potent it was, but he speculated that it was at least as potent as an immortal male's. He said that the venom provides intense pleasure to the female and other benefits, but I already knew that because Bridget explained it to me."

Jasmine nodded. "It's intensely pleasurable."

How did she know? Had she enjoyed immortal partners? Or maybe she'd heard it from her friends?

Jasmine was human, and she had stumbled upon the world of immortals only recently. Her former partners must have been human, and they didn't have fangs or venom.

Ell-rom found it hard to believe that she'd been intimate with an immortal male in the short time she'd been exposed to the immortals' world, but it wasn't his place to ask. If she wanted to share details about her past with him, she would do so of her own volition.

"Julian also told me what Dormants are, and that you are almost certainly a Dormant, and that if we are together, I will be your inducer." Ell-rom felt his cheeks heat up again as he thought about the next thing Julian had told him, but he also remembered the medic's advice to share his thoughts with Jasmine and not shy away from intimate topics. "He said that I needed to ask for your consent to induce you, and if you didn't wish to become immortal, we would need to use what he called protection."

Julian had described that protection as a very thin barrier that was worn over a male's erection so his seed couldn't enter the female. Venom alone was not enough to induce transition in an adult female, and by preventing the insemination, it could be prevented. It was also a good method to prevent an unwanted pregnancy, although Ell-rom couldn't understand why a pregnancy would be unwanted.

Perhaps when he regained his memories, he would remember why having babies was not always a good thing.

"I know all that," Jasmine said beside him on the bed, her legs dangling over the edge, and she put a hand on his knee. "We are not anywhere near where that is a concern." She turned to look at the camera. "Not in here. I'm going to start advocating for you to stay with me in my apartment at the top of the building, not just because I want us to have a comfortable big bed and privacy, but because I know that you will get better when you have fresh air and a view that is more exciting than the color of this wall."

Ell-rom's excitement rose to such a level that his heart was galloping like a wild animal, but then he remembered that his sister was still unconscious and couldn't leave the clinic. "That sounds so enticing, and I crave that with a frightening intensity, but I need to stay close to Morelle, and I don't think the medical team will approve moving her up to the top-floor lodging."

"No, they won't." Jasmine let out a breath. "I'll think of something. Where there's a will, there's a way, right?"

Ell-rom nodded. "I went to see her while you were gone. Her color is better, and her cheeks are not as hollow. I also like to think she knows I'm there, talking to her."

"I'm sorry I was gone for so long and couldn't come with you," she said. "I had coffee with Margo, the one who helped save me from those bad guys I told you about. She needed my help with something."

"I wasn't complaining." He took her hand. "Well, maybe a little. I miss you when you are gone, even for a short while. But I can't be greedy. Your friends also deserve your company."

Jasmine's lips lifted in a half smile. "Speaking of my friends, they would like to meet you. I told Margo that I would check with you and with the doctors before inviting them."

Her friends had accompanied Jasmine, the gods, and Julian to Tibet and helped in various manners in the search. He owed them a debt of gratitude.

Glancing at the pile of new clothes stacked on the corner of the bed, he nodded. "I would be delighted to meet them, especially since I don't have to do that in these medic clothes." He looked down at the loose, pale blue pants. "Not that there is anything wrong with them, but they are more suitable for sleeping than receiving guests."

"I'm glad that you are happy about the clothing." Jasmine leaned in, wrapping her arms around him in a warm embrace before pressing a soft kiss to his cheek. "Now all that's left is to get the medical team's approval and check whether your other sister plans to visit you today."

"Yes. I would like to know that as well. I forgot to ask Julian if he knew whether she was coming."

"I'll ask him." Jasmine hopped off the bed. "In the meantime, you can put on the swimming trunks. We need to hit the pool and start working your muscles."

"We?" He arched a brow. "Are you coming in with me?"

"If that's okay with you. I have my swimming suit on already." She pulled her shirt up and her pants down, revealing something so sinfully sexy that it took his breath away.

Literally.

He had trouble catching a breath.

"What is this thing?" he mumbled.

Two red triangles with some gold design on them covered the very tips of her breasts and were connected with strings that looped behind her neck and her back. The bottom part wasn't much better, with a small red triangle covering her feminine mound and connecting with strings to the back.

Laughing, Jasmine pulled her shirt down and her pants up, covering the swimming attire. "It's called motivation."

She left the room before he could ask what she'd meant by that.

32

JASMINE

J asmine was still smiling when she left the room. The expression on Ell-rom's face had been priceless, and the erection that had sprung up between his legs was the best sign of health.

Her prince was really getting better by the hour rather than by the day.

She was glad that Julian had told him about her being a Dormant and that it hadn't come from her. She'd dreaded telling Ell-rom that she needed him to induce her.

Why?

Jasmine wasn't sure.

He would love to be able to repay her for all she had done for him, but perhaps that was the problem. She didn't want him to do it out of gratitude. She wanted him to do it because he accepted her as his one and only, his fated mate.

She was already quite sure that a bond was forming between them and that they were meant to be together, but she had proven not to be the best judge of character, and she was going to take it slow and not jump to premature conclusions.

"Julian." She waved at the doctor, who was about to duck into Morelle's room. "Wait up."

"How can I help you?" he asked.

"Ell-rom wonders if you know whether his other sister plans to visit today. Well, I want to know that too because my friends want to see him."

"I don't know," Julian said. "But I can find out. I'll text Kian and ask. The Clan Mother is probably spending a lot of time with her daughter and new grandson. That's why she didn't come yesterday."

"The same thing occurred to me, but Ell-rom was disappointed that she didn't come. I know that she is a goddess and all that, but she could have sent a message to him that she couldn't come instead of just letting him wait and worry."

Julian smiled sheepishly. "You are right, but neither of us is going to point it out to the Clan Mother. She doesn't have to explain herself to anyone."

"Of course." Jasmine smiled. "I would never dare. By

the way, Ell-rom is ready for the pool. Should we grab some towels and go?"

"There are plenty of towels by the pool, so you don't need to take any from here, and I don't want you going alone. Wait for me. I'll show you both what Ell-rom needs to do, and then I can leave you there to practice."

"I don't even know where the pool is. We will wait for you."

"It will only take me a few minutes to check on Morelle, and then to put on my bathing suit."

She nodded, imagining what the hunky doctor would look like in almost nothing at all. He was a gorgeous male specimen and a physician, which made him even sexier, and yet she hadn't felt attracted to him even before Ell-rom consumed every cell in her brain.

Perhaps the bond Julian had with Ella worked not just to ensure that he felt no desire for other females but for other females not to find him desirable either. It was a nifty trick to keep marriages intact. Hopefully, she would one day have it with Ell-rom.

When she opened the door to his room, she found him sitting on one of the chairs with the robe she'd gotten wrapped around him.

"It was a little cold to sit here in just the swimming pants." He regarded her with his intense blue eyes. "Do you also have a robe to cover your bathing suit?"

"I don't, but I will walk over there in my clothes and remove them when we are about to enter the pool. Julian is coming with us to show us what to do."

Ell-rom frowned. "I don't want other males to see you nearly naked."

Jasmine grinned. Finally, he was showing some jealousy. "There will be no males there other than Julian, and he's happily mated, which makes it impossible for him to be attracted to any females other than his mate."

"He can't? Why?"

Jasmine sat down in the other chair. "It's the result of the bond that forms between mated immortals. Once they find their truelove mates and form that connection, they become physically incapable of being attracted to anyone else. It's a wonderful way to ensure fidelity."

"Is that true for all immortals?"

Jasmine nodded. "As far as I know, yes, and it's also true for the gods. That's where they got it from. But from what I heard, finding a truelove mate is supposed to be very rare, so in days past, the gods and many immortals mated for political reasons and economic convenience, and those couples were not known for their fidelity. It's only true for truelove mates."

"How do the immortals and gods know if their partners are their trueloves?"

Jasmine shrugged. "I'm almost as ignorant about this world as you are, but if I had to guess, it's the inability to feel desire for anyone other than their fated mates."

"That makes sense."

He looked at her with a question in his expressive eyes, but she wasn't ready to answer it yet. She believed that they were fated for each other, but he needed to believe it too, and without being influenced by her.

The knock on the door saved her from having to evade an answer, and when the door opened and Julian walked in, she was relieved to see him wearing a medical coat over his bathing suit.

She wasn't attracted to him, but she had eyes, and she appreciated beauty in all its forms, including a perfect male form like Julian's. Ell-rom would not have reacted well to that.

"Everyone ready?" Julian asked.

"We are." Jasmine looked at Ell-rom.

Holding on to the walker, he pushed to his feet, which were clad in the flip-flops she'd gotten him for just this purpose.

Julian followed her gaze and shook his head. "Those won't do for someone who is still unsteady on his feet. You will need to take them off." He walked over to the bed and lifted a pair of sneakers. "These are better for now." He crouched at Ell-rom's feet and helped him put them on.

33

ELL-ROM

Ell-rom didn't say much on the way to the pool.

Having the medic kneel at his feet and change his footwear should not have felt so awkward. After all, Julian had probably seen more of him than anyone alive and had helped him shower when he could barely stand, but it had still been a very unsettling experience.

It had felt like a setback.

Ell-rom had been so proud of his accomplishments and his modicum of independence, and the medic's gesture had shattered the illusion. He could have sat down and exchanged the flimsy footwear for the more substantial type himself. Julian didn't have to humiliate him like that. But he couldn't even be angry at the medic because his actions had come from a place of goodness and not malice.

Something buzzed, and Julian stopped walking and pulled out his phone from the coat he had put over his bathing suit. After reading what had been sent to him, he lifted his head and smiled at Ell-rom. "You will have visitors later today. I told Kian that you would need a long nap after exerting yourself at the pool, so the evening would be a good time for the Clan Mother to visit you."

Ell-rom's heart rate accelerated. "Did he tell you why she had not come yesterday?"

Julian shook his head. "She was probably busy fawning over her new grandson. The Clan Mother adores babies."

"She is incredible," Jasmine blurted. "Knowing she loves babies just makes her even more magnificent in my view. It means that she has a good heart."

Julian nodded. "The Clan Mother is all heart."

Ell-rom loved the way Julian talked about Annani. He did not fear her, and he did not even worship her. He just loved and admired her. If Ell-rom ever got to perform any princely duties, he wanted to be like Annani. Loved and appreciated by his people instead of feared.

Not that he was going to be a prince of anything. He was a very long way from Anumati, and even there, he would have never ascended to the throne even if he had not been an abomination.

His sister would.

Ell-rom frowned. Was that something he'd remembered? Or had he deduced it from what he had been told? Only females could rule Kra-ell. Males were not even allowed to be priests, and the belief that twins share a soul was the only reason he could have been conscripted.

That part he remembered being told and not actually living it.

He also had no memory of ever being in water before, but he was not afraid of the pool. Jasmine had explained that it had a sloping bottom and that they would stay where he could stand. There was nothing scary about that. It was like standing in a bathtub, only with cold water instead of warm.

What he was anxious about was Jasmine parading in that bathing suit that left most of her skin bare, and his reaction to that. He also planned to watch Julian's reaction to verify that what Jasmine had told him about the medic's inability to feel desire for her was true.

He didn't doubt Jasmine, but she might have been told things that were not true or were just partially so.

Why did he think that?

Ell-rom had no answer for that except a deep-seated knowledge that not all people were well-meaning and that it was naive to accept every statement as true.

"Here we are." Julian pushed open a set of double doors that had a small round window at the top of each panel.

The sharp scent that Ell-rom had been smelling ever since they had stepped out of the elevator intensified ten-fold, and he sneezed.

"Forgive me. The chemical smell is irritating my nose."

Jasmine turned to Julian with a worried look on her face. "What if Ell-rom can't tolerate the chlorine?"

"We need to test it." The medic took off his coat and toed off his shoes. "Let's start by just putting our feet in the water."

He led Ell-rom to the edge and helped him sit down on the floor, which was much more difficult than sitting on a chair.

"Do you need help taking your shoes off?" Julian asked.

"No, I can do it." Ell-rom copied what the medic had done with his own shoes and used the leverage of the floor to pull out his foot from one shoe and then removed the other with his toes.

Next to them, Jasmine pulled her shirt over her head, but Julian paid her no attention.

"You can keep your robe on if you are cold," Julian told him. "Pull it up if you don't want it to get wet." He scooted to the edge and put his legs in the water.

Ell-rom wasn't keen on removing the robe and letting Jasmine see the stark difference between his and the medic's physiques. Julian was covered with lean muscle, while Ell-rom looked like a deflated version of that. His skin wasn't stretched taut over his muscles, and he was gaunt and sickly-looking.

How could Jasmine be attracted to him?

If not for the scent of her desire, he would have thought that she had only pretended, but that enticing aroma had been unmistakable even for an inexperienced male like him.

Some things were innate.

Now was not the time to think of those things, though, and if he didn't want to embarrass himself, he needed to keep his eyes off Jasmine, who had removed her pants as well and was sitting at the edge of the pool with her legs dangling in the water.

Ell-rom scooted forward, imitating the way Julian had done it, and when he got to the edge, he scooped the robe behind him and put his legs in the water.

"How does it feel?" Julian asked.

"Strange. My legs feel as if they weigh less, and they float up."

The medic grinned. "That is why exercise in water is easier than outside of it."

Jasmine leaned forward so she could see Julian on

Ell-rom's other side. "Do you know if Anumati's gravity is the same as Earth's?"

"It should be stronger by a good measure, I would think," Julian said. "The planet is much bigger, and gravity is directly proportional to mass. That should also explain, at least in part, why the gods, and by extension the immortals, are so much stronger than humans."

"Like Superman," Jasmine said.

"Who is Superman?" Ell-rom asked.

"He is a fictional character." Julian hopped into the water, which reached only to his waist. "You seem to have gotten used to the chemical smell, and your skin looks fine. We can proceed with the exercises."

"What about the teardrop?" Jasmine asked. "I meant to ask you if it was waterproof but given that you jumped into the pool with it around your neck, it must be okay."

"It is. The earpieces are waterproof, too, but we need to keep the teardrop out of the water for it to broadcast sound. That's why I shortened the string. I suggest that you do the same once you join Ell-rom in the water."

"I will."

Ell-rom had no choice but to remove the robe, and he dreaded the moment Jasmine saw him like that.

Was there any way he could ask her to leave without offending her?

That was so cowardly that Ell-rom was ashamed of even thinking it. Jasmine was kind, and she had feelings for him. She wouldn't make comparisons between him and Julian and find him lacking. She knew he was still recovering and wouldn't always look like an animated skeleton.

As he untied the belt and shrugged off the robe, Julian offered him his hands.

"Grab on to me, and I will pull you in."

Reluctantly, Ell-rom followed his instructions and used the medic's hands to balance, but instead of waiting for Julian to pull him in, he slid into the water.

When his feet touched the bottom, the sensation was unlike anything he could remember experiencing. The water embraced him, supporting his weight in a way that immediately eased the strain on his muscles.

"Congratulations!" Jasmine clapped her hands. "One more step toward victory."

Was it?

Ell-rom was afraid to look at her, but his eyes were drawn to her of their own accord, and he saw her sitting on the edge of the pool, her lovely brown hair cascading down her front, hiding the fronts of her covered breasts, but leaving the swells exposed.

"Eyes on me," Julian said, most likely saving Ell-rom from doing something stupid.

34

JASMINE

As Julian explained, the exercises were designed to build strength without putting too much strain on Ell-rom's recovering body, and Jasmine memorized them as best she could so she could continue the therapy with Ell-rom later.

As Ell-rom's eyes kept shifting to her and roaming hungrily over her body, she preened under his attention, feeling a boost of confidence. But then she remembered he'd never seen a woman so scantily clad before, so of course he was excited. In many ways, Ell-rom was like a boy experiencing these feelings for the first time, but knowing how much he hated that comparison, she wasn't going to give voice to her thoughts.

It took a while for her prince to give his undivided attention to Julian instead of sneaking peeks at her, but as the exercises demanded more and more of his focus and effort, his covert glances became less and less frequent.

"Do ten repetitions of this exercise," Julian told Ell-rom. "Then rest for a few breaths and repeat it. You should do three rounds of each exercise for a total of thirty repetitions for each."

When Ell-rom proceeded to do as instructed, Julian turned around and waded over to where Jasmine was sitting. "Do you think you will be able to guide him through it if he forgets?"

Jasmine nodded. "I memorized all the exercises."

"Good." Julian put his hands on the edge of the pool and, in one powerful move, jumped out of the water, splashing droplets over Jasmine.

"Show-off." She laughed, grabbing a towel.

"You need to get in the pool," he told her as he took the towel from her hands. "Keep a close watch on Ell-rom."

Jasmine stifled a smile. "I will."

"I'll be back in half an hour to help him get out of the pool. Don't do anything I wouldn't do." He winked.

"Oh, yeah? And what wouldn't you do if Ella was here?"

"Good point. Then don't do what I would have done." He wrapped the towel around his shoulders, picked up the coat he had discarded before entering the pool, and walked out.

Jasmine got into the water and stood next to where Ell-rom was doing his leg lifts.

He stopped, his eyes roaming over her again. "It is difficult to concentrate on the exercises with you looking like that."

"You seemed to be doing well up until now. Julian is really good at what he does, isn't he?" She hoped to distract Ell-rom from his obvious fascination with her body. "The exercises he has shown you are excellent for building your strength without putting too much strain on your muscles."

To her surprise, Ell-rom's expression darkened. The light that had been in his eyes moments ago dimmed and was replaced by something that looked almost like resentment.

"What's wrong?" Jasmine moved closer to him.

Ell-rom dropped his gaze to the rippling surface of the pool. "It's not important," he muttered.

"Hey," Jasmine said softly, placing a hand on his arm. "Talk to me."

He shook his head. "I'm ashamed to admit that I find myself jealous of Julian's healthy looks."

"Ell-rom." Jasmine lifted her hands and cupped his face, pressing a soft kiss to his lips. "When you're back to yourself again, you'll be even more handsome than Julian. You're half-god and a royal, after all. As I think you can tell, I find you very attractive as you are. But I also have no doubt you'll be absolutely stunning when you're fully recovered."

The words weren't just platitudes to make him feel better. Even in his weakened state, Ell-rom was beautiful in the way of the gods—a perfection that was nearly impossible to look away from.

Her words seemed to have the desired effect, and a spark reignited in Ell-rom's eyes. Wrapping his arms around her, he lifted her, which was made possible by the buoyancy of the water, and held her against his chest.

With her feet dangling above the pool's floor, she had no choice but to lift them and wrap them around his hips. His swim trunks and her bikini bottoms were not much of a barrier, and feeling his hard length pressing against her soft core was delightful.

The glow in his eyes intensified. "Jasmine," he breathed as he put his hands under her bottom to support her.

"Yes?"

"What am I supposed to do now?"

Still cupping his cheeks, she leaned in. "Kiss me."

The look in Ell-rom's eyes shifted from insecurity to something darker, more intense, and then his lips were on hers, kissing her with a fervor that threatened to turn the pool's water to steam.

She responded in kind, her hands wrapping around his neck as she deepened the kiss.

With her clinging to him like a monkey, Ell-rom could support her weight with one hand, and he used the other to explore. As he traced the curves of her body with newfound confidence, cupping her breast, Jasmine arched into his touch, a soft moan escaping her lips.

She knew that they should stop and that this wasn't the time or place, but it was so hard to think clearly when Ell-rom was holding her like this, kissing her like she was the air he needed to breathe.

Desperate for friction, she started rubbing her core against his erection, moving herself up and down with the muscles of her thighs.

Ell-rom pushed one of the bikini top cups aside and teased her nipple in sync with her rubbing motion below.

As things were starting to get truly heated, the sound of the double doors swinging open jolted them back to reality. They sprang apart just as Julian's footsteps sounded on the tiled floor of the pool deck.

"Hello," he called out, seemingly oblivious to what he had walked in on. "Time to wrap it up. We need to get Ell-rom back to the clinic to get showered, eat lunch, and rest before the Clan Mother's visit."

Ell-rom looked at her, his eyes still glowing and his fangs still a little elongated but retracting. "I need a moment," he whispered, but her earpieces had no trouble picking it up.

Thinking quickly, she turned to Julian. "Before we get out, I have a few questions about the physical therapy regimen," she said, her voice a touch too bright. "I was wondering about the long-term goals and how we might be able to continue some of these exercises outside of the pool. I took Pilates back in the day, and it's done lying down. I think it could be very beneficial to Ell-rom. Is there a chance we can get a Pilates reformer in here?"

As Ell-rom shot her a grateful look, Jasmine kept Julian engaged in conversation for a few minutes, giving him time to compose himself.

"A Pilates exercise machine is a great idea, especially since Morelle will have to go through rehabilitation. I'll discuss it with my mother. How long have you been practicing Pilates?"

"Oh, not long. Just a few weeks. It was too pricy for my budget."

Jasmine had a feeling that Julian was perfectly aware of what she was doing and was cooperating with her.

He really was an awesome guy, and Ella was a lucky girl for having him. They would have beautiful babies one day.

"I'm okay," Ell-rom whispered.

She smiled. 'Let's get you out of here before you turn into a prune."

He frowned. "A fruit?"

She chuckled. "It's just another expression that the teardrop can't translate."

"Oh." He held on to her hand as she led him to the pool steps, where Julian was waiting.

"Don't get out yet," she said as she rushed out and grabbed his discarded robe from the floor. "We don't want you to catch a cold." She wrapped it around his shoulders.

"Thank you," he murmured, his voice low enough that only she could hear.

Jasmine offered him a warm smile. "Any time," she replied, giving his hand a quick squeeze.

Julian chuckled. "Just a reminder, Ell-rom can't catch a cold."

"I'm not sure about that." She wrapped her arm around Ell-rom's middle and helped him up the first step. "Maybe the miraculous healing ability is also diminished after seven thousand years in stasis. Human viruses can be deadly to an alien."

Julian stepped forward to help Ell-rom up the rest of the steps. "The healing ability is part of our DNA. It's not something that comes and goes."

"Oh, well. Good to know."

As they made their way back to the clinic, Jasmine thought about how far they'd come in such a short time. Just days ago, Ell-rom had been unconscious, barely clinging to life, and now he was walking, albeit with assistance, engaging in physical therapy, and, well, engaging in other activities as well.

The thought brought a smile to her lips. The road to full recovery was still long, and he had yet to face the complexities of integrating into a new world, but moments like the one they'd shared in the pool were the best proof that things were heading in the right direction.

35

KIAN

As Kian and Brandon made their way through the village toward Kalugal's section, the sun was high in the sky, casting dappled shadows through the lush canopy of trees that lined the path. But despite the beautiful day, Kian's mood was darkened by clouds.

"This is impressive," Brandon said as they crossed the bridge to Kalugal's quarter. "It looks like Kalugal's spared no expense to create an oasis for himself and his men."

Kian cast him a sidelong glance. "Are you seriously saying that you have never even come to take a look?"

Brandon shrugged. "I saw it during construction, but you know me. I'm not as interested in developing and building as you are."

Kian chuckled. "Unless there is a movie to be made

on those subjects, and then you dive right in and learn everything you can about it."

Brandon had been instrumental in protecting the village site during development and construction, staging the area as a movie set. Once the first phase had been completed, William's camouflage systems and other measures had replaced the staging.

"That's in my past. I lost interest in making movies. The studios are run by morons and cowards who don't understand the market, and I'm not allowed to thrall them to influence them." He flashed Kian a smile. "My charm and persuasion techniques stopped working. So unless you want to fund a new studio and find someone who can run it, I'm done wasting my time there."

That was why they were on their way to see Kalugal. Brandon had decided that the big screen was dead, the small screen was dying, and all that was left was social networks with their steady stream of poison, brainwashing young and old minds alike. Luckily for them, social media was open to manipulation, especially when one of the most successful platforms was owned by one of them.

Kalugal had had some world domination aspiration of his own back in the day, which was why he had built InstaTock, but it ran away from him, and nowadays he was in it just to make money, and a lot of it.

Or so he claimed.

Sometimes, it was hard to tell with Kalugal. He liked to appear as if he didn't take anything seriously, but that was a façade. The guy was super smart, super cunning, and morally gray, having no qualms about using his power of compulsion to gain an unfair advantage. Still, Kalugal never used his power or his wealth to promote evil. Besides, desperate times called for desperate measures, and sometimes a guy like Kalugal was the last shield against the forces of darkness.

"The world keeps changing," Kian murmured. "And I'm not sure which direction it's taking. Advancements in technology promise a bright future, with a servant robot in every house and people having to work much less, but I'm afraid that social pressures and world demographics are going to drag it down a dark path again."

Brandon slowed down. "You mean Navuh and his army of drug-dealing traffickers and evil influencers?"

Kian frowned. "You think he is behind the wave of hate-filled influencers?"

"Of course." Brandon waved a hand. "The wave of evil is not coincidental. Someone is organizing and financing it, and usually, that someone is Navuh. Although, to be frank, this time I suspect that other sociopaths with way too much money to spend are involved because we know that Navuh is short on cash."

"I'm not sure that's still the case. Drugs bring in a lot of money, and so does trafficking." Kian stopped walking and turned to Brandon. "We know what Navuh's goals are, but what are theirs if we assume that they are human?"

Brandon shrugged. "The same as Navuh—world domination, or maybe they just want to see the world burn. A cabal of sociopathic anarchists."

Kian chuckled. "That sounds like a plot for a blockbuster movie."

"Or a streaming series. The market is no longer about big-budget productions. People don't go to movies as much as they used to, and they prefer to wait until it's available on one of the streaming services."

Kian let out a breath. "I'm so sick of this. Lately, it seems that everything I do fails. Even this village, which I believed was going to be a sanctuary for our entire clan, is failing because I invited Kalugal and his men and the Kra-ell to join us. I thought that we could all live in peace and that we would be stronger together, but the integration I was hoping for is not happening. Someone has been stealing packages from the mailroom and sabotaging the security shutters and trash incinerators."

Brandon was silent for a moment. "The village is like a microcosm of the world. Integration is difficult when people are fundamentally different from each other."

They paused under the shade of a large oak tree, its branches spreading wide above them.

Brandon continued, "Even in the United States, which was founded predominantly by European Christians, integration is only partially working. Many people stay true to their roots. Italians stick with Italians, Greeks with Greeks, and so on. But at least everyone believes more or less in the same things and holds similar values."

Kian nodded. "The former Doomers have adopted our loose belief in the Fates, and they've forsaken their belief in Mortdh, who they weren't fans of even while in the Brotherhood. That's why they escaped. They didn't believe in Mortdh's patriarchal, misogynistic ideology that sought the enslavement of humans."

Brandon's brow furrowed. "Not all of that came from Mortdh. Navuh expanded on his father's teachings."

Kian waved a dismissive hand. "Does it matter who came up with which part of their poisonous ideology? What matters is the end result and the hellholes that the countries under Navuh's influence have become. In the past, I believed that we could reach them and plant seeds of democracy and respect for human life and equal rights for all. We've made modest progress with a few of them, but many have gotten even worse, and lately, I've given up on ever trying to reach these populations. They're too brainwashed to be saved."

They resumed walking, the sound of gravel crunching under their feet filling the silence between them.

"So, what's the solution?" Brandon asked.

Kian let out a bitter chuckle. "Maybe we should leave, settle on Mars, and paint a big target on Earth for the Eternal King to do away with it."

Brandon snorted. "And I thought that I was in a funk. What's gotten into you?"

Kian stuck his hands in his pockets. "Failure," he admitted. "In the world at large and in our midst. I invited strangers into our village, thinking I was doing the right thing, but I was wrong, and now I'm stuck, and I don't know what to do about it."

"Integration takes time," Brandon said. "It's not going to happen overnight or even over a few years. It's a process."

"It can be a process when you have new generations born that are not indoctrinated in the old ways and can be taught new things. We are immortal, the Kraell are long-lived, and we stay the same. We don't change."

36

KALUGAL

Kalugal watched his guests arrive through the camera mounted over the front door. Kian wore his usual office attire of slacks with a button-down, but it was a bright sunny day, which made it too hot for the tie and jacket that he normally wore during work hours. Next to him, Brandon was as suave as usual, his brown hair styled to perfection, his shoes polished, and his slacks tailored to fit.

They both wore dark sunglasses, protecting their eyes against the glare of the sun. For Kian it was a necessity, but for Brandon, it was more of a fashion statement. He was further removed from the source, and his eyes were not as sensitive as Kian's.

Curiously, Kalugal, who had more god than human in him, had much less trouble with the sun than Kian. Come to think of it, Kian's eyes were more sensitive than his sisters'. Perhaps the different fathers that each of them had influenced their genetics more than they chose to admit.

Jacki peered over his shoulder at the screen. "Do you want me to open the door, or are you going to do it?"

"I'll do it." He rose to his feet, walked to the front door, and opened it for his guests. "Welcome, gentlemen."

"Hi," Jacki said. "Please, come in."

"Hello." Brandon dipped his head. "Your home is lovely."

She frowned. "You've never been here before?"

"I only saw it during construction. I live in the city, and I'm rarely in the village, but that's going to change soon."

"How come?" Jacki asked as they walked toward the dining room.

"I'm changing directions." He looked at Kalugal. "Which is what I came to talk to you about."

"I'm happy to help in any way I can." Kalugal motioned to the seat he wanted Brandon to take. "Please, sit down."

The way he had it planned, he and Jacki were sitting on one side of the table, and Kian and Brandon were across from them.

"Where is Darius?" Kian asked.

"With Shamash." Jacki smiled apologetically. "I wanted an adult-only lunch for a change, and Darius loves spending time with his Uncle Shamash."

Kalugal didn't like that Jacki elevated his assistant's status to a family member, but he knew better than to argue with her. He was going to lose no matter how good his argument was.

"I love the scale of this dining room." Brandon glanced up at the ceiling.

"Thank you." Kalugal reached for the wine bottle he'd prepared and uncorked it. "Jacki and I put a lot of thought into this house. The size was constrained by the security requirements, so most of the square footage is underground, but we have skylights all over to let in natural light." He poured the wine into everyone's glasses. "At night, unfortunately, we can't enjoy the starry sky unless we want to sit in the dark. The automatic shutters cover all the windows at the same time that the rest of the village goes into dark mode."

Kalugal lifted his hand and motioned for Atzil to start serving lunch.

"You are in for a treat, Kian. I don't know what Atzil whipped up for you, but it smells delicious."

As the cook walked in with a tray laden with dishes, his usually confident demeanor was tinged with a hint of nervousness. He served Jacki first, then Kian,

Brandon, and Kalugal last, following the instructions Kalugal had given him beforehand.

Poor Atzil had been fretting over the vegan dishes he'd prepared for Kian, and Kalugal hoped his cousin would be kind in his assessment.

Once everyone had thanked the chef and he departed, Kalugal lifted his glass. "To family!" He clinked his glass with Jacki's and then Kian and Brandon's. "*Bon appétit.*"

He watched Kian take the first bite of whatever the thing on his plate was. "How is it?"

"Delicious," Kian said. "Decadent."

Brandon cast a glance at the dish. "I love polenta with wild mushrooms. I always order it at *Maria's*."

Kalugal chuckled. "Thanks for telling me what this dish is. I could smell the mushrooms, but I didn't know what that yellow thing was."

After the first course was done, Brandon leaned back with his wine glass in hand. "I would like to hear more about InstaTock and your vision for its future."

Kalugal had been waiting for this opening. "Well, my original plan was to use it as a steppingstone to take over the world." He paused to wink at Kian. "But I've changed my mind. I decided that the world was not worth conquering. Who needs that headache?"

He'd expected Brandon to laugh, but instead, the media specialist nodded solemnly. "Couldn't agree more, and it seems that Kian shares your opinion. On the way over here, he was talking about taking the clan to Mars and abandoning Earth to the mercy, or rather the lack thereof, of the Eternal King."

Brandon said that with such a straight face that Kalugal wasn't sure whether he'd been serious or jesting. It was probably the latter because Kalugal had never heard Kian talk like that. The guy might be paranoid, but he wasn't fatalistic or nihilistic.

Affecting a horrified expression, he turned to his cousin. "Kian! I'm shocked. What happened to your unwavering dedication to humanity?"

Kian rolled his eyes, but Kalugal could see a hint of a smile tugging at his lips. "It's been a trying few weeks," he admitted.

Seizing the opportunity, Kalugal leaned back. "Finally, you're seeing things my way. As I've been saying, humans are sheep. They are too easy to manipulate and control, so it's better if someone who wants what's best for them is in charge rather than letting some crazy billionaire with a bizarre dystopian agenda do it and kill millions because he wants to depopulate the planet."

"Right." Kian smirked. "You know what I think of that. No one person should decide what's best for everyone else. It should be a democratic process."

"Pfft." Kalugal waved a dismissive hand. "As if the sheep know what is good for them. A democratic process just means that the same billionaires pay for the campaigns of politicians who know how to look distinguished, say all the right things, and make promises they have no intention of delivering on. The system is rigged. You know it, I know it, and Brandon knows it, so why pretend that it's a sacred cow?"

37

BRANDON

At first, Kalugal's words resonated with Brandon, but he wasn't ready to give up on democracy just because the system was rigged. It needed to be fixed, that was true, but it didn't need to be replaced by an autocratic rule. That was never a good idea.

Any student of history should know that, but Kalugal was a young immortal, and his education was probably lacking. He was an extremely smart guy, but he might have focused on other subjects and hadn't studied history and politics in depth.

Brandon didn't have formal education in those subjects either, but since his job was to spread positive influence to the world, he had read extensively on both subjects. It wasn't an easy task to discern truth from propaganda or to remain objective when a particular historian happened to be very persuasive, but Brandon had developed a few simple rules to help him in the sifting process.

The easiest litmus test was to look at the results. So far, democratic regimes produced the highest quality of life for their citizens and the least suffering. Human rights were largely respected, and people felt safe. That didn't happen in totalitarian regimes, whether they were based on ideology or religion, which Brandon considered to be the same.

It made no difference what the belief system was as long as those who had put themselves in charge could use it to control and abuse their citizenry with impunity.

Given Kian's shifting expressions, he was probably doing a similar analysis, and Jacki looked like she had heard the argument before and had opinions about it but wasn't going to voice them in the name of showing solidarity with her mate—at least in public.

Before any of them could respond to Kalugal's statement though, Atzil appeared with the main course, effectively pausing their conversation.

The chef lingered by the table, waiting for Kian to taste the dish he had prepared for him and watching for his reaction.

"This is excellent, Atzil," Kian said. "Thai cuisine is one of my favorites, and you have gotten the flavors perfectly."

Atzil puffed out his chest, beaming with pride. "Thank you. I'm glad you enjoy it."

"You made his day," Jacki said as Atzil retreated to the kitchen.

"I meant it." Kian dug into his curry.

The conversation lulled as they all focused on the meal, the only sound the gentle clinking of cutlery against fine china, and Brandon took the opportunity to admire the fine art adorning the walls. It was all original, he had no doubt, and the eclectic mix of styles worked for the space, as it was decorated in an odd combination of traditional and contemporary. The interior design wasn't Ingrid's work, that was for sure, and he wondered who Kalugal could have hired to do it.

Perhaps one of the younger immortals had recently graduated from a design school.

As Brandon finished his main course, Kalugal put down his fork and knife and leaned back in his chair. "I've been considering incorporating more immersive elements into InstaTock. What are your thoughts on virtual reality experiences?"

"I think it's the future of entertainment. The potential for storytelling in a fully immersive environment is incredible. And with your resources and existing platform, you could really push the boundaries of what's possible. People will shift from being consumers of stories to being participants and co-creators."

Kian nodded. "We already have the technology courtesy of acquiring Perfect Match, but it requires being hooked up to a very expensive machine and having medical supervision. It's not suitable for home use."

"True." Kalugal reached for the second bottle of wine he'd opened. "But at the rate artificial intelligence applications are advancing, the technology might catch up in only a few years. The other part of the equation would probably be a brain implant that would allow people to hook into the game without the need for a multimillion-dollar machine and techs to supervise them. The chip will replace both." He poured into their glasses.

Brandon chuckled. "That would be game over for humanity and the start of the zombie apocalypse. Imagine what governments could do if they could hack straight into the brains of their citizens. It would be *The Matrix*."

"The masses will live inside an illusion," Kian murmured. "Or die. What would the elites want to do with them? Especially if all the manufacturing could be done by robots, including building the robots themselves?"

Brandon considered that for a long moment. "Entertainment. They will enjoy watching them in the simulated reality they live in. Like *The Hunger Games*."

"It didn't happen on Anumati," Kian said. "I'm sure they have the technology. I guess the Eternal King didn't want to turn his people into zombies who lived inside a simulation. He must have prohibited the installation of chips inside people's brains."

Kalugal nodded. "That's interesting. He does things the old-fashioned way, with charisma, propaganda, and a healthy dose of compulsion. The guy is super smart, so he must have realized all the possible downsides of too much control. Or maybe he just likes the challenge of controlling his civilization with the power of his personality and his talents. It's no fun doing something if it runs on autopilot and requires no effort."

"That's precisely why he disallowed it," Jacki said. "Anyone can control a population of chip-powered zombies, but only the Eternal King, or someone as capable as he is, can control several trillions of free-thinking gods, not only on Anumati but in all of its colonies as well."

Kalugal nodded. "That's one hell of a power rush. It gives me the shivers."

38

KIAN

Jacki made a lot of sense.

The Eternal King's main objective was to hold on to his throne, and he didn't need an implant in his citizens' heads to ensure that. Why would he have made it easy for any mediocre bureaucrat to take over?

The king would have been murdered in a blink of an eye. The reason he was still in power after ruling for hundreds of thousands of years was that his people were mostly content, and no one thought that there was a viable replacement for the king. The only one who had ever come close had been his heir, Kian's grandfather. That was why the king had gone to such lengths to get rid of him while making it look as if he had no choice and was doing the right thing.

Manipulative, smart bastard.

As Atzil brought out dessert—a beautifully presented array of fresh fruits and pastries–Kalugal raised his glass in a toast.

"To new beginnings," he said. "And to the power of collaboration."

"We haven't even discussed InstaTock yet." Brandon leaned over and clinked his glass with Kalugal's. "But I'll drink to that."

Once everyone was done with the toast, Kalugal set his glass down and looked at Brandon. "Tell me what you want to do on my platform."

"You know what my job is, right?"

Kalugal nodded. "You are in charge of spreading the clan's gospel through movies, literature, television, etc."

Brandon's brow furrowed. "We don't preach, and we don't claim that our worldview is of divine origins."

Kalugal arched a brow. "I beg to differ. Where did the religions of old get their ideas from? And what shaped the monotheistic religions?"

Brandon leaned back in his chair and crossed his arms over his chest. "Not all monotheistic religions share the same principles and ideology. Surely you agree with me on that."

"Yeah." Kalugal sighed. "I do."

"Anyway," Brandon continued. "Ahn's idea of a free, self-governing society, with equal rights and dignity for all, was originally taught to the humans as a religion because it was easier and faster to do it that way. These days, influence is happening on social media, and that's what I want to do with InstaTock. I will provide the content, but I need your algorithm to push it to become viral."

Kalugal regarded him for a long moment, smoothing his fingers over his goatee. "What kind of content are you thinking of?"

"I'll start with influencers. Perhaps I'll use clan members for that. Good-looking people trend faster. I'll write the scripts for them and either film them myself or delegate this to Ella and Tessa. They are good at this. But I might also come up with some fresh ideas for different kinds of short-form content. Today's audience has the attention span of a gnat."

"I want to see each piece of content before you post it."

Brandon didn't look impressed by Kalugal's stubborn expression. "That might work in the beginning, but if it's effective, I plan to flood the platform with it, and it will not be practical in the long term. You will be spending your days looking at amateur-style videos."

"I'm great at delegating." Kalugal turned to Jacki and smiled. "Is that something you would be comfortable doing?"

"Sure. I would love to help turn the world into a better place. You were complaining about the hateful trash that people post on our platform."

"I was." Kalugal huffed out a breath. "InstaTock was supposed to be educational and motivational. But instead, it turned into a cesspool of depravity, and I'm not a prude. But some of that stuff is just wrong. I take down the worst offenders, but they find ways around the bots that look for trigger words. It's a never-ending pursuit."

"The answer is not to take them down but to make them less popular," Brandon said. "And also, to flood the platform with positive content, and I can help a lot with that."

"What about compensation?" Kalugal asked. "The platform makes me way more money than I have ever expected, and I don't want to lose the income."

"You won't," Brandon promised. "I have decades of experience producing content that consumers want to watch. Your ad income will grow, not shrink, and by a large margin."

"So, no payment for using my platform?"

Brandon laughed. "You should thank me for not charging you for all the content I'm going to provide you with that you can profit from."

"Tough negotiator." Kalugal shook his head, but it was more for show than real dismay.

Brandon was right, and the production costs of what he had in mind would have to be covered by the clan. If this was a deal between unrelated parties, Brandon could have charged a lot for the content.

"So?" Brandon arched a brow. "Do we have a deal?"

Kalugal nodded. "Six months trial. If we all get along and it works as well as you expect, we can negotiate a longer-term contract. If not, we part ways as friends."

"Deal." Brandon offered him his hand.

After shaking it, Kalugal turned to Kian. "Should we shake on it as well? After all, Brandon works for the clan."

"Sure." Kian shook his hand. "Do you want to draw up the contract, or should we?"

"I'll do it. I want to spell out everything so there will be no misunderstandings."

39

SYSSI

Syssi walked into Amanda's office and pulled out a chair. "Cheryl Bastia called to cancel."

Amanda looked up. "That's the third one today. What's going on? Is there a football game everyone is watching, or is there a super sale somewhere?"

"I don't know." Syssi sat down. "People used to love volunteering for the testing. Everyone wanted to find out whether they had paranormal abilities. Nowadays, I have a difficult time getting anyone to come, even when we promise to pay them."

Their paranormal research used to draw in the most people, and it had been harder to get volunteers or even paid subjects for regular brain research. Now, it was the other way around. They had no trouble filling the two fMRI stations but couldn't get enough people for simple precognition and telepathy tests.

Even though the procedure was completely noninvasive, Syssi was surprised that people didn't mind a tech using a machine to peek inside their heads and watch how their brains worked in real-time.

Perhaps it was the allure of the sleek, cylindrical devices gleaming under the lab's fluorescent lights, or maybe the students were fascinated by the mysteries of the human brain. Or what was more likely was that they preferred to get paid for taking a long nap. Amanda was currently focusing her official neuroscience research on brain activity during different sleep states.

"Do you want to grab a coffee now that we have an unexpected break?" Amanda asked.

Syssi smiled. "I'd rather visit the girls."

She missed the days when the daycare was in Amanda's old office, and they could just pop in to see their daughters whenever they wanted. But she had to admit that it had been far from ideal for their babies to be cooped up in that windowless room, especially with all the toys that Amanda had kept buying. The new space on the first floor was much better for the children as well as for their mothers, who managed much more work without the constant distractions.

Amanda shook her head. "We were just there less than an hour ago. It's not good for them to see us so often. It undermines the nanny's authority."

As if on cue, Syssi's phone buzzed with a notification. She glanced at the screen to see a photo of Allegra and Evie playing in the sandbox outside, with Karen's boys a few feet behind them.

"Look at what Jenna sent right now." Syssi showed the photo to Amanda.

Her boss's expression softened. "Oh, how adorable. And look at this. Allegra is posing for the camera. She's just like me."

Like Amanda, Allegra was an extrovert who liked dressing up and had very firm opinions about most things. But she also had a lot of Syssi in her, most notably her precognition talent.

"I am still having a hard time with Allegra exhibiting foreknowledge at such a young age," Syssi admitted. "I shouldn't be surprised though. She communicated telepathically with me from the womb."

Amanda's eyebrows drew together, forming a slight furrow above her nose. "It could be a coincidence that she said the initials of Alena's baby name before any of us knew what it was going to be. She might have meant Ethan."

Her sister-in-law hadn't said that Syssi might have hallucinated the communication with Allegra while she was still in the womb, but Syssi knew that Amanda thought that. Some paranormal abilities were easier to accept than others.

"That's always possible." Syssi sighed. "I don't know what to do."

Amanda tilted her head. "About what?"

"The vision I promised your mother I would court after the twins were found. She hasn't mentioned it yet, but I'm sure she will remind me soon."

Amanda arched a brow. "And the problem with that is?"

"The problem is that I'm scared of what I'm going to see—or rather, what I might not see." Syssi ran a hand through her hair. "As long as I don't attempt it, hope remains. But if the Fates show me that Khiann is dead..." She trailed off, unable to say it out loud.

"I don't think you have a choice." Amanda pursed her lips. "She has not forgotten, and she is probably waiting for you to bring it up. When you don't, she will remind you, and you will have to come up with some lame excuse for why you didn't do it right after the twins were found as you had promised."

Amanda's directness helped crystallize things for Syssi. "Maybe you can help me find an excuse that wouldn't be lame?"

Amanda just arched a brow. "Really?"

"Ugh." Syssi groaned. "I don't want to be the bearer of bad news. Besides, my visions are not always clear, and deciphering them often happens after the event occurred."

Amanda reached out, placing a comforting hand on Syssi's arm. "The Fates will show you what you need to see. You might once again be granted a vision that has nothing to do with my mother, and she will understand that the Fates don't want her to know what happened to Khiann."

That was a comforting thought. Maybe the Fates would spare her the pain of having to tell Annani that her mate had been dead for the past five thousand years.

Syssi took a deep breath. "Okay. I'll do it. But I need either you or Kian to be there when I induce the vision. I promised Kian I would never do that without someone watching over me."

"I know, darling. Of course, I will be there for you." Amanda patted her arm. "Do you want me to come over this weekend?"

"I have to check with Kian and see what his plans are. If he is home, he can watch over me."

"Even if he can, call me. I want to be there."

It dawned on her then that Amanda was just as anxious about what the vision would show as she was.

Her mother's well-being was on the line.

"You know what? I think now is the perfect time to do it. Even if the results are not what your mother hoped for, she won't sink into depression because she just got a new grandson and a new pair of siblings. There won't be a better time for this than now."

"True," Amanda said. "That's a very valid argument. I'll pray to the Fates that you find he is alive."

Syssi nodded. "Perhaps we should ask Alena, Sari, and Kian to pray along with you. Khiann needs all the help we can provide."

40

JASMINE

Ell-rom was sleeping soundly, and Jasmine was back in the chair scrolling through videos about gorillas, which she found surprisingly entertaining and encouraging for some reason. Their expressions were so human, as were their reactions to things like rain or finding things funny. Knowing that they were peaceful and ate mostly leaves, stems, fruit, and bamboo shoots made watching them a relaxing experience.

If only humans could be more like gorillas, the world would be a better place.

As an incoming message banner popped up on the screen, she switched applications and was surprised to see that it was a text from Frankie.

Usually, communications from Frankie came through Margo, and a flutter of concern rippled through her as she wondered if something had happened with Margo's brother. Had she told him instead of arranging a meeting where he could see Lynda being cozy with her ex? Or had the meeting taken place already, and WWIII erupted?

Glancing at Ell-rom's peaceful sleeping form, Jasmine stepped out of the room and then out of the clinic and walked down the corridor a few steps before stopping and leaning against the wall.

As she dialed Frankie's number, her call was answered right away.

"Jasmine! I'm so glad that you called me back. How is Ell-rom doing?"

"Great. He had his first rehab session in the pool today."

"How did it go?"

"Better than expected." Jasmine smiled even though Frankie couldn't see her.

"And how are you doing, girl?"

"I'm doing amazing." She looked both ways to make sure that no one was out in the hallway. "After Julian was done showing Ell-rom the exercises, he left, and we stayed a little longer. Things were just starting to get interesting when he returned and almost caught us making out."

"Ooh," Frankie cooed. "I want details, honey. Tell me more."

"All I can say is that Ell-rom is improving by the hour," Jasmine said, lowering her voice despite the empty hallway. "His body is responding as a young male's body should."

Frankie's laughter echoed through the phone. "That good, huh? Where are you now?"

"In the hallway." Jasmine glanced back towards the clinic. "Any activity is exhausting for Ell-rom, and I'm not talking about making out in the pool. Taking a little walk or doing easy exercises in the water drains him. That's why he spends so much time sleeping."

"Must be boring," Frankie said. "I mean, it's fine playing nurse and doing naughty things with the patient, but what are you doing while he's out?"

"Well, sometimes I join him. We slept the whole night in each other's arms."

"Aww, that's so sweet," Frankie cooed. "Listen, the reason I'm calling is that my cousin Angelica is coming over, and I was wondering if you'd like to join us. I need someone human-looking for balance, so Angelica doesn't get overwhelmed in case Dagor, Negal, and Aru decide to leave their tinkering for an hour and come say hi."

"Are they still working on the salvaged equipment?"

"They've been holed up in that room for days. I don't know what else they are hoping to find."

It suddenly occurred to Jasmine that inviting Angelica to the penthouse wasn't the best idea. "Are you sure it's okay to allow your cousin to visit? I mean, did you ask Kian if it was okay with him? After all, the penthouse is his."

"We are not meeting in the penthouse. We are meeting at the café. We still need to pretend to be human, though. The story is that we work for Perfect Match, and they have insane nondisclosure requirements. That's why I thought that having you there was a good idea."

Jasmine laughed. "As the token human?"

"No, as an actress who can spin a tale better than me. Angelica and I practically grew up together, and she will know right away that I'm fibbing. Besides, you know that your humanity is just a temporary condition. Once your prince has everything working properly, you will enter transition in no time."

Jasmine bit on her lower lip. "It might take a little longer than that, but I really shouldn't be discussing this in public or anywhere else for that matter. It's private."

"Then come to the café. I can be there in five minutes."

It would be nice to spend time with her friends and meet the feisty Angelica. Ell-rom would probably be asleep for hours, and if he woke up, she could ask

Julian to call her, and she could be back down in the clinic in minutes.

"When will your cousin get here?" Jasmine asked.

"She was supposed to already be here, but Angelica is always late. It's an Italian thing."

Jasmine laughed. "I thought it was a Russian thing, and then I thought that it was an actors' thing. Is anyone punctual?"

"The Germans," Frankie said. "They pride themselves on their punctuality and work ethic. Do you know that they turn off their phones at the start of their workday and don't turn them back on until it's time to go home?"

"I didn't know that. Makes sense, though."

"No, it doesn't. What if there is an emergency with their kids or something?"

"I'm sure there is a system in place for that."

"Maybe, but that doesn't lend itself to a joke. I have tons of jokes on every ethnicity under the sun, and Dagor just doesn't get them. Come to the café, and I'll share my best ones with you."

"I will in a few minutes. I need to tell Julian that I will be gone for a little bit."

"A long bit. Come on, you need a break, girl. It's not healthy to spend every minute of the day with your guy, no matter how fabulous he is."

When Frankie ended the call, Jasmine put the phone in her pocket and headed back to the clinic.

Once inside, she knocked on Julian's open door. "I just wanted to let you know that I'm going to the café for a while to hang out with Frankie and her cousin. Could you call me as soon as Ell-rom wakes up?"

He looked up. "No problem. Enjoy your break and don't rush back. He can survive without you for a couple of hours."

As Jasmine turned to leave, she nearly collided with Edgar, who had appeared seemingly out of nowhere. "What are you doing here?"

He flashed her a charming smile. "I was in the building to deliver something that the gods needed, and I thought I'd stop by to say hi." Leaning in close, he whispered, "I wanted to see Morelle."

Jasmine hesitated for a moment, then nodded. "I'm on my way to meet Frankie in the café, but I can take you to Morelle's room for a quick peek."

As they walked toward the princess's room, Julian arched an eyebrow at them, but he didn't stop them from entering.

The princess lay still and pale, her chest rising and falling in a steady rhythm.

Edgar walked over to the bed and leaned to look at her face up close. "She's stunningly beautiful," he breathed. "She looks like the statue of Nefertiti." He turned to look at Jasmine. "She was also bald."

"Maybe it's their regality that makes them look similar."

"No, I'm telling you. She looks a lot like Nefertiti. I'll show you." Edgar pulled out his phone and started a search for a picture of the ancient Egyptian queen. "Aha!" he exclaimed when he found it. "Told ya."

He held it up next to Morelle's face, and there was some resemblance, mainly in the prominent cheekbones and the shape of the lips.

"Is that statue even authentic?" Jasmine asked. "There are so many fakes, and in people's minds, Nefertiti looks like Elizabeth Taylor playing Cleopatra. Very few remember Jeanne Crain or Geraldine Chaplin playing Nefertiti."

Edgar chuckled. "I'm old enough to have seen those movies, but I don't remember who played what part in which movie or even what the plot was."

"Because you are not an actor."

Jasmine needed to go, but she felt bad about bailing on Edgar. "Frankie invited her cousin Angelica. Do you want to meet her?"

Edgar's face lit up. "Sure, I'd love to meet Angelica. Heard a lot of good things about her."

The way he said that indicated interest, and Jasmine regarded him with a wry smile. "I thought that your heart belonged to this sleeping beauty, or rather the sleeping Nefertiti."

He affected an innocent expression. "I'm intrigued, but I'm not yet taken. For now, I'm still a free agent."

Fair enough. Jasmine had hooked up with Edgar even though she had longed to meet her prince. The difference was that once she had seen Ell-rom, she couldn't even think about another male. From that moment on, he was the only one for her.

She had a strong feeling that the princess was not meant for Edgar. If she was his fated mate, he would know it on a subconscious level and wouldn't be so eager to check out Frankie's cousin.

41

EDGAR

As they made their way to the elevator, Edgar tried to imagine what Angelica looked like. For some reason, he didn't think she was anything like Frankie.

Maybe he was thinking about a character named Angelica he'd seen in a movie who was blond and curvy, but he didn't remember it. It was just what his mind conjured when he thought about her.

The truth was that he didn't have a preference for a specific hair color or even body type. As long as the female was attractive and fun to be with, he was game.

Well, he might have a slight preference for strong-willed females, but perhaps he should compromise and choose someone who was more easygoing.

After all, Jasmine had a strong, independent personality, and it hadn't worked out between them.

"I feel like I'm in a movie," Jasmine said once they got into the elevator. "Only weeks ago, I was living my mundane life, thinking that the best thing that would ever happen to me would be landing a major role, and now I'm living among immortals and gods and falling in love with an alien prince."

He arched a brow. "Falling in love?"

Only a few days ago, it would have hurt hearing her say that, but Edgar had made peace with their breakup and was actively looking for a new partner, so it was all good.

Jasmine shrugged. "I know it's too soon, but I can't help it. Ell-rom is just so sweet."

"Sweet?" Edgar felt like a parrot, repeating what she'd said, but what could be sweet about a half-Kra-ell prince who had been raised as a celibate monk?

"Yes. He's sweet. Innocent. I find it endearing."

He would never understand women. He was a young immortal, but he was ancient in human terms, and he knew that sweet and endearing were antonyms to sexy and desirable when referencing a male.

The elevator doors slid open, and as they walked up into the building's elegant lobby, Edgar smiled and waved at the human security guards. "Good afternoon, fellows. How is it going?"

"Good. It's a slow day," said the one whose name tag proclaimed him as Officer Roger Brown.

When they passed them, Edgar leaned to whisper in Jasmine's ear. "It's funny. They have no clue who I am."

"They don't? I thought that they worked for the clan."

"They do, but they don't know who their employer actually is, and they have no idea that there are additional levels below the parking garages. They think that we came from one of those."

Jasmine cast him a sidelong look. "I thought that they were part of the clan."

He laughed. "Have you ever seen an immortal who looked to be forty-something and had a beer belly?"

"Yeah, I did. The butlers. Sans the bellies. They are stocky and short but not fat."

He'd forgotten that she had seen Okidu and Onidu on the cruise.

"They are…well…they are immortal but not in the way we are."

"What do you mean?"

He was about to answer, but then they passed the wall of greenery that separated the café from the rest of the lobby, and Frankie greeted them with frantic arm waving.

"Over here!"

As if they could miss her.

"I brought Edgar," Jasmine stated the obvious. "I hope it's okay."

"Of course." Frankie rose to her platform-clad feet and hugged Jasmine and then Edgar. "I've missed you. Why haven't you come to hang out with us?"

Edgar wasn't aware that they wanted him to come, and he wasn't sure that Frankie meant it.

"I have a job to do." No one had required him to fly them anywhere recently, but his job was to be on standby for when he was needed. "I've just seen your guy and his buddies. They are still slaving over that equipment, hoping to find the black box."

Frankie rolled her eyes. "Tell me about it. Between that and my Perfect Match training, Dagor and I barely see each other. As you know, it's difficult for a newly mated couple to be apart."

Edgar grimaced. "I wouldn't know. Did you order already, or are we waiting for your cousin to arrive?"

"I didn't order. I grabbed a table first. But now that you are here, I can go. What would you like?"

Edgar gave her an incredulous look. "Don't even think about it. I'll order for us. Tell me what to get for you and for your cousin."

"You are such a macho guy." Frankie rolled her eyes. "As if I can't place an order by myself."

"I'm sure you can, but do you want to stand in line in those shoes?" He looked down at them pointedly.

They were pink, glossy, and at least five inches high. He had no idea how she even managed to walk in them.

"Good point. I'll have a grande latte with skim milk and a scone. Angelica will have the same, just with soy milk. She's lactose intolerant."

He turned to Jasmine. "What about you?"

"I'll have what Frankie is having. I'll help carry things when they fill the order."

"That's okay." He patted her shoulder. "I'll manage."

42

JASMINE

As Edgar walked away, Frankie waited until he was out of earshot to lean over the table with a mischievous smile lifting her lips. "He seems in a good mood. Is he finally over you?"

Jasmine cast a sidelong glance at Edgar, making sure that he wasn't looking their way. "He's infatuated with the princess, but it's not serious. He was very eager to meet your cousin."

Frankie's eyes lit up. "That's awesome. I would love to match those two." She narrowed her eyes at Jasmine. "You don't mind, right?"

"Not at all. I want Edgar to find his happily ever after. I will feel less guilty about ending things between us. He was good to me, and I feel like I didn't treat him right." She sighed. "But I just knew that he wasn't my one and only, and I think he knew that as well, but it has taken him longer to accept it."

Frankie frowned. "So, why are you still feeling guilty?"

"Because I have Ell-rom, and I'm happy, while Edgar doesn't have anyone yet."

"I get it." Frankie turned toward the wall of greenery segregating the café. "Here she is." She jumped to her feet and rushed over to hug a blond woman who looked nothing like her.

Angelica was a little taller than Frankie, but not while Frankie was wearing five-inch platform heels, and she was a little fuller in all the right places. She looked young, carefree, and sweet.

Nothing like the daredevil that Jasmine had imagined her to be. But then looks could be deceptive, and with a face like hers, Angelica could get away with murder, and no one would suspect her.

"Jasmine," Frankie said as she led her cousin to the table with an arm around her waist. "Meet my cousin, Angelica."

"Hi." Jasmine offered the woman her hand. "It's a pleasure to finally meet you. I've heard so much about you."

"Like what?" Angelica shook her hand with surprising strength for a delicate and feminine-looking girl like her. In comparison, Jasmine felt almost masculine.

"That you are fearless and that you are the queen of bikinis. Frankie told me that she borrowed three sets from you."

Shaking her head, Angelica pulled out a chair and sat down. "I found this place that sells factory rejects for peanuts. I paid five bucks per set, and the defects were barely visible."

Frankie mock-glared at her. "Don't reveal all of our secrets."

Angelica snorted in a very unladylike fashion. "You have more secrets than Margo has conspiracy theories. What's the deal with you staying in this fancy building? Is your new boyfriend that rich?"

As Frankie cast Jasmine a pleading look, she quickly thought of a story that wouldn't sound too outlandish. "The apartment is owned by the Perfect Match Virtual Studios. Lodging is provided as part of the compensation package for those who need it during training."

Angelica looked skeptical. "Why would they do that? People are willing to sell their mothers to get a job at that place. They don't need to tempt them with fancy apartments."

Jasmine shrugged. "They have been investing a lot of resources into recruiting and training their employees. They want them to stay, and there is no better way to do that than to provide them with lodging that is close to the studios."

Frankie looked impressed with her answer, but Angelica still looked skeptical. "Do you work for them too?"

"I'm about to start soon. I'm working on another project for them right now."

"What kind of project?" Angelica asked.

Jasmine smiled. "I'm sorry, but I'm not allowed to talk about it. The confidentiality agreement they had me sign is a monster. If I break any of their rules, I'd be in big trouble."

Angelica nodded sagely. "Frankie told me about it. It's crazy, but I can understand why they need it. As long as they have no competition, they can have good profit margins, and if they are publicly traded, their share price goes up. They need to ensure that no one steals their tech."

"Precisely."

The way Angelica talked about profit margins, Jasmine wondered if she worked in accounting or maybe in investments.

"What do you do for a living, Angelica?"

"Nails." She lifted her hands and turned them around to showcase the small masterpieces that were painted on her nails. "I'm a beautician. For now, I work in someone else's salon, but I'm saving to open a place of my own. Then I can profit from renting stations to others."

"I admire your entrepreneurial spirit."

"Thank you." Angelica beamed. "People don't realize how much money there is in this business." She reached for Jasmine's hand. "Oh boy. You need help. These are atrocious. What have you been doing, mountain climbing?"

Jasmine chuckled. "I think you are in the wrong business. You should be a detective. That was a classic Sherlock Holmes observation."

43

EDGAR

"Here you go, Edgar." The barista leaned toward him as she handed him a tray with four lattes. "Do you need sweeteners?"

"I can get them myself."

Amy had been flirting with him since the moment she'd spotted him standing in line, and the preferential treatment she was giving him was embarrassing. He was surprised that the other customers were not complaining.

Normally, he wouldn't have minded the attention, and he probably would have taken her phone number and called her later, but not today.

Amy was pretty, and Edgar liked assertive women, but he didn't like how strongly she was coming on to him. He hadn't given her any indication that he was interested, and she should have backed off instead of continuing to push.

"Don't be silly," Amy cooed. "I'll get them for you. The scones should be all warmed up by now as well."

"Thank you."

He glanced in the direction of the table and noted that Angelica had arrived while he was busy thwarting Amy's advances. She was sitting with her back to him, so he couldn't see her face, but he noted with satisfaction that she was indeed blond as he had imagined.

Maybe he needed a break from brunettes.

Jasmine was gorgeous, but the thing they'd had going was over, and the princess was still in a coma, so nothing had started with her yet, and he was a free agent.

"Here you go, Ed." Amy handed him the paper bag with the warmed-up scones and dropped a bunch of sweeteners of all types in the middle of his tray with several stirrers. "Can I get you anything else?"

"Napkins would be nice."

"Sure thing." She grinned.

Turning around, she lifted a stack of napkins from a pile on the counter, pulled out a pen from her pocket, and wrote a number on the top one.

"I get off at eight. Call me." She put the small stack on top of the pile of sweeteners.

"Thank you." He forced a smile before turning around.

"Call me," she said loudly to his back.

He didn't answer.

The woman hadn't asked if he was single or even if he was interested in women. He had never been as pushy as she was, not even as a young and inexperienced male. He'd always waited for a signal that his advances were welcome before continuing.

Shaking his head, he walked over to the table. "Hello, ladies. Your lattes and scones are served." He put the tray and the bag down and then turned to look at Angelica.

Wow.

What a face.

"Angelica, I presume?" He finally found his voice and offered her his hand. "I'm Edgar."

"Hi." She put her hand in his. "You are the pilot, right?"

"That's me." He pulled out a chair and sat down.

Angelica looked at him, then at Jasmine, and then back at him. "Frankie told me that the two of you were an item."

"Not anymore," Jasmine said. "Edgar is a free agent."

"What happened?" Angelica asked.

He didn't know how to answer that and looked to Jasmine for help. It wasn't as if he could tell Frankie's cousin that Jasmine was nursing an alien prince to health and falling in love with him in the process.

"It just wasn't meant to be," Jasmine said. "Edgar is an amazing guy, and we had a lot of fun together, but we both realized that we weren't meant for each other."

Angelica looked into his eyes as if she could read the truth straight from the depths of his soul. "Is that so? Jasmine is stunning."

Not as stunning as you, Angel.

He nodded. "On the inside as well as on the outside, and we will always be friends. But we couldn't be everything to each other."

For a long moment, she just looked at him, and then her gaze shifted to the stack of napkins. She snatched the one on top. "Who gave you her phone number?"

"How do you know it was a she and not a he?" Edgar teased, pissed at himself for not getting rid of the napkin earlier.

Although, given that he had only two hands and both were carrying things, that would have been a little difficult.

Angelica chuckled. "It's a she. I can tell by the handwriting."

"You see?" Jasmine waved a hand. "You are in the wrong business. You should be a detective."

"No, thank you." Angelica handed him the napkin. "I prefer to immerse myself in beauty and tranquility."

Edgar made a production of tearing up the napkin into small pieces and stuffing it inside one of the bays on the cardboard tray. "What do you do?" he asked.

She eyed the pile of shredded paper, and a small smile tugged at her lips. "Nails." She offered him her hand again, this time so he could admire the work that had been done to her nails. "I didn't do these, my friend did, but that's what I do for a living."

He held her fingers in his and brought her hand closer to examine the decorations someone had painstakingly painted on each nail. "Beautiful." He lifted his eyes to Angelica's face. "But not nearly as beautiful as you are."

Angelica blushed as if to demur. "Thank you." She pulled her hand back, but her reaction was a definite *yes, please continue*.

"Ooh," Frankie cooed. "Should we leave the two of you alone?"

"Don't you dare," Angelica hissed.

As the conversation flowed easily, touching on everything from the latest fashion trends to stocks and bonds, Angelica proved to be sharp, witty, and in possession of a good sense of humor.

In short, she was a delight to be with, and Edgar was seriously smitten.

44

ELL-ROM

As Ell-rom stirred awake, it took him mere seconds to become aware of Jasmine's absence. The realization sent a pang of disappointment through his chest, but he quickly shoved it aside. He couldn't expect her to just sit there all day long. Not when he was no longer on the verge of death, and she didn't fear that he would slip away when she wasn't there.

As sleep further faded away, his bladder awakened as well and signaled that it needed to be emptied, and Ell-rom no longer needed to wait for anyone to assist him to the bathroom.

The walker was parked next to the wall, a few steps away from his bed, but he believed he could reach it by holding on to the bed for stability.

When his objective was achieved, and his hands gripped the handles, it felt like another step on his journey of recovery had been traversed.

Turning the walker around, he started toward the bathroom, but a knock on the door halted his progress.

Bridget entered. "Good evening, Ell-rom. I see that you are feeling good, given that you are up and about."

He was glad that she wasn't reprimanding him for taking the initiative.

"Yes, thank you. I was just on my way to the bathroom."

"Then I won't delay you. Julian asked me to tell you that Jasmine is with Frankie at the café and that she wants to be called as soon as you wake up. Do you want me to let her know that you are awake?"

He shook his head. "I want her to enjoy her time with her friends. I can manage without her for a little while." He smiled. "Not for too long, though."

Bridget gave him a knowing look. "I know precisely what you are talking about. That's what happens when you find your one and only. It's hard to be without them." She waved a hand. "We will talk about it later. I don't want to keep you." She opened the door. "Don't forget that the Clan Mother will be here in a little over an hour."

"Thank you. I hadn't forgotten, but thank you for reminding me."

He was excited to see Annani again but also a little nervous. She was just such a big personality. His newfound sister was intimidating not because she was aggressive or hostile but because she exuded power. It was mitigated by her loving character, charm, and humor, but she was still a lot to handle.

Ell-rom had already showered, but he wanted to get dressed for the occasion—something nicer than the clothes the medics probably wore when they handled wounds, because he hadn't seen Bridget or Julian wearing them. Usually, they had a white coat over their regular clothes, and in Bridget's case, it was mainly to store items in its big pockets.

After taking care of his bladder, he walked over to the sink without relying on the walker and washed his hands. He brushed his teeth and then spent a moment examining his reflection in the mirror. His cheeks were hollow, but his skin looked better, and the dark fuzz on his head indicated that his hair was growing. He didn't look bad bald, but he would have preferred to have his hair back.

The clothes Jasmine had bought him were stored in a tall, narrow cabinet in the bathroom. She'd called it a thing that was locked, but it wasn't. It was open, and he pulled out the nice pants and shirt she'd gotten him. He also took out the shiny black shoes and a pair of black socks.

Ell-rom took his time getting dressed, occasionally pausing to catch his breath, and left the socks and shoes for last because it required sitting down, and he wanted to finish what he had to do standing up first.

It was odd how he didn't even have to pause to think about keeping his movements economical to preserve his energy. It had become second nature to him in the short time since he was awakened, but it would have probably been difficult for his old, healthy self to accept or even fathom.

Still, he would take today over yesterday any time. In his previous life, he had been lonely and had to be covered from head to toe at all times so he wouldn't be recognized for what he was.

Returning to the mirror, he leaned against the vanity as he tackled the small buttons on the shirt, and when he had them all done, he tucked the shirt into the pants the way he'd seen Kian's.

As a finishing touch, he reached for the cologne Jasmine had bought. He applied it sparingly, not wanting to overwhelm himself or anyone else with the scent. The fragrance was pleasant, crisp, and clean, with hints of citrus and wood.

Now it was time for the socks and shoes. Closing the lid on the toilet, he sat on it and wondered whether he should try to lift his foot to his hand or bend down to put the sock on. There was also a third option of not wearing socks and just pushing his bare feet into the shoes.

That was the easiest, but Ell-rom didn't want to make things easy for himself. He wanted to do them right. By the time he managed to pull the socks on, he was out of breath and sweaty and regretted his decision, but it was done.

He pushed his sock-covered feet into the shoes, put his hand on the grab bar, and hoisted himself up. Feeling dizzy, he had to take a moment to steady himself before reaching for the walker.

45

JASMINE

"Why did no one call me when Ell-rom woke up?" Jasmine accused.

It was possible that Julian had forgotten to tell his mother, but Jasmine doubted that. The guy wasn't forgetful.

"Ell-rom didn't want me to call you," Bridget said. "He wanted you to enjoy your time with your friends, and I agreed with him."

Ell-rom was all alone in the bathroom, without anyone to stand by the door in case he needed help.

"What if he falls down and hurts himself?"

Bridget smiled. "We would know and go help him. Stop worrying." She opened the clinic door for Gertrude, who walked in with two trays.

"Dinner time." Bridget took one of the trays from the

nurse and turned to Jasmine. "Can you please get the door?"

"Yes, of course." She opened the door to Ell-rom's room and held it open for Bridget and Gertrude to go in.

If Bridget was okay with Ell-rom being alone in the bathroom, then there was no reason for him to remain in the clinic.

After the doctor and nurse placed the trays on the side table, Jasmine followed Bridget to her office. "When do you think Ell-rom will be ready to move out of the clinic? I don't think he should be here anymore. He can stay with me in the penthouse, and we can come down here every day for the rehabilitation."

For a long moment, Bridget seemed to be mulling it over. "What happens the next time you want to go to the café and there is no one in the penthouse to keep an eye on your prince?"

That was a good point. "I'll take him with me."

Jasmine expected Bridget to laugh at the ludicrous suggestion, but the doctor seemed to take it seriously. "Give him one more night here, and tomorrow he can move to the penthouse."

"Thank you." Jasmine felt like hugging Bridget, but the doctor didn't seem to be the type who enjoyed that sort of thing. "I owe you and Julian and Gertrude so much. You have all basically put your lives on hold to care for Ell-rom and Morelle."

Surprisingly, that was the part that got a chuckle out of Bridget. "Thank you. We like being appreciated, but we are not doing this for you."

"I know. But still, I need to express my gratitude."

Bridget nodded. "You are welcome. Now, go eat dinner with your prince before it gets cold."

"Yes. I will." She rushed back into the room.

Ell-rom should have been out by now. Was he showering again?

She was about to ask if he was okay in there, but when the door opened, a transformed prince came out of the bathroom.

"Wow, Ell-rom." Jasmine put a hand over her heart, and tears misted her eyes. "You look so handsome, so dignified."

"Thank you." He smiled shyly. "I wanted to look more presentable for my sister's visit."

Jasmine lost the war with the tears, and they spilled out of her eyes in a gush.

Ell-rom's expression turned horrified. "What happened?"

"Nothing." She waved a hand. "These are happy tears. I'm just overwhelmed with joy."

She was overreacting, and she blamed the actor in her. Jasmine had been trained not to stifle her feelings. She was taught to embrace and amplify them so she could reenact them, but it didn't work with every emotion. She didn't do that with negative emotions because she knew instinctively that it was dangerous to let those feelings loose. But happy ones, well, they could get as wild as they wanted to go.

Ell-rom walked toward her as fast as the walker allowed, and when he reached her, he cupped her cheek and leaned over to take her lips in a gentle kiss. "I'm glad you are so happy about me wearing the things you got for me."

Jasmine shook her head. "It's not about that. It's just that seeing you dressed like this indicates how much you have improved in such a short time. It's silly, but I feel as if it's in part my achievement."

"It is certainly your achievement." He kissed her softly. "I would not be here without your help."

Jasmine took a long, shuddering breath. "Let's eat before the Clan Mother gets here. We need to be done with dinner and clear the space."

As they sat down, she unfolded the big paper napkin and draped it over her lap, then looked at him pointedly, hinting that he should do the same.

"Is this part of the dining etiquette?" he asked as he followed her example. "Or is it just prudent to protect my nice clothing?"

She was glad that Ell-rom wasn't shy about asking. There was still so much he had to learn, and the best way to do that was by asking a lot of questions.

"Right now, it's just practical." She started removing the lids from the various dishes. "It's part of the etiquette when you dine with cloth napkins and real utensils."

Ell-rom removed the lids from the dishes on his tray and frowned at the scoops of hummus in three different colors. "What is this?"

It was nearly impossible to explain, assuming that none of the ingredients grew on Anumati. "It's a paste made from a kind of bean and mixed with different flavors. The green one is spicy, and the red one is probably spicy as well. The purple and the yellow are fine." She took one of the pita chips that came with it, dipped it in the wasabi-flavored hummus, and put it in her mouth.

It delivered a nice punch but wasn't too spicy.

"Is that how people usually eat this dish?" Ell-rom picked up one of the pita chips.

"There are many ways to eat it, but I like scooping it up with the chips."

For several moments, they focused on sampling all the dishes, with Ell-rom asking what was what, and Jasmine explaining as best she could.

"How is Frankie?" Ell-rom asked when they were half done with dinner.

"I got to meet Frankie's cousin, Angelica. She's a beauty technician and quite the character. But the really interesting part was that Edgar showed up, and the two of them unexpectedly clicked. There was definitely chemistry there."

Ell-rom frowned. "Edgar is the pilot, right? The one who helped search for our pod?"

"That's the one."

She still hadn't told Ell-rom about her fling with Edgar, but it never seemed like the right time.

"If he's immortal, I assume that he is a member of Annani's clan?"

"He is."

"Then how come he has never met Angelica before? Is the clan so big that not everyone knows everyone else?"

"Angelica is human, and so was Frankie until not too long ago. I'm not sure if she's a Dormant, though. If Frankie and Angelica's mothers are sisters, then she definitely is. Otherwise, she probably isn't."

Ell-rom tilted his head. "What determines if someone is a Dormant?"

"To be honest, I'm not entirely clear on all the details," Jasmine admitted. "The Clan Mother would be able to explain it much better than I can, so save that question for her."

46

ELL-ROM

At the mention of Annani, Ell-rom felt tension creep back into his shoulders. He glanced at the clock hanging on the wall, realizing how close it was getting to her visit. "We should clear the table, and I should brush my teeth again."

Jasmine reached across the table, placing her hand over his. "Relax and finish your dinner. I'll take care of clearing up while you clean your teeth."

"We don't have much time, and this room now smells of the food. I should have thought of that beforehand, and we should have eaten out in the reception room."

Jasmine's eyes suddenly lit up. "I have an idea. There is no reason for you to meet your sister here. You are no longer bed-bound, and you can meet her in a much more dignified manner." She waved a hand over him. "Especially since you look so suave."

"That is a great idea. We can all fit in the reception area."

Jasmine shook her head. "I have something better in mind. Kian has an office in the underground, and it has a nice conference table. We can all sit around the table, drink coffee and tea, maybe even get desserts from the café if it's still open." She reached over and took his hand. "You'll feel much more comfortable talking with your sister while sitting in a chair instead of lying in bed."

The idea of meeting Annani in a more formal setting appealed to him. After all, wasn't that the reason he had gotten dressed up?

Ell-rom wanted to look dignified, to be considered more as an equal, even if it was an illusion. He had nothing to offer Annani except his loyalty and friendship, and there was so much that he needed from her.

There was nothing equal about them.

"I like your idea."

Jasmine grinned. "Today it's the office, and tomorrow it's the penthouse. I convinced Bridget to let you go tomorrow. We will come back for rehab sessions and checkups a couple of times a day, but you can spend the rest of the time on a beautiful rooftop terrace, breathing the questionable city air and admiring the blue, cloudless sky." She gave his hand a light squeeze. "But most importantly, we will get to spend our nights in a big, comfortable bed." She gave him a sultry look that had the blood heat up in his veins.

"I can't wait." He squeezed her hand back. "But please refrain from making suggestive comments until after my meeting with the Clan Mother."

Her laugh sounded a little evil, which made it doubly sexy, and as he rose to his feet and reached for his walker, he was already sporting quite the bulge in his pants.

He shook his head. "What am I supposed to do now?"

"Think of something else," Jasmine said as she collected the empty dishes and put one tray on top of the other. "Think about what Annani told you about the history of the gods on Earth."

That was good advice. He needed to remind himself of the things his sister had already told him so he wouldn't ask them again, and by doing so, he would distract himself from thinking about spending the night with Jasmine in a big bed and without a surveillance camera overhead.

Frankly, it was terrifying.

He had no idea what he was doing.

After brushing his teeth and making sure that his clothing was still clean, Ell-rom walked out of the bathroom, leaning only lightly on the walker. His leg muscles were still underdeveloped and weak, but he was gaining confidence in their ability to support his weight and enable his mobility.

When he emerged from the bathroom, Jasmine was waiting for him with a big smile on her face. "I asked Bridget to text Kian with my idea of meeting in his office, and he loved it. He and Annani are heading straight there, and since we need to allow more time for the walk over there, we should leave right now."

Ell-rom nodded. "Do you know the way?"

"I've been there only once." She wrapped her arm around his torso. "Before the Clan Mother came to see you, I was summoned to Kian's office for an official introduction. She probably didn't want me to start hyperventilating in front of you when I saw her. There is no mistaking what and who she is."

Ell-rom slanted her a glance. "But you've met gods before. You traveled with Aru and his companions to look for my pod. It shouldn't have been such a shock to meet Annani."

Jasmine chuckled. "Your sister is not like Aru and his friends. First of all, she glows, and they don't. Annani looks like what I imagined an angel would look like." She canted her head. "How does the word angel translate in your language?"

"Emissary, messenger, guardian spirit."

"That's about right. Anyway, she was very nice and welcomed me into her clan even though they can't be sure I can become immortal. The Clan Mother believes that I am a Dormant because of my witchy powers."

"I have no doubt that you will turn immortal."

By the time they arrived at a set of glass doors, he was a little out of breath, and the nice shirt was clinging to his back.

"Hold on," he said to stop Jasmine from going in. "I need to catch my breath."

"Of course." She smiled encouragingly. "You look so good that I keep forgetting that you are still recovering."

It was a very nice way to say that he was still weak without actually saying it and, at the same time, adding a compliment on top. It occurred to him that Jasmine had a natural knack for making people feel good about themselves.

He was so lucky to have her.

After a lifetime of misery, the Mother of All Life had rewarded him with a female who promised an eternity of joy.

47

ANNANI

"I am surprised by this request to meet in your office." Annani sat down at the head of the conference table. "Why not in the clinic?"

The last thing Annani wanted was to tax Ell-rom's frail body with having to sit through her visit instead of comfortably lying down in a hospital bed.

Was this his idea or Bridget's?

"Bridget says that Ell-rom is feeling better and that he wants to demonstrate how well he's doing."

Annani hmphed. "What it will actually mean is I will have to keep the meeting even shorter than the last, but so be it. I can wait until he and Morelle are in the village to continue our talks." She smiled. "I am looking forward to it. I will host them in my house so they will have the Odus to assist them and so we can talk as much as and whenever we wish." She was getting excited by her idea. "Perhaps they will become my companions."

Kian shook his head. "You are forgetting that at this point, Ell-rom is a package deal with Jasmine, and I doubt Jasmine will feel comfortable staying with you in your house. Ell-rom would want Morelle with him, so they will probably get a place of their own."

Annani regarded her son from under lowered lashes. "I expected your opposition to be about them coming to the village in the first place, not about the particulars of their lodging."

"I knew you would want to do that sooner or later, and I knew that fighting you over this would be futile. I resigned myself to doing my best under the circumstances. Although, I have to admit that I don't know how to mitigate the potential risk of the twins manifesting formidable compulsion powers. We risk them taking over the village and using every clan member as a puppet to do their bidding."

Annani nodded. "I do not disregard your concerns. We will not move them until Morelle is also awake and both Ell-rom and Morelle regain their memories. We will be better equipped to assess the potential risk of moving them to the village then."

"Thank you, Mother." The look of relief on Kian's face was almost offensive.

What had he been thinking? She had not gotten to live for over five thousand years and form a clan of her own by ignoring reason. She was just much less risk-averse than him, so he thought that she was impulsive.

The sound of footsteps in the corridor outside made her turn toward the door, and when the knock sounded, Kian motioned for Okidu to welcome their guests.

The fact that he had brought his Odu along indicated that Kian did not fully believe that Ell-rom was harmless in his current state. He had claimed that he needed Okidu to do some cleanup work in the office and the clinic, but Annani had a feeling that it was just an excuse to bring the Odu when Kian had seen that she had not brought one of hers.

"Good evening, Mistress Jasmine, Master Ell-rom." Okidu bowed. "Please come in."

"Thank you," Ell-rom said, not showing any reaction to the Odu.

Perhaps he did not even know what an Odu was. Well, he did not remember what he had known before entering stasis, but if he had been taught to fear the Odus, his response would have been instinctive.

Leaning on a walker and wearing slacks, a button-down shirt, and dress shoes, he looked handsome and distinguished. The difference between how he had looked only two days ago and now was amazing.

It was not just the clothes but the way he carried himself. Despite his obvious physical weakness, there was a dignity in his bearing that reminded her of their father.

Ahn had been silver-haired and pale, while the fuzz growing on Ell-rom's head was dark brown, and his skin was a shade darker, even though he was probably paler than he would be once he recovered. But the prominent cheekbones and the shape of the mouth and nose were so similar to their father's that Annani's heart squeezed with the old pain of losing him. A pain she had mercifully almost forgotten over the millennia since. Yet, where Ahn's features had been hardened by centuries of rule, Ell-rom's were still soft.

Like a child's.

It was sweet, but it would not last. Not if she could help it.

Ell-rom needed to learn that showing softness was okay when surrounded by family but not to the outside world. People would take advantage of him, or worse, think that it was okay to harm him. It was a sad fact of life, especially for males but also for females. Those who showed strength were less likely to be attacked.

"Hello, brother of mine," she said. "It is so good to see you up and about and looking well."

Ell-rom dipped his head. "Hello, sister. I've been looking forward to seeing you again."

"Hello, Clan Mother." Jasmine executed the most elegant curtsy Annani had seen in a long while.

She smiled. "Oh, Jasmine. There is no need to bow or curtsy to me, but I must say that you did it beautifully, which was quite a feat given that you are wearing pants. It was a pleasure to see such perfect form."

Jasmine's eyes sparkled. "Thank you, Clan Mother. I was taught how to do it properly by a wonderful choreographer working for one of the theatrical productions I participated in."

Annani did not know if it was common practice for actors to share credit for their successes with their production teammates, or if it was just Jasmine's way, but Annani liked that she had credited the choreographer.

"You also have innate grace and talent," Annani said, and meant it.

Jasmine dipped her head. "Thank you, Clan Mother."

Anandur pulled out two chairs for Ell-rom and Jasmine, and waited patiently until everyone exchanged greetings and sat down before helping Jasmine push the chair in.

She smiled brightly at him. "Thank you."

"You are most welcome." He walked around and sat across from her.

As Annani had requested, Ell-rom was seated to her left and Kian to her right, so her brother and her son were facing each other. Anandur sat across from Jasmine, and Brundar sat on the other side of the table closest to the door.

Okidu was still standing. "Shall I bring refreshments, Master Kian?"

"Good thinking. Is the café still open?"

Anandur looked at his watch. "It's closed, but we can use the vending machines, which should be fully stocked." He rose to his feet and clapped Okidu on the back, wincing when he encountered the hardness of the Odu's frame. "You should stay here."

So Annani had been right. Okidu was there to provide added security for her, not to clean up.

She cast Kian a reproachful look, to which he responded with a rueful smile and a shrug.

48

KIAN

A lesser male would have crumpled under Annani's hard gaze, but Kian was used to it, and she was used to him being vigilant about her safety. They just played their respective parts.

As his mother turned to her brother, her scowl turned to a smile. "How are you feeling? Did any more memories return?"

He shook his head. "Regrettably, I have nothing significant to report. I was hoping that today you would tell me more about what you know of my past."

"I do not know what your past is, but I can tell you what I know about our father's rebellion, what led to it, what happened after it was quashed, and continue from there to the events that happened on Earth. I covered some of it in our previous talk, but I can fill in the gaps and go on from where I ended the story."

"I wish I could write it down." Ell-rom sighed. "I don't trust my memory."

"Do you remember how to write?" Jasmine asked.

"I'm not sure."

"Let's test it." Kian rose to his feet.

He walked over to his old desk, and when he opened the drawer in which he used to keep his writing pads, he wasn't surprised to find a new stack that was dust-free. He had no idea when Okidu had the time to do that. He hadn't done it today because he hadn't brought a stack of yellow pads with him.

He pulled out one, found a pen, and brought it over to Ell-rom. "Give it a try. Writing is a muscle memory."

On second thought, Kian didn't know if they wrote by hand on Anumati. A civilization so advanced must have mastered voice-to-text eons ago, or they might have found another way to keep records.

Ell-rom took the pen, and by the way he held it, it was obvious that he had used writing instruments before. What he didn't know was how to release the ink and he looked the pen over with obvious confusion.

"Press the little lever on the side," Kian said. "That's how the cartridge containing the ink is released."

"Thank you." Ell-rom cast him an embarrassed smile and did as Kian had instructed. He began to write on the page. "I don't know if I'm inventing a new script or if I am actually writing in the Kra-ell language."

"Easy to find out." Kian pulled out his phone, snapped a picture of what Ell-rom had written, and was about to send it to Jade when it occurred to him that Ell-rom might have written something private. "Is it okay if I send it to Jade?" he asked.

"Yes, please. I am very interested in finding out whether I remember how to write."

Kian typed up his question and sent the text, and the response came just as Anandur entered the office with everything he'd gotten from the vending machines.

"She says that you have lousy handwriting, but she forgives you given your injury. She asks if I require a translation."

The smile on Ell-rom's face could illuminate the room, at least to the extent that the glow from his eyes did. "I wish to learn more about my past. That was what I wrote."

"Let's check." Kian answered Jade's text with a thank you and a yes.

Her reply came back right away, confirming what Ell-rom had said.

"You were correct." Kian put his phone on the table. "Congratulations on another victory. You remember how to write."

"It is quite remarkable," Annani said. "Although I should not be surprised. The gods of my time used to write with a stylus on a tablet. But given the advances in human technology, I would have expected an advanced civilization like the Anumatians to come up with a better way to record things."

Suddenly, Kian remembered Syssi's visions about Aria scribing by hand for the Supreme Oracle. "Maybe it's a religious thing," he said. "Syssi had a vision about the Anumati's head oracle, and she saw another goddess writing her predictions by hand. It's possible that temples are the only places where things are still recorded manually."

"I would like to visit Anumati and see all of its wonders." His mother smiled at Ell-rom. "But only if I could do so while invisible. I do not wish to be detained by our grandfather."

Ell-rom nodded. "From what you told me about him, none of us want to be discovered by him, and especially not my sister and me."

"About that," Kian said. "At some point, we will need to fake your death so the Eternal King will stop looking for you. The less he's interested in Earth, the better, and right now, you are the only reason he keeps sending patrol ships to the region."

The prince and his sister still had a long way to go before they would appear to be in the same state as the Kra-ell, who had perished in their stasis chambers, but it was better for Ell-rom to start thinking about this now than to spring it on him when the time came.

49

ELL-ROM

Ell-rom didn't like the sound of that.

"How do you propose to fake our deaths?" he asked.

Kian shifted in his chair. "I'm not sure yet. We had several ideas floating around, each with its drawbacks. But we are waiting for you to look like your fellow pod mates, so you don't look like you entered stasis unaided and survived. Bridget saved the uniforms that she cut off you, but fixing them so they look like new will not be easy, especially given Anumati tech, which will discover every imperfection no matter how small."

Ell-rom had another question. "How is the Eternal King going to discover that we were found?"

Once again, Kian looked uncomfortable. "Aru and his teammates were sent to Earth to look for the missing pods. Thankfully, they are part of the resistance, so they are as eager as we are to hide the fact that you were found. Their commander on the patrol ship is also a member of the resistance, but they all have to keep up the pretense that they are doing their job. If the Eternal King suspects that they are not, another ship will be deployed to this sector, and everyone serving on Aru's ship will be declared a traitor. We don't want that."

"No, we do not." Ell-rom rubbed a hand over his face. "I do not want anyone dying to protect me and my sister. Isn't it better to pretend that we were never found than to try a deception that might backfire? You all keep talking about how advanced Anumati is and what amazing technology they have. They might be able to see through anything you try."

"Ell-rom's right," Jasmine said. "Do they need to send a DNA sample to their commander?"

"I don't know," Kian said. "Aru didn't mention that."

Jasmine crossed her arms over her chest. "I'm sure it will be required. DNA testing can even be done on burnt remains. It can be extracted from remaining bone fragments." When everyone looked at her with curiosity in their eyes, she shrugged. "I read about it in a detective novel, and it sounded so out there that I checked, and it's true. They really can do that."

What Ell-rom wanted to know was how it was connected to his and Morelle's faked deaths.

Kian reached for one of the packaged desserts that Anandur had brought and tore open the container. "I can check with Aru, but since it is premature to discuss this, it can wait. We are here to talk about more pleasant topics like the clan's history and how my mother created it."

Ell-rom decided that he needed to talk with Aru himself. Arranging a meeting wouldn't be a problem since he was joining Jasmine in the penthouse tomorrow, and Aru lived there as well.

"Actually, I've been curious about something Jasmine mentioned," he said. "I was hoping to learn more details about the Dormants. In particular, I'm interested in finding out who can become a Dormant and how they are discovered."

Kian snorted. "We have been trying to solve that mystery for a long time. I mean the one about finding Dormants. We know how they come to be."

So that was why they weren't sure that Jasmine was one. They had no way to test for it. Earth seemed to be much less technologically advanced than Anumati.

Ell-rom nodded. "Then I would love to hear how Dormants are created."

"That is part of what I planned to tell you today," Annani said. "It all started when our father allowed the gods to take human partners and the first immortals were born. After that, some of these immortals also took human partners, but to their great dismay, their children were born human. After further examination, it was discovered that the children of female immortals carried the godly genes, but the children of male immortals did not. Those who possessed the genes could be activated."

"I know that part," Ell-rom said quickly, to stop Annani from explaining it again. "Julian told me how it's done."

"Excellent." Annani smiled. "As it turned out, the genes kept passing from a mother to her children, but only the daughters kept passing them on. We believe that there are many humans who possess them and do not know it. The problem is finding them. We tried various methods of attracting potential Dormants so all of my clan members could have the lifelong mates they long for, but it seems that all our efforts are futile, and we have to trust the Fates to deliver them to us."

Ell-rom shook his head. "Why couldn't your clan members find their mates inside the clan? Are the numbers too small? And who and what are the Fates?"

"Ah." Annani leaned back in her chair and took her coffee cup with her. "Those are two very important questions, and I am impressed by how sharp your brain is that you immediately focused on them."

Ell-rom felt like preening but composed himself and dipped his head instead. "Thank you."

"To answer your first question, you need to understand how I formed the clan. After my beloved Khiann was murdered, I fled the assembly, fearing Mortdh would come after me next. In the frozen lands of the far north, I mourned my Khiann for many years. I did not know that all the other gods had perished as well until rumors started filtering even to that remote region. Thankfully, I had my loyal Odus to help me, so I did not starve or lack shelter." She turned to look at the servant, who smiled and bowed nearly in half to her.

He did not look immortal, but Ell-rom instinctively knew that the male was not human. He was something else, but what? Something tickled the back of Ell-rom's mind, a feeling of unease, but he could not fathom why. The male seemed harmless.

"Are the Odus a different race of people?" he asked.

50

ANNANI

Annani smiled. "Yes. This is a very good way to describe them. They were created, not born, so some think they are not people, but I disagree. They are just a different kind."

Ell-rom frowned. "What do you mean by created, not born?"

"The Odus were built with both mechanical and biological components and provided with an artificial intelligence. But since they can learn over time, and they interact with people, they mimic like children do, and they learn about emotions." She turned to Okidu and motioned for him to come closer.

When he did, she took his hand in hers. "Okidu and his brothers were sent to Earth when their kind was outlawed on Anumati. They are the last seven of their kind, and they were given to me by my Khiann as an engagement present. I am sure he did not foresee what an enormous part they would play in my life, but I am not sure I would have survived without them." She gave Okidu's hand a light squeeze before letting go of it.

Jasmine looked shell-shocked, but she did not say anything. Instead, she gaped at Okidu as if she was seeing him for the first time.

"When my children were born," Annani continued. "I entrusted each baby to the care of one of the Odus. Four are currently accompanying my four surviving children, and three are still with me. Okidu is Kian's companion."

Ell-rom leaned forward. "Why were the Odus outlawed on Anumati?"

Annani smiled sadly. "They were originally built to be house servants, but when the riots started, the Eternal King ordered their reprogramming. They were turned into soldiers and used to fight the Kra-ell and the rebel gods. The king must have realized that they posed a danger to his rule, so he came out with a propaganda piece, claiming that he was eliminating them in the name of the peace agreement with the Kra-ell queen."

Ell-rom shook his head. "I am afraid that all of this political maneuvering is difficult for me to understand."

Annani sincerely doubted that her brother struggled to understand anything she told him. He seemed exceedingly bright, but he was also soft of heart, and he did not like to talk about upsetting subjects. That was why he had not asked how the Odus were eliminated. He must have guessed the sad truth.

"You have plenty of time to learn about the intricacies of politics, and especially the complicated Anumatian society. The truth is that what I know I have learned from Jade and Aru. Until we saved Jade from Igor, we did not know much about the Kra-ell or the gods, and we did not know anything about their planet. The rebel gods never shared information about their past with their offspring, the gods who were born on Earth. We did not know that our parents were rebels and exiles." Annani paused to take another sip from her coffee.

"Where did you think they came from?" Ell-rom asked.

She shrugged. "A different place in the universe was one of the possibilities I entertained. Another one was that they were the lone survivors of an ancient Earth civilization that was wiped out by some cataclysm. Before meeting my Khiann, I was more inclined to believe the second hypothesis. The marvelous devices the gods possessed, like flying aircraft and tablets that stored information, were few and falling apart without the ability to fix anything because there were no spare parts. We also did not have the materials and machines required to make them, so I reasoned that the knowledge had been lost.

Later, when I started seeing Khiann, he told me what his father had told him, which was a little bit more than what I knew, but it still did not make sense to me that people who belonged to an advanced civilization across the stars had lost contact with their home world and could not get replacement parts for their equipment. That was why I had a hard time accepting the alien origins hypothesis."

Next to her, Kian chuckled. "I've always wondered whether you really did not know where the gods came from or were hiding it from us to enhance your allure or something of that nature. Now I finally realize that you were conflicted on the subject, and that is why you never talked about it."

"That was part of the reason," Annani said. "The other part was what you have suspected all along. Shrouding my origins in mystery worked better than admitting how little I knew." She turned to Ell-rom. "We keep veering off the subject because there is so much to talk about, but let us get back to how I created my clan and why most of my clan members cannot mate amongst themselves."

Annani adjusted the folds of her gown. "After I found out that my people were gone, I spent several more years in mourning, but then I realized that I was the only one left to carry on their legacy. I could not do that alone, so I decided to have children. I took many human lovers, but it took a long time until I became pregnant with my first daughter, Alena. After her I had Kian, Lilen, Sari, and Amanda. They alone were not enough, but Alena was a miracle of fertility for a goddess, and through her, most of the clan came to be. Her daughters took human lovers and had more children, and their daughters continued to do the same, and so on. But since everyone was my descendant, they were forbidden to each other even when generations removed. I did not know why the taboo existed, but if the gods forbade unions between matrilineal descendants, I knew that they must have had good reasons for that."

"We spent centuries searching for Dormants," Kian said. "Relationships with humans could only be fleeting, and we all longed for life-long companions."

"How did you end up finding them?" Jasmine asked.

"The Fates," Annani said. "They are trickling them our way. The first one was Syssi, Kian's mate. She came to work for Amanda, and Amanda immediately realized that there was something very special about her and tried to convince Kian to woo her."

The glow in Ell-rom's eyes flared bright. "Are we going to hear how you met your lovely mate and fell in love?"

Annani's heart swelled with joy. Her brother was a romantic like she was.

Kian sighed dramatically, but his lips quirked up in a smile. "I didn't want to hear about it, and flat out refused to meet her, but when the Fates decide to match you with your one and only, they don't give up. The net they weave is so intricate it sometimes takes many different threads to intersect to bring truelove mates together."

51

JASMINE

Jasmine listened with great interest to Kian's tale of falling in love with Syssi. The poor guy had had some scary moments when Syssi had been transitioning, and then his sister had gotten kidnapped by a Doomer. That story had a happy ending, though. Amanda and Dalhu had turned out to be truelove mates and were now the proud parents of a baby girl.

It was so obvious that Kian still loved his wife passionately and she was his everything. Having a baby girl together had only made their marriage better.

Jasmine wanted what they had and what Aru and Gabi, Ella and Julian, Margo and Negal, and Frankie and Dagor had. She had never before seen people so fully committed to each other and who truly loved being together.

When Ell-rom reached for her hand under the table and gave it a light squeeze, Jasmine wondered if similar thoughts had been going through his head even though all he had been exposed to was Kian's sweet love story. He hadn't seen the other couples and how they interacted with each other, but he would, starting tomorrow.

"That was a lovely tale," Ell-rom said. "But I am a little worried about my ability to induce Jasmine's transition. I am only half god, and I don't know what my Kra-ell half will do. Did the Kra-ell also take human partners?"

The goddess settled back in her chair, her fingers laced around her coffee cup. "The Kra-ell situation is similar, but not identical. They too have hybrid children with humans, and these offspring often exhibit strong Kra-ell characteristics. When these hybrids have children with humans, however, their offspring are born human. It is the same pattern as with gods and humans."

Jasmine had heard the explanation about how gods came to have immortal children and how the second generation was born human, but she knew next to nothing about the Kra-ell.

"There was one notable case of a human female whose mother was a hybrid Kra-ell," Annani continued. "Her transition was induced by an immortal, but she did not turn immortal. She developed the same characteristics of a Kra-ell and human hybrid, and we assume that she will be long-lived like them. That is not good enough for her immortal mate, though. I hope our science will one day solve the problem of turning humans immortal."

Ell-rom leaned toward his sister. "Is it significant that she was induced by an immortal male and not a Kra-ell hybrid?"

The goddess smiled. "You are so astute, brother of mine. A Kra-ell male's venom isn't potent enough to induce transition. Only the venom of an immortal or a god can do that."

Ell-rom's face fell. "What if my venom takes after my Kra-ell half rather than my godly half?"

Jasmine felt a flutter of anxiety in her stomach. She hadn't considered this possibility, and now that it had been brought up, she was worried. The thought of having to approach Edgar for help to facilitate her transition was uncomfortable, to say the least.

Before Ell-rom had entered her life, she would have done that without much hesitation. But now? The idea of being with anyone other than her prince was intolerable.

Annani placed a reassuring hand on Ell-rom's arm. "The Fates would not have brought you and Jasmine together if there was any chance you lacked what was necessary to induce her transition."

"The Fates?" Ell-rom asked. "You've mentioned them before. What exactly are they?"

Annani's eyes lit up at the question. "Gods and immortals loosely believe in the three Fates who shape destinies. It is not a religion per se, and some believe more strongly than others. Supposedly, the Fates are in charge of truelove matchmaking and personal development, but sometimes they meddle in more than just that."

Jasmine nodded, recognizing the concept. She'd heard Edgar and the other gods invoke the Fates often enough, but this was the first time she'd heard a proper explanation.

"The Fates must answer to someone, though, right?" she said. "Since the scope of their duties and what they are in charge of is limited, they cannot be the creators of the universe or the ultimate arbiters of all the different worlds."

Annani turned to her with an encouraging smile. "What do you believe in, Jasmine?"

"The Goddess, the Mother of All Life." Jasmine pushed a strand of hair behind her ear. "I mean, it's just another spin on the belief in an omnipotent creator. Most people think of the creator in masculine terms, but Wiccans worship the Goddess, and I'm more comfortable with that image than the guy with the long beard."

Ell-rom regarded her with a puzzled expression. "What guy with a long beard?"

She waved a dismissive hand. "That's how many people imagine God."

"Interesting." Ell-rom frowned. "I wonder how that started. Does the Eternal King have a long beard?"

Annani laughed. "I do not think so, but we can ask Aru or Jade later."

"It was just a thought." He turned to Jasmine. "I am glad that we share a belief in the same deity. I don't know what that belief entails, but you can tell me. A shared belief should be a good foundation for a relationship." He seemed embarrassed for a moment. "I don't know where that came from. Maybe my priestly training is starting to come back to me."

Annani let out a laugh, the sound so rich and melodious that it raised goosebumps on Jasmine's arms. "Many different things contribute to a good relationship." Her eyes twinkled with amusement. "Respect, patience, the ability to compromise, and great sex."

Jasmine couldn't help but laugh along. "I couldn't agree more, Clan Mother."

She glanced at Ell-rom, expecting to see him join in their mirth, but instead she noticed a nervous expression flitting across his face, and she suspected the reason for that was fear. Ell-rom was a novice, and he was afraid of not meeting her expectations, which was natural.

Wanting to change the subject and ease his embarrassment, Jasmine turned back to the Clan Mother.

"You mentioned that the Fates are responsible for truelove matchmaking. How does that work exactly? Do they just push people together?"

Annani looked pleased by the question. "The Fates weave intricate webs of circumstances and coincidences. Sometimes, it takes years for their plans to come to fruition. They might influence a person's career choice or prompt them to move to a new city, all to set up the perfect meeting between trueloves."

52

ELL-ROM

Ell-rom didn't know whether his sister was stating facts or being sentimental. She seemed to believe that coincidences were actually not coincidences at all but the Fates working in roundabout ways to bring mates together.

"How can you be sure it's the Fates and not just random chance?" he asked, looking at Kian.

The male seemed far too cynical and jaded to believe in magical beings.

"That is an excellent question." Kian leaned forward. "The truth is, we can't be certain. For a long time, I scoffed at the idea of the Fates arranging matches, but when I witnessed time and again highly improbable coincidences, I became a believer."

Jasmine nodded. "Take us, for instance. The events that put me on the path to finding you were so convoluted that believing they happened at random is even more far-fetched than believing in divine intervention. On the other hand, though, what about free will? If the Fates are manipulating everything, does that mean we don't have a choice?"

Annani shook her head. "The Fates may set the stage, but we still make our own decisions. They might bring two people together, but it is up to those individuals to choose to be together." She smirked. "Although truelove mates do not have any choice in the matter. In a way, it is like Perfect Match, but instead of an algorithm finding the best possible match for you, it is the Fates who do the matching, and since their database is much larger than the one on Perfect Match's servers, they can do a better job."

Everyone around the table was nodding their heads, but Ell-rom was stumped. Something must have been lost in translation because what Annani had said made no sense.

"Forgive me, sister, but the translation device must have gotten it wrong. I did not understand what you just said."

"Speaking of translation devices." Kian reached into his pocket. "I have earpieces for you so you can communicate with people who don't have the pendant." He leaned across the table and put them in Ell-rom's hand. "They are already configured to translate from our language to yours, and Jasmine can show you how to operate them."

"I should do so now and make everyone's life easier."

They all had translation earpieces, and because he didn't, they used teardrop devices to broadcast what they said in Kra-ell. Since the teardrops also canceled the sound of what they said in their own language, the others had to hear it through their translation earpieces as it was translated from Kra-ell back to their own language. He could only imagine what a mess the two-way translation made of the original words.

"It's very simple." Jasmine took one of the devices and put it in his ear. "Give me your finger." When he did, she tapped the device with it and then tapped her teardrop. "I deactivated my translator. What do you hear?"

"I hear you speaking directly in one ear and the translation in the other." He smiled at her. "I like your real voice better."

"I'm glad, but you should put the other one in as well. Listening to both languages at the same time will give you a headache."

Reluctantly, he put the second device in his other ear. This time, he did not need to tap it to activate the translation feature. It was already doing so. Evidently, they both started working as soon as one was turned on.

"They are impervious to water," Kian said after deactivating his teardrop. "You can shower and swim with them, and since they mold to your ears, you can even sleep with them. I suggest you just don't take them off until you learn our language."

As the others also deactivated their teardrops, Annani explained that Perfect Match was the name of a service that found perfect matches for people, but only from the database of others who applied for the service and filled out the questionnaire. The Fates had no such limitations.

"Now I understand. It is an interesting concept to find one's mate with the help of artificial intelligence."

"It is much more than that. When they meet, they do not meet in person. They meet in a virtual world and go on an adventure together. Aru told me that Anumatians use virtual reality extensively and that every patrol ship is equipped with several virtual rooms. I do not know if the Kra-ell use it as well, though, and even if they do now, I do not think that they did seven thousand years ago."

"I have no concept of such functionality," Ell-rom said. "So, I believe that you are correct about that." He thought about his statement for a moment. "I wasn't surprised by the translation devices or by the medical equipment in the clinic. So, I must have had a concept of such things, at least subconsciously."

"That's an interesting topic." Kian tore another piece off his dessert. "I think we've covered how our clan was created and why we need to find Dormants. Do you have any other questions?" He put the piece in his mouth.

Ell-rom chuckled. "I have hundreds, but I don't want to keep you here all night."

The truth was that he was getting tired again, and thinking about how long the trek back to the clinic was, he wasn't sure he would make it.

"Well," Kian said, glancing at his watch, "This has taken longer than I expected, and I need to head back." He shifted his gaze to Ell-rom. "You should probably rest."

Ell-rom nodded. "I probably should." He looked at Annani. "When will I see you again?"

Leaning over, she reached for his hand. "Tomorrow, I have family obligations, but I will come on Saturday. Kian will coordinate the exact time with you. This will give you time to process what you have learned before we continue."

"I will miss you," Ell-rom blurted out. "I enjoy your company."

Smiling, Annani patted his hand. "And I enjoy yours, brother of mine." Her smile grew wider. "I do not tire of hearing myself say the word brother. It is such a delight."

Jasmine cleared her throat. "About the location of the next visit. Tomorrow, Ell-rom is moving in with me to my room in Kian's penthouse. So, we should probably meet there."

"Congratulations," Kian said. "That's one more marker in your journey to full recovery."

53

JASMINE

As they left Kian's office, Ell-rom's steps were slower, more deliberate. The long meeting had clearly taken its toll on him, and now that the adrenaline rush was over, exhaustion seemed to descend on him all at once.

Nevertheless, Jasmine was proud of him for lasting as long as he had, sitting up straight and keeping his head up. He was naturally dignified as if it was encoded in his DNA.

Heck, maybe it was. He was the Eternal King's grandson, the son of the unwanted heir to the throne. She wondered what happened to Ahn's mother, the king's official wife. She must have been devastated when her son died.

Oh, well. Misery apparently wasn't restricted to humans. Even the gods experienced it.

Ell-rom managed not to shuffle and stoop until the last stretch of the corridor leading to the clinic, but eventually, he gave up the fight and leaned heavily on the walker.

"They should provide scooters for people working here," Jasmine joked. "These corridors are endless."

Ell-rom smiled tiredly. "It's not difficult for the immortals, and I doubt they entertain many humans down here."

"You are probably right." She opened the clinic door for him. "I wonder how many humans have ever seen this place and lived to tell the tale."

Ell-rom turned a pair of horrified eyes on her. "Do they kill humans to preserve their secret?"

She laughed. "It's just another expression, Ell-rom. They can thrall humans to forget whatever they don't want them to remember. They don't need to kill anyone for that."

"That's good to know." He slumped against the walker. "I want to sit with Morelle for a little bit before I get into bed. Do you want to come with me?"

Jasmine hesitated, not sure whether he really wanted her there or was inviting her to join him because it was the polite thing to do.

There was only one way to find out, and that was to be upfront about it and ask. "Only if you want me to. If you want to be alone with her, that's fine with me."

"Of course, I want you there." He continued shuffling to the door and leaned over his walker to open it. "Maybe you could sing something for Morelle?" He smiled. "And for me. I want to test these new devices. Perhaps they are better at transmitting melody and translating poems."

He probably meant lyrics, but perhaps there was no word for that in Kra-ell. Maybe they called all songs poems.

"Let's do it." She followed him into the room.

As they sat on the two chairs Julian had thoughtfully left in the room, Jasmine thought of a song she should sing, and the first one that popped into her mind was 'The First Time Ever I Saw Your Face.'

As she began singing the first verse, Ell-rom looked at her with awe. "That's beautiful, and I can hear you singing perfectly. These devices must be much more sophisticated than the teardrops."

Jasmine's eyes widened as a realization hit her. "Oh! Why am I so dumb? If I could hear myself singing through the earpieces, then, of course, you could hear me too."

Ell-rom's expression shifted from wonder to concern. "Don't say that about yourself. You're incredibly smart, Jasmine."

"I'm not." She rolled her eyes. "But thanks for saying that."

"I mean it. You come up with observations and suggestions that no one else does. It's like your mind is not constricted by preconceived notions. You are a free thinker."

Touched by his words, Jasmine leaned in and placed a soft kiss on his cheek. "Thank you. That's very sweet of you."

"And very true," he added.

Clearing her throat, Jasmine resumed singing the song she had started, then continued with 'Can't Help Falling in Love,' her voice carrying in the quiet room. As she finished the last notes of that one, she transitioned smoothly into 'The Way You Look Tonight,' letting herself get lost in the romantic lyrics and well-known melody.

At some point, she noticed Julian leaning against the doorframe with his arms crossed over his chest and an appreciative smile on his face.

She finished the song and gave him a mock bow.

"That was beautiful," he said. "You should give concerts."

Jasmine felt her cheeks warm at the compliment. "Thank you, but I don't have any original pieces or even a style of my own," she admitted. "I'm just good at covers."

Julian shook his head, pushing off from the doorframe to enter the room. "You're selling yourself short," he insisted. "Once you get to the village, I'll personally introduce you to composers and poets who can write songs for you. Your talent deserves to be showcased."

Jasmine felt a flutter of excitement at the idea but also a twinge of nervousness. She'd never considered pursuing music seriously before. "That's very kind of you," she said. "I'll definitely think about it."

"Can you sing that first song again?" Ell-rom asked. "It was hauntingly beautiful."

"Of course."

She sang 'The First Time Ever I Saw Your Face' again, and as she finished, Ell-rom's eyes were glistening with unshed tears.

She put a hand on his arm. "Are you okay?"

He nodded. "Yes. I'm just a little emotional."

Jasmine had a feeling that he needed a moment or two alone with his sister and rose to her feet. "I need a cup of tea to soothe my throat. Would you like some, too?"

He nodded.

"I'll make it and bring it to your room." She patted his shoulder before leaving.

As she stepped out of the room, she heard Ell-rom begin to speak softly to his sister, his words too quiet for her to hear.

54

JASMINE

Out in the hallway, Jasmine pulled out her phone and typed out a text to Margo. *I just wanted to give you a heads-up. Ell-rom will be joining us at the penthouse tomorrow. Bridget is going to release him into my care, so he will be staying with me until further notice.*

Margo called back almost immediately. "We should throw him a party, but I don't know whether it should be a *Welcome Back to the Living* party or *Congratulations on getting Better*. Any preferences?"

Jasmine laughed. "I don't know. Both sound off. What do you have in mind, though? Lunch?"

"Yeah. It'll be a good excuse to get the guys to leave the equipment alone and come for lunch in the penthouse. We should make it a surprise for Ell-rom. So, don't tell him."

Jasmine bit her lip, considering the suggestion. While she appreciated Margo's enthusiasm, she wasn't sure that a surprise party was the best idea. "I'm not sure about that. Ell-rom might be overwhelmed. He's not used to being around a lot of people, and that was true even before he got on the settler ship. He and his sister lived in isolation."

"That's so sad," Margo said. "Well, it's up to you whether to surprise him or tell him ahead of time so he can be ready. Either way, I think a little gathering would be good for him. It might help him get used to being around people. Besides, we need to be introduced. Out of the whole team that went to Tibet, he only knows you, Julian, and Aru."

"Oh, right. If we are having a party, we should invite Julian and probably Edgar too."

"Are you sure?" Margo sounded like she thought that was a bad idea.

Jasmine leaned against the wall, mulling over the options. On the one hand, she wanted to make Ell-rom feel welcome and celebrated, but on the other, she didn't want to cause him any unnecessary stress or discomfort.

As she was considering, Julian walked by and noticing her pensive expression, raised an eyebrow. "Everything okay?"

Jasmine sighed. "Margo wants to throw a welcome

party for Ell-rom tomorrow when we bring him to the penthouse. I'm just not sure if it's a good idea."

Julian considered this for a moment. "It's a kind thought, but you're right to be cautious. Ell-rom is still easily overwhelmed and gets tired quickly."

Jasmine nodded. "That's what I was thinking. But he needs to meet the people he will be living with."

"Then just keep everything mellow and quiet."

"Will do, doc." She saluted him. "You and Ella are invited."

He shook his head. "I can't. My mother is taking the day off tomorrow, so I am on duty the entire day."

"That's a shame."

He smiled. "It will make the gathering smaller."

It also meant that she didn't need to invite Edgar. For now, she didn't want her former and current boyfriends to meet. Men had a tendency to start showing off and being obnoxious in situations like that, and Ell-rom wasn't in any shape to engage in male posturing.

When Julian continued on his way, she returned her attention to Margo. "Sorry about that. Did you hear Julian?"

"Of course, I did. We will keep it quiet and simple. I'll order delivery from the Golden Dragon, and we will use the dining room for a change."

She doubted Ell-rom could eat any of the Golden Dragon's heavy dishes. She would probably need to bring him lunch from the vegan delivery service that Bridget had found.

"Great idea, but Ell-rom is on a restricted diet, so I'll bring his lunch from the clinic."

"Poor guy," Margo said. "So, I guess I will see you both tomorrow. Around noon?"

"More or less. I will call you tomorrow so we can coordinate. By the way, any news about the Lynda saga?"

Margo sighed. "She hasn't talked with her ex since the last time we spoke, so maybe it's over between them."

"Given everything you told me about her and what the cards foretold, I doubt it."

"I know. It's just that I don't want to step into that hornet's nest and unleash all this ugliness. Rob will be crushed, and even though it would be better for him in the long run, I'm still cringing when I think about it."

"I get it. Let me know if there is anything I can do."

"Thank you, but there isn't."

"If you think of something, don't hesitate to ask, just don't ask for a hex. I don't do those."

Margo laughed. "I would never wish anything bad to happen to Lynda. I wish her all the happiness in the world, just with someone who isn't my brother."

"You are a very good person, Margo. Better than me, for sure. Thank you for organizing a nice welcome for Ell-rom."

"My pleasure. Good night, Jasmine." She ended the call before Jasmine had a chance to say good night back.

As she turned back toward Morelle's room, Jasmine could still hear Ell-rom's soft voice, now interspersed with long pauses, and she wondered what he was saying to his sister. He couldn't talk about their shared past because he didn't remember it, so all he could tell her was what he had recently learned. There was a lot of it, and telling his sister was probably helping him absorb all that information and internalize it.

Jasmine leaned against the wall, content to wait as long as Ell-rom needed, when she remembered that she had promised to make tea and bring it to his room.

Rushing out, she headed to the kitchen.

As she waited for the water to boil, Jasmine hummed the melodies of the love songs she had sung earlier. She loved singing, and Julian's offer to introduce her to composers and lyricists was intriguing.

Maybe this new chapter in her life would bring unexpected opportunities in more ways than one.

55

ELL-ROM

Ell-rom sat by Morelle's bedside, his eyes fixed on her still form, her hand clasped in his. Her body was slowly becoming restored, and he had to believe her mind was just taking longer and would eventually do the same.

The chief medic had assured him Morelle would recover. The brain scans showed low-frequency waves interspersed with moments of higher-frequency activity, which Bridget claimed hinted at preserved brain function.

Ell-rom had no idea what the medic was talking about except the last part about brain function.

Bridget also said that the scans she'd done on Morelle's brain revealed activity in various regions, with most functional connectivity still intact. He understood that and the part about Morelle's pupils responding to stimuli. Her heart rate and respiratory patterns were stable, reflecting her body's resilience.

Those were all positive indicators, and Ell-rom took comfort in these assurances, holding on to hope that his sister would soon awaken, but he still couldn't shake the worry gnawing at his insides.

"Come on, Morelle. You need to wake up."

As the room remained silent, Ell-rom sighed, and his shoulders sagged. For days, he'd been hearing the same reassurances that Morelle was improving and that her body was healing, but without seeing her eyes open and hearing her speak coherently, it was becoming harder to believe.

With a grunt of effort, Ell-rom pushed himself to his feet, using the bed for support. His stiff body protested the movement, but he didn't care. He'd been pushing himself hard, and he wasn't about to quit. He was tired of being restricted in so many ways.

He leaned over and placed a gentle kiss on Morelle's forehead. Her skin felt cool beneath his lips, but he reminded himself that it was likely due to the room's air conditioning. Bridget had repeatedly assured him that all of Morelle's vitals were stable and improving.

"I'll be back tomorrow morning," he promised. "Please, try to wake up for me."

If only he could glimpse the future and know for sure that his sister would be returning to him.

Maybe he could. Hadn't Jasmine promised him to do a reading on Morelle?

She had promised to read Morelle's future using the tarot cards that had helped her find him. Somehow, they had never gotten around to it, but tonight, he would ask her to do that.

He was tired, but because of how worried he was, he wouldn't be able to fall asleep.

Entering his room, Ell-rom was surprised to find it empty. He had half-expected Jasmine to be there, waiting for him with the tea she had gone to make.

Maybe she had met one of her friends in the kitchen or called someone on the phone. She had a life that she had put on hold for him, and he could not expect her to be there for him every second of the day.

Ell-rom had no doubt that she would be back, though. Those fears were finally gone.

Eyeing the distance from where he stood to the bathroom, he contemplated leaving the walker by the door and attempting to make it across without relying on the thing, but in the end, common sense prevailed, and he decided not to take chances.

If he fell and broke something, his recovery would take even longer. He needed to build muscle and get stronger.

Once in the bathroom, he carefully removed the nice clothes he'd worn for the meeting and hung them neatly in the closet.

Next, he reached for the sleep clothes Jasmine had bought for him. The soft fabric felt soothing against his skin, and as he pulled on the shirt, a wave of emotion washed over him. It was such a simple thing, just some comfortable sleepwear, and yet it meant so much to him because it represented Jasmine's thoughtfulness, her kindness, and the way she took care of him.

After brushing his teeth, Ell-rom stepped out of the bathroom, and as he made his way to the bed, the door opened, and Jasmine entered, balancing a tray with two steaming cups of tea and some sort of baked dessert.

"Sorry it took so long," she said, setting the tray down on the small table by the window. "I got caught up talking with Margo."

Ell-rom settled into one of the chairs and reached for one of the cups, cradling it in his hands. "How is Margo doing?"

Jasmine's smile seemed a touch forced as she replied, "She's fine. Just busy with training for her new job."

Ell-rom sensed there was something she wasn't telling him, but he pushed the thought aside. He hadn't earned the right to be privy to all her secrets yet.

One day, he would, though.

Instead, he focused on the matter that had been weighing on his mind. "Do you remember when you promised to do a tarot reading for Morelle? I was wondering if we could do that tonight."

Jasmine's eyes widened. "I forgot about that. I'll get right to it." She pushed to her feet and pulled out the bag that she was hiding under his bed.

"You know that there is plenty of room in the closet in the bathroom, right? And everyone knows that you are staying with me all night. You don't need to keep your things under my bed."

Pulling out a blue fabric pouch, she shoved the bag back under the bed and rose to her feet. "It doesn't matter anymore. We are both moving out of here tomorrow."

He'd forgotten about that. His memory was still not functioning well.

"True. I hope that's okay with the other occupants of the apartment."

"The two apartments." Jasmine moved the tray to the floor to make room for her cards. "We took over what used to be Kian and his sister's personal lodgings. There are three bedrooms in each and an additional room that can serve as an office or a studio." She pulled a stack of cards out of the pouch. "I can't wait for you to get out of here and finally see the blue sky, the sun, the clouds, the city. And when you feel better, I'll take you out on a tour." Her eyes widened with happiness. "I'll take you to the beach. I bet you and Morelle have never seen an ocean."

"Unless the temple was right on the edge of one, probably not."

Nodding, she put the stack of cards on the small table. "I hope I have enough room to do a spread. If not, we will have to do it on the floor."

"How does this work exactly?" he asked, his eyes fixed on Jasmine's hands as she shuffled the cards.

Her movements slowed as she considered her response. "Tarot is just a tool for channeling what's inside of me. I must have some foresight, but it's a weak ability, and I need something to help me focus it."

Ell-rom nodded, trying to wrap his head around the concept. "So, it's not like Syssi's visions. From what you told me, she doesn't need any tools to bring them about, and they play out like scenes from real life."

"Yeah. Her talent is in a different sphere than mine. She gets her visions from the universe or the Fates or some other external force. I just interpret what I see in the tarot. Also, different people can read different things from the same spread."

Jasmine resumed her vigorous shuffling of the cards. "Each card has its own meaning, but the interpretation can change depending on its position in the spread and how it relates to the other cards. It's not just a talent but also a skill. It's important to remember that whatever I glean is open to interpretation and therefore shouldn't be taken verbatim."

Ell-rom's heart sank. The cards were not a portal into the future, and they might not tell him whether Morelle would wake up with her mind intact. Still, they would show what Jasmine's intuition was telling her, and she had a proven track record of being right.

56

JASMINE

Jasmine set the stack of cards on the table. "Put your hand over the stack, close your eyes, and think about your question."

Ell-rom did as she instructed and then opened his eyes. "Do you want me to tell you what I asked for?"

She shook her head. "I don't want it to influence the reading. I already know that it's about Morelle, but I want to see what the cards say before I know the specifics."

As Jasmine began to lay out the cards in a pattern on the table, Ell-rom leaned forward, his curious eyes darting from card to card as he tried to glean meaning from the images.

"This spread is called the Celtic Cross," she said. "It's good for getting a comprehensive view of a situation before diving deeper into specifics."

Ell-rom nodded, although at this point, this information must all be meaningless to him.

Jasmine's hands moved with practiced ease as she laid out the spread, the familiar weight of the cards in her hands bringing a sense of calm even as she felt Ell-rom's anxious gaze upon her.

She turned over the first card. "This card is called the Six of Wands," she said. "It represents the present situation, and it symbolizes victory and recognition. It suggests that Morelle is overcoming obstacles, even if we can't see it yet."

Ell-rom leaned forward, his eyes fixed on the card. "That's good, right?"

Jasmine nodded, offering him a reassuring smile before turning over the next card. "The Empress. This card crosses the first, showing influences affecting the situation. The Empress represents abundance, fertility, and nurturing. It could mean that Morelle is being well cared for, her body healing and preparing for what's to come."

As she continued through the spread, each card seemed to build upon the last. The Queen of Wands, in the position of the recent past, spoke of confidence and charisma, but the Emperor, in the position of potential outcome, made Jasmine pause.

"The Emperor represents authority, structure, and leadership. In this position, it could suggest that

Morelle is destined for a position of great responsibility."

Ell-rom's brow furrowed. "Do the cards elaborate on what kind of responsibility?"

Jasmine hesitated, then decided to voice the interpretation forming in her mind. "Combined with the other cards, especially the Six of Wands and the Queen of Wands, it could indicate that Morelle will be a queen. It could also mean that she should have been a queen because I don't see how she can become one on Earth. It also indicates that she will thrive, which is the most important for us at this time because it gives us hope that she will have all her faculties when she wakes up, or soon after." Jasmine lifted her eyes to Ell-rom's and smiled. "I know that is your biggest concern."

He nodded. "It echoes what my mother told me and my sister. She said that the seer foretold our future and that our destiny awaited across the stars. The seer also said that we would thrive and be safe."

Jasmine reached out, squeezing his hand gently. "That's awesome. The cards have just confirmed what the seer saw seven thousand years ago." She turned over the final cards, each one seeming to further confirm her interpretation. "The Star in the hopes and fears position speaks of hope and renewal. The World as the final outcome suggests completion and harmony." She smiled at Ell-rom. "The cards are very positive. They indicate that Morelle will not only recover but thrive. She'll be safe and achieve great things."

"That's the one part that is confusing to me. The seer didn't say anything about Morelle becoming a queen."

Jasmine shrugged. "Maybe you only remember a fragment of the prophecy. Perhaps there was more."

"It's possible." He leaned back in the chair and closed his eyes. "I feel such great relief but also anxiety. The queen part worries me."

She collected her cards and started shuffling them again. "What was your question?"

He opened his eyes. "I asked what Morelle's future was."

"That's what I thought. Queen can mean more than a monarch. It could be that she will find a mate who will treat her like a queen, or that she will start some online business and call herself the queen of something. The cards shouldn't be taken too literally."

He nodded. "Perhaps we need to do another reading and ask that specific question."

Jasmine put her cards inside their pouch. "Not today. You look like you are going to fall over." She walked over to the bed, crouched next to it, and pulled out the bag to put the cards back inside.

When she got up, Ell-rom was already asleep on the chair, his breathing deep and slow.

She chuckled. "Come on, big guy. Let me help you get in bed." She wrapped an arm around him and pulled him to her. "The good news is that you are getting heavy, and the bad news is that you are getting heavy. I can't hold you up for long. You need to help me."

He immediately awoke and straightened up, taking the load off her arm. "I'm sorry." He took a stumbling step toward the bed and climbed in with lethargic limbs.

"Come lay beside me." He held the blanket up.

"I need to change into my comfy clothes."

"I will be asleep by the time you get here. Can you do it later?"

"Sure." She turned off the lights using the remote, toed off her shoes, climbed in, and cuddled close to Ell-rom. "I can't refuse an invitation like that."

"I forgot to thank you for this sleep clothing. It is very comfortable and soothing."

"You're welcome." She kissed the underside of his jaw. "Would you like me to sing you to sleep? It will help you relax."

A small smile tugged at Ell-rom's lips. "Actually, I'd rather you kissed me to sleep."

Jasmine laughed softly. "I can do both."

She wrapped her palm around the back of his neck and then glanced at the security camera on the wall behind him. Ell-rom was lying on his side with his back to the room's camera, and the darkness provided a false sense of privacy, but Jasmine didn't mind if anyone saw what they were doing. If anyone wanted to watch her kissing her prince, they were welcome to do so.

She leaned into him and pressed a soft kiss to his lips. Ell-rom responded eagerly, his arm wrapping around her waist to pull her closer.

What started as a gentle good night kiss quickly deepened, becoming more passionate, and as Ell-rom's eyes began to glow, casting a soft light in the darkness, Jasmine felt a thrill run through her.

When his fangs started elongating, a visible sign of his arousal, that thrill turned into a throb.

Regrettably, her exhibitionist tendencies did not run deep enough. She was fine with being seen kissing Ell-rom, but not much more than that.

Sighing, she pulled back slightly. "Save this for tomorrow, big guy, for when we'll have a real bed and real privacy."

"Why are you calling me big guy?" Ell-rom murmured. "Is it another term of endearment?"

She chuckled softly. "It is in this context." She planted another quick kiss on his lips. "You didn't like it when I called you lover boy."

Ell-rom groaned quietly. "I don't mind it now. I just can't seem to get enough of you."

Jasmine felt her heart swell at his words. "I feel the same way, but we need to save it for tomorrow."

As she began to hum softly, a lullaby she remembered from one of the plays she'd appeared in, Ell-rom's breathing evened out, and sleep claimed him. She continued humming while thinking about what the cards had revealed.

They had suggested a grand destiny for Morelle, but what did that mean for Ell-rom?

57

KIAN

Kian leaned back in his chair, his fingers steepled under his chin as he listened to Onegus's report.

"The thefts have stopped," the chief said. "The sabotage as well. It seems our increased surveillance has scared off the culprits."

Kian shifted his gaze to Jade. "Your opinion?"

"They're just biding their time," she said. "The moment we lower our guard, they'll be back at it, probably in some new form we haven't anticipated."

"Did your interrogation of Borga and her group yield any clues?"

Jade shook her head. "They deny any knowledge of the incidents. I used my modest compulsion power to force them to tell me the truth, but my ability was limited. Perhaps someone more powerful should interrogate them."

Onegus cleared his throat, looking uncomfortable, which wasn't like him. "Did you speak with Drova?"

Peter had reported that Kagra suspected Jade's daughter and her friends of being involved in the so-called pranks, and Kian could just imagine how Jade had taken it.

Jade's posture stiffened. "I did, and she also denies having anything to do with it."

Kian felt a surge of frustration. He could deal with enemies from without, but enemies from within were a different story. He hated policing his own people, and even more so, he hated investigating them for committing crimes.

"We need answers, and we need them now. I'm tired of tolerating saboteurs in our village."

Onegus shifted in his seat. "What do you suggest we do? Question everyone who lives here?"

"That's precisely what I'm going to do. I asked Toven to come over, and I'm going to ask him to help in the investigation. He can question each resident of the village and use his abilities to force them to tell the truth. We'll start with the Kra-ell and then move on to clan members."

"What about the humans?" Onegus asked.

"You can assign them to any of the guardians. Arwel, with his empathic abilities, would probably be the best choice. He should also assist Toven when he's compelling the Kra-ell and immortals to answer him truthfully."

"That will take forever," Jade said.

"Not necessarily." Kian leaned back in his chair. "He will ask each person two simple questions." He lifted one finger. "Did you take anything that didn't belong to you from the mailroom or anywhere else in the village?" He lifted a second finger. "Did you deliberately cause malfunctions of our security shutters, garbage incinerators, or any other equipment?"

Jade nodded. "That's good. First, find the ones who did it and then find out why."

"Precisely," Kian said.

Onegus shifted his gaze to Kian. "Have you spoken with Toven about this?"

"He's on his way here now," Kian said. "I have no doubt he'll offer his help."

Jade leaned forward. "Do you need me to stay for the meeting with Toven?"

Kian shook his head. "No, you and Onegus can go."

A short while after the two had left, a knock on the door announced Toven's arrival, and Kian rose to his feet to greet him.

"Good morning, Toven. Thank you for coming."

"You sounded like you needed me urgently. What's going on?"

Kian felt a twinge of guilt for causing the god to be unnecessarily alarmed. "We are not under attack, and for now, the situation is under control, but I need your help to prevent it from escalating." He walked to his desk and opened the drawer where he kept his cigars and cigarillos. "How about we take this to the roof? I could use a smoke, and it's a nice day out there for now. Later, it will get too hot to venture out there."

Toven shrugged. "I'm not much of a smoker, but the last cigar I had was on the cruise, so why not."

After climbing the one flight of stairs, Kian opened the door to his rooftop oasis. A large umbrella provided shade, and two comfortable lounge chairs flanked a small table.

"Please, take a seat." Kian motioned to one of the lounges and sat on the other one.

"Nice setup you have here," Toven commented, looking around. "Do you often entertain up here?"

Kian opened the cigar box and offered the selection to Toven, and then picked one as well. Once Toven had lit his, Kian shook his head as he lit his favorite Opus X. "Usually, it's just me, and occasionally I bring a guest over, but I'm trying to cut down on the smoking. Allegra makes a face when she smells it on my clothes, so I have to shower and change before I can play with her. That kind of puts a damper on the fun."

Toven chuckled. "Ah, the sacrifices we make for our children." A shadow passed over his eyes. "I didn't know I had children, so obviously I wasn't involved in raising them. I hope Mia and I will have a child someday, and I will experience being a father."

"It's the best thing in the world," Kian said. "Challenging, terrifying at times, but absolutely worth it. Watching Allegra grow, getting to know her as a person is a joy and a privilege. I hope Syssi and I will be blessed with more children, but I don't want to be greedy and anger the Fates, so I leave the decision up to them."

Toven tilted his head. "So, no more fertility potions for you?"

"Not unless my wife demands it." He frowned. "Are you and Mia taking them?"

"Not yet. Mia is eager to have children now that she is all healed, but I want to show her the world first. We have eternity ahead of us. We can afford to take a couple of years just to enjoy each other."

"I agree." Kian paused as he savored another flavorsome mouthful of the blue smoke. "Syssi and I were married for a while before we were blessed with Allegra, and I think that it was good for our marriage."

After they'd spent some time in quiet companionship, enjoying their smokes, Toven put his cigar down. "So, what's the story? What's got your panties in a wad?"

Kian laughed. "That's such an old phrase that humans would say it dates you. The joke would be on them, though, as it really doesn't."

The god smiled. "All the more reason to use it."

"Yeah, you are right. Anyway, I don't know if you've heard, but we've had a wave of petty thefts and sabotage in the village." He continued to tell Toven about the suspects that they had investigated so far and the lack of results they had gotten.

Toven's eyes narrowed. "What exactly are you expecting me to do?"

"I want to question everyone in the village, and I need you to compel them to tell the truth. We'll start with the Kra-ell, and if the culprit is not one of them, we will move on to clan members."

Toven was quiet for a long moment, his cigar forgotten. "I'm not going to win any popularity contests after something like that. I would rather not do it."

"I know, and believe me, I wouldn't ask if I saw any other way. But this needs to end."

Toven sighed, rubbing a hand over his face. "I owe you, so I won't say no, but I want it on record that I'm not happy about it."

"If you have a better idea of how to deal with this, I'm all ears."

Toven shook his head. "I wish I did. The only thing that comes to mind is assembling everyone in the big assembly hall, giving them a speech about unity, solidarity, integration, etc., and offering them a way to voice their grievances without fear of retaliation. Maybe an anonymous letter or something like that."

"I can try it, or you can stand before the assembly and compel the saboteur to come forward. That will save us time asking each person separately."

"I can't," Toven said. "The purebloods are incredibly difficult to crack, and I need to do it one-on-one with them and involve Mia to enhance my power."

"Right. I forgot that. It's such a nasty business when it has to do with my own people, and I include every resident in the village under that umbrella. But I can't allow this to fester. Right now, it's a small cancerous growth that can be cut out easily without much damage to the body. But if we neglect to address it, the cancer will spread until there will be nothing left to save."

Toven took a puff of his cigar. "Many of the decisions a leader must make are unpleasant. But someone needs to make them." He smiled. "I'm just glad that this someone is you and not me. When do you want to start?"

"I'll have Onegus prepare a schedule, starting with the Kra-ell."

58

ELL-ROM

The dream enveloped Ell-rom, vivid and visceral. He and Morelle were in what looked like an office or a small reception room. The head priestess sat on a large pillow on the floor, with a low desk in front of her. He and Morelle stood in front of her, and all three were unveiled, so he could see his sister's face.

They were still children, twelve or even younger. Morelle's features were delicate, her blue eyes fierce but tinged with worry as they faced the stern head priestess. The older woman looked distinctly Kra-ell, and she was angry, her piercing gaze flashing dark red as it moved between them.

"Which one of you did it?" she demanded, her pointy tongue darting out of her mouth, the dark triangle at the tip indicating that she was of royal blood.

That was one more thing that he and Morelle were missing. Their tongues were pink and rounded. That alone was enough to betray their mixed heritage and get them killed. But it wasn't the only thing. They didn't look even remotely Kra-ell. In fact, they could easily pass for gods.

Morelle glanced at him, her eyebrow rising. He responded with a shake of his head and then addressed the priestess with as much formality as he could muster. "We do not know what you are referring to, Holy Mother."

"Which one of you killed Ro-buh?"

The priestess's response sent a chill through Ell-rom.

"I did not even know that he was dead," Morelle said, turning to Ell-rom with surprise. "Did you?"

"I did not," he said with much less conviction.

The head priestess narrowed her eyes at him. "Out with it, Ell-rom. What did you do?"

Shame and fear washed over him as he lowered his head. "I wished he was dead," he murmured. "Did the Mother of All Life grant my wish?"

The obnoxious guard wasn't supposed to enter the temple garden grounds where Ell-rom and Morelle spent most of their time, but he was allowed at the temple, and as acolytes, they had duties to perform there.

Ro-buh had liked to taunt Ell-rom mercilessly for being a priest, calling him a coward hiding behind the acolytes' veils and pretending to be a female.

When Morelle tried to intervene, Ro-buh had treated her with thinly suppressed disdain, asking what deformities she was hiding under her veil and threatening to yank it off.

They had complained to the head priestess, but she had dismissed their concerns, telling them to deal with the problem themselves. It was the Kra-ell way, but they weren't ordinary Kra-ell. They were being hidden in the temple for a reason, and he couldn't understand the head priestess's dismissive attitude. The guard could discover their secret and attack them with the intention to kill.

Both Ell-rom and Morelle carried daggers on them and were well-trained in their usage, but they were several years younger than Ro-buh.

Last night, as Ell-rom had been thinking about the best way to deal with Ro-buh, he had wished for the ability to kill the guard with a thought, but he hadn't expected his wish to come true. He hadn't known that he possessed such power.

To Ell-rom's surprise, the head priestess's anger melted away, replaced by a smile that sent shivers down his spine. "I was wondering when your powers would manifest," she said, her voice filled with pride and satisfaction. "Congratulations, Ell-rom. You are the first and only compeller who can kill with a mere thought and without using your voice."

Mortified, he looked at Morelle for support, but she wasn't looking at him. Her eyes were blazing blue light at the priestess. "You did that on purpose. You sent Ro-buh to taunt us to see what we could do. You sacrificed him."

The head priestess acknowledged the statement with a nod. "I did. The queen and I have realized that the two of you have been too sheltered to ever manifest your powers. You needed to be prodded, and Ro-buh was chosen to do that. He was never a real threat to you because I had him watched by loyal guards."

Ell-rom couldn't breathe.

He had killed a male with a mere thought, and the priestess had no problem with that. The male had been disposable. How could she be so callous?

How?

Ell-rom jerked awake, gasping for air and sweat beading on his forehead. He felt disoriented, the dream still clinging to the edges of his consciousness.

That dream couldn't have been a memory. It was impossible. He couldn't kill anyone with a thought. He couldn't even compel, so the very idea was preposterous. It might have been the wish of a vulnerable youth, and he must have been carrying the guilt of wishing for the guard's death in his subconscious.

It was just a nightmare.

It hadn't been real.

Beside him, Jasmine stirred, her eyes fluttering open. "Ell-rom?" she murmured. "What's wrong?"

He took a deep breath, forcing his features into what he hoped was a reassuring expression. "I had a dream."

She perked up. "A memory?"

"Yes. Maybe."

Jasmine sat up, fully alert now. "What was it about?"

Ell-rom hesitated, the full weight of the dream pressing down on him. He needed time to think about that dream to examine whether it could have been true. He wasn't ready to share the horrifying revelation about his supposed powers, but he could focus on the less disturbing aspects.

"I saw my sister's face. We were young, maybe twelve or so. And the head priestess was there. We were in her office, and she was reprimanding us for something. We all had our veils off, and I remember thinking that Morelle and I could pass for gods. The priestess looked very Kra-ell, and she had that dark triangle on her tongue that indicated she was of royal descent. Morelle and I have rounded pink tongues."

"What did Morelle look like?" Jasmine asked.

Ell-rom closed his eyes, picturing his sister's young face. "She was beautiful," he said, a small smile tugging at his lips. "Delicate features, big blue eyes very much like mine. She looked fierce, but she was a little scared of the priestess. I was scared of her, too. She was intimidating."

If the dream was true, the head priestess was also heartless and manipulative. How could she have sacrificed the life of the guard just to discover what Ell-rom and Morelle could do?

Could his sister kill with a mere thought, too?

Mother above, it was terrifying. He should never think negatively about anyone.

No, it just wasn't true. No one could do that. It had just been a nightmare.

Jasmine cupped his cheek. "You look shaken by the dream. What did you and your sister do that got you in trouble with the head priestess?"

Ell-rom felt a pang of guilt as he forced a smile and prepared to lie. "The dream ended before I found out."

Jasmine chuckled. "You were probably too scared to find out and woke yourself up. I sometimes do that when I have bad dreams. I wake up with a headache, but it's worth it to end the nightmare."

Ell-rom wished that his dream was just that.

A nightmare.

59

JASMINE

Ell-rom seemed pensive while they were getting ready for the day, his brow furrowed as if he was wrestling with some internal conflict. Her prince certainly didn't have a poker face, and when he tried to lie or hide something, it was written all over it.

There had been more to that dream than he had admitted to, but she didn't want to pressure him into talking about it if he wasn't ready.

"You said you've had nightmares," he suddenly said. "What were they about?"

The question caught her off guard, and she hesitated for a moment, memories of countless restless nights flashing through her mind. "They're mostly about my mother." Jasmine sat on one of the chairs flanking the bedside table that they had turned into their dining table. "She died when I was a little girl, and I don't know exactly what happened to her. I can barely remember her, and my father refuses to talk about her. He claims that the less I know, the better it is for me. So, I keep dreaming about her dying in hundreds of different ways, and sometimes it is me who is dying instead of her. I haven't had them lately, but I know they'll come back. They always do."

Ell-rom sat on the other chair and leaned forward to take her hand. "I feel so guilty for not asking you about your family before. I was projecting my situation onto you, so if I had no past because I couldn't remember it, you didn't have a past either. It was like our lives started in this room. I'm so sorry for being so self-absorbed."

"Don't apologize." She gave his hand a light squeeze. "It's not like I encouraged a conversation about my dysfunctional family. It's not something that I like to talk about."

"Good or bad, your family is still a part of you, and it shaped who you are as a person, even if their contribution was showing you how not to be like them."

She laughed. "You are very astute for a newborn."

Thankfully, he got the reference and smiled. "I was born with preexisting programming."

"That's not a joke. I think people are born with genetic memory. Like fear of snakes. Even those who have never seen a snake are afraid of them."

"You are diverting the conversation away from your family. Tell me about them."

"There's not much to tell," she said with a shrug. "I don't remember much about my mother, and after she died, my father married a woman with two sons who hated me and made my life miserable."

"Why?"

"They'd gotten into their stupid little heads that my father stole their mother from their dad, and they resented us both for it. They should have stayed with their father if they loved him so much."

"Did they?" he asked quietly. "Love their father?"

"They hardly saw him. Their mother got full custody of them, so the father had either washed his hands of them or was so bad that the court decided he wasn't a fit parent. I think it was the second one, and they inherited their bullishness from him. They were nasty punks who picked on a little girl who had lost her mother because she was an easy target. By giving it the spin of blaming my father for their parents' divorce, they avoided being punished for how they treated me, because my father and their mother felt sorry for them or guilty or whatever."

Ell-rom's eyes started glowing, and his fangs descended over his lip. "What is the Earthly custom for avenging a female mistreated by the males whose duty it was to protect her?"

Jasmine loved that question for multiple reasons.

The first one was that Ell-rom felt compelled to avenge the wrongs inflicted upon her, and the second was that he was asking what the proper way to do that was according to local custom. He didn't just assume that it was to inflict bodily harm, as it would have been in his old world, but his elongated fangs suggested that was precisely what he would like to do.

"Earth's population has many different cultures, and each has its own customs. In the West, most people will say that as long as my brothers didn't physically harm me, I should just let it go. And that was what I did. Now that we are adults, I only have to suffer their presence for a few hours once a year, and I forget about them the rest of the time."

He shook his head. "I don't understand people like that. Even though they are not your brothers by blood, it is their duty to protect you, not to torment you."

Jasmine shrugged. "Not all people are good, Ell-rom. But don't take it to heart. My life got much better after I left home. I loved acting, and I found a community of people who were like me. I met many good people in the productions I was in."

While she had enjoyed the camaraderie of her fellow actors, none of those relationships had been particularly deep or lasting. She had tried to keep in touch with people after the productions, but it had never lasted long. People drifted apart.

The friendships she had formed with Margo, Frankie, Gabi, and Ella felt more genuine and meaningful than any she'd had before. And then there were the gods, Julian, and yes, even Edgar, who had become an unexpected but welcome part of her life.

"Do you miss them?" Ell-rom asked. "Your friends from your acting days?"

"Not really," she admitted. "I like the new friends I've found here. They feel more real, somehow." Her eyes widened. "It's the affinity Amanda talked about. Immortals, gods, and Dormants feel a special affinity for one another. That's why these friendships feel more meaningful to me."

"I'm glad that you've found people you can connect with. I hope they will accept Morelle and me as well."

"They will." Jasmine patted his hand. "You are adorable."

He grimaced. "I am no such thing."

She rolled her eyes. "It's amazing how males are the same no matter what species they are. You want people to think of you as powerful and dangerous, and you are embarrassed to show your sensitive side."

"For all we know, I might be dangerous. I need to regain my memories to know who I really am."

Their conversation was interrupted by a knock on the door, announcing Gertrude carrying a tray laden with their breakfast.

"Good morning," she said cheerfully. "I hope you're both hungry because the service sent a lot of food." She put the tray down on the table. "Also, Dr. Julian wanted me to tell you that he wants Ell-rom to do another pool session before you two head up to the penthouse. He knows that after you go, there is no chance you'll be back today." Gertrude winked at Jasmine from behind Ell-rom's back.

Julian knew about the surprise welcome party, and that was why he didn't expect them to return for the rehab session later today, but Jasmine reconsidered her decision to keep it a surprise. Given Ell-rom's unsettling dream and his comments about it, perhaps he was still too emotionally fragile for surprises.

"I'm looking forward to it," Ell-rom said. "The hardest part for me is actually walking all the way to the pool and then back to the clinic. I will probably need to rest before I'm ready to move to the penthouse."

That meant that the lunch party would have to become a dinner party, and Jasmine needed to let Margo know right away.

As Gertrude and Ell-rom continued talking about the pool exercises Julian had planned, Jasmine pulled out her phone and sent a quick text to Margo. *Need to move the welcome party to dinner. Ell-rom has a pool rehab session this morning and will need to rest before coming up.*

Margo's reply came almost instantly. *No problem! It'll*

work even better. I'll order delivery from the Golden Dragon. Does Ell-rom have special preferences?

Jasmine typed back. *He's strictly vegan, but even though they have some vegan dishes at the Golden Dragon, they are too rich for him at this stage of his recovery. I'll get his custom-delivered dinner from the clinic.* She sent the text and then typed up another. *Thank you for being an awesome friend and organizing this for him.*

As she put the phone down, Jasmine made a mental note to speak with Bridget about arranging food deliveries to the penthouse for Ell-rom.

"Is everything alright?" he asked.

Jasmine smiled. "Everything's fine. I was texting Margo about arranging a little get-together at the penthouse. It's going to be us, the three gods, and their mates. Nothing too fancy, just a welcome dinner to help you feel at home in the new place."

To her relief, a smile spread across Ell-rom's face. "That sounds lovely. I'm eager to meet your friends and thank them in person for their contribution to rescuing Morelle and me."

60

ELL-ROM

Exhausted from the pool session, Ell-rom rested his body on the hospital bed, but his mind refused to slow down and go quiet. He was excited about moving to the penthouse, scared of not meeting Jasmine's expectations, and disturbed by the dream he'd woken from that morning.

It lurked at the edges of his consciousness, casting a dark shadow on all the good things he was looking forward to, like meeting Jasmine's friends, seeing what this world looked like topside, and spending his first night with Jasmine without a surveillance camera hanging overhead.

He tried to push the disturbing dream aside and focus on the positive aspects of the day ahead, but it clung stubbornly, refusing to be dismissed. The best he could do was to let it fester in a corner of his mind while he thought of other things.

He hoped that Jasmine's friends would like him. They seemed important to her, and Ell-rom was determined to make a good impression.

But how?

Ell-rom had no idea how to interact with people, especially in a large group. His encounters with Annani and Kian had gone well enough, but that was different. Annani, his half-sister, was his blood, and so was Kian, although it would take much more to gain the confidence of his nephew. Still, he was family, while Jasmine's friends were strangers to him, and they were under no obligation to befriend him.

Ell-rom sighed, turned on his side, and tucked his arm under the pillow.

Social interactions were the least of his worries. He was much more concerned about disappointing Jasmine.

Tonight would be their first night together in complete privacy, with a large, comfortable bed at their disposal. Jasmine would have some expectations, and he wanted nothing more than to fulfill them, but his knowledge of intimacy was limited to what Julian had told him, and he feared it wouldn't be enough.

Yet even this paled in comparison to his greatest fear. What if, in a moment of anger or frustration, he unintentionally killed someone with his mind?

The possibility seemed absurd, and yet the dream had felt so real. He couldn't simply dismiss it and hoped it would never manifest. He would need to be constantly mindful of his emotional state, never allowing himself to become agitated, angry, or even fearful. He had to remain calm.

Perhaps that was the reason his mother had consecrated him and Morelle to the priesthood?

Perhaps the seer had seen his ability developing as he neared puberty, and she had warned his mother that he needed to learn self-control and stay away from conflict? Becoming a priest was the best way to achieve that.

No, that didn't make sense.

The head priestess wouldn't have tested them if their mother had wished for their talents to remain dormant. The reason he and his sister had been put in the temple was the way they looked and not some prophecy about his powers manifesting. But after they had, he might have reached the same conclusions as he just did, deciding that priesthood was the best path for him.

The probability of that was disturbingly high.

Still, even if he had decided that in his past life, he didn't need to stick to this decision now. In a way, he had been reborn, and none of his previous vows and convictions remained in effect.

It was a flimsy argument, but there was no way he was giving up on being with Jasmine in every way a male could be with a female. He wanted a future with her, perhaps even children, and it was all possible in this new world he found himself in. Things he could have never dreamt of on Anumati.

"Thank you, Mother," he whispered. "Thank you for smuggling Morelle and me onto the settler ship and giving us a chance at life."

The sound of the bathroom door opening pulled Ell-rom from his spiraling thoughts, and as Jasmine emerged with a neatly folded stack of his clothes in her arms, he cast her a smile. "What are you doing?"

"Packing." She walked over to him. "Can't fall asleep?"

"I'm too excited."

Jasmine's face lit up. "Then let's go up to the penthouse now." She crouched and pulled a bag from under his bed. "There's no reason for you to spend more time here than necessary." She placed his clothes inside.

Ell-rom nodded, pushing himself up to a sitting position. "True, but I want to visit Morelle before we go and spend some time by her side."

Jasmine's expression softened. "Of course. Take all the time you need."

"Did you pack my nice clothes?" He shifted his weight to his feet and stood up.

"Do you want them?"

"I want to look good when I meet your friends." He reached for the walker and used it for support.

"I kind of hoped that you would put on a pair of jeans and a T-shirt, but if you want a dressier outfit, it's fine with me." Jasmine dug into the bag and pulled out the items he'd requested. "You do you, Ell-rom."

"What does that mean?"

She put the clothing on the shelf of his walker. "It means that you should have your own style, and it shouldn't be dependent on what I like."

"But I want to please you."

Jasmine smiled. "That's so sweet. You can wear jeans for me some other time. When meeting new people, you should wear what makes you feel comfortable and confident."

By the time Ell-rom was done getting dressed and came out of the bathroom, Jasmine finished packing and even took the bedding off.

"Why are you removing the bedding?"

"It needs to be laundered in preparation for the next patient, and I want to make things easier on Gertrude. She was so nice to us."

"We are going to keep seeing her every day until Morelle wakes up and goes through rehabilitation."

"Still, if I can save her some work, I'm happy to do so." Jasmine put her large bag next to the door. "Let's go to your sister. I'll pick this up on our way out."

Ell-rom took a long look at the room that had been his entire universe since he had woken up in this world, and he felt a surge of anxiety at the prospect of leaving it behind. It wasn't a particularly nice room, and there was nothing he would miss about it, but he had created good memories with Jasmine in there, and he would always feel a little nostalgic about it.

At Morelle's room, Ell-rom approached her bedside and gently took her hand in his. "Hey, Morelle. I'm moving out of the clinic today, but don't worry. I'll still visit you every day. You just focus on getting better."

Jasmine stood quietly by the door, giving him space, and Ell-rom appreciated her ability to sense when he needed a moment alone with his thoughts.

"The place I am moving to is right here in the building. It's on the top floor, and it has lots of windows, and I can't wait to see the sky and the sun in this alien world we arrived at. It is nothing like the world we expected to encounter. Seven thousand Earth years made a big difference, and humans are an advanced civilization now. You will enjoy it here. I think." He lifted her limp hand, turned it palm up, and put it on his cheek. "I need you to wake up, Morelle."

As usual, there was no response, not even a finger twitch or the slightest change in her pulse.

With a sigh, Ell-rom returned her hand to her side and rose to his feet. "I'll be back soon."

61

JASMINE

As Jasmine and Ell-rom emerged from his room, they were greeted by the warm smiles of Julian and Gertrude.

"Congratulations, Ell-rom." Julian clapped him on his back. "Another milestone achieved. You've graduated to independent living."

"Thank you," Ell-rom replied with a shy smile. "I wish your words were true and I was really independent, but it's a step in the right direction."

Julian's expression softened. "Every journey is made one step at a time, and you are taking a big one today." He gently clapped Ell-rom on the back again. "Enjoy your new lodging and come back tomorrow at ten for our daily checkup and pool physiotherapy session. Don't forget your swimming trunks."

As Ell-rom nodded, Jasmine made a mental note to talk to Julian later and write down the prince's appointment schedule. It would be her job to stay on top of that and make sure that he showed up on time, wearing the proper attire for the activity.

"I'll make sure he is here." Jasmine moved the strap of her heavy duffel bag to her other arm. "I left some of my things under the bed. I'll come back later to get them."

Julian's eyes twinkled with amusement. "I'll help you get everything up to the penthouse in one go."

She hesitated. "That's okay. I can come back for my stuff later." She didn't want him to see the sleeping bag and rolled-up camping mattress that she'd hidden under the bed.

He laughed. "We all know what's under the bed. I would have offered you a cot, but I didn't want to embarrass you."

She should have known they'd be aware of her makeshift sleeping arrangement, and she would have thanked him for the cot, not been embarrassed by it, but it was too late for that now.

As Julian ducked into Ell-rom's room, Gertrude stepped forward and enveloped Jasmine in a warm hug. "We're going to miss having you perform for us. It's going to be boring without you." She moved to gently hug Ell-rom next. "Don't worry about your sister. We will take good care of her."

"I know. Thank you. You were incredible."

Jasmine laughed. "Isn't this a bit much? It's not like we're parting ways forever. We'll be back here tomorrow, and I will sing again. I'll even do requests."

Gertrude's eyes brightened. "Can you sing 'I Will Always Love You'?"

"With pleasure. It's one of my favorites."

"Thank you." Gertrude looked as giddy as a little girl.

Jasmine swallowed the lump that had formed in her throat. This place had been their safe haven, a cocoon where Ell-rom had begun his recovery and where their relationship had blossomed. Leaving it felt significant, like finishing one chapter and starting another.

Julian emerged from the room with the sleeping bag and the rolled-up mattress and reached for her duffle bag. "Allow me."

"It's okay. You are already carrying enough."

He snorted. "Don't be silly. I'm an immortal. I could carry you on one arm and Ell-rom on the other if I needed to. This is nothing."

"Well, if you put it that way." She handed him the bag.

Ell-rom sighed. "I can't wait for the day I will be able to say that. Right now, I can barely carry myself." He leaned on his walker.

"Patience, my friend," Julian said as Gertrude opened the front door of the clinic for them and held it open.

As the door closed behind them, Jasmine felt a flutter of excitement. This was it, the start of their new life together.

Julian led them to the elevator that would take them directly to the penthouse.

Ell-rom had only ridden it one floor down, so he wasn't prepared for the speed as the elevator surged up, accelerated, and then seemed to be slowing aggressively. As the doors slid open, he was unsteady on his feet.

Julian glanced at him. "Dizzy?"

"A little. I didn't expect that." He followed Julian out and gasped as he saw the opulent vestibule.

Jasmine turned to watch his reaction, following his eyes as he took in the mosaic floor and then the domed ceiling with its elegant mural.

At the center stood a massive stone table, and atop it sat an enormous marble vase with fresh flowers, their vibrant colors and heady fragrance filling the space.

Ell-rom approached the flowers, leaned in, and inhaled deeply. "Wow, this is incredible."

Jasmine remembered how she'd felt the first time she had seen the space, but after passing through this vestibule countless times, she'd grown accustomed to its grandeur. Seeing it again through Ell-rom's eyes reminded her of her own first impression.

"Is this how everyone on Earth lives?" Ell-rom asked.

Jasmine laughed. "Not even close. This is exceptionally luxurious by Earth's standards. And you haven't seen anything yet."

She strode towards the large double doors at the far end of the vestibule, pausing for a moment with her hands on the ornate handles and savoring the moment. Then, with a flourish, she flung the doors wide open.

"Welcome to your new home, Ell-rom." She gestured for him to step through.

62

ELL-ROM

As Ell-rom stepped through the double doors Jasmine had flung open, he found himself rooted to the spot, overwhelmed by the sight before him. The most striking feature was the vast expanse of glass that seemed to make up an entire wall of the room. Through it, he could see the darkening sky, a canvas of deep blues and purples.

Was the sky above Anumati as magnificent? Was it the same color?

Jasmine wrapped an arm around his middle. "Do you want to go outside?"

"Can we?"

"Yes. That's a terrace. It's meant to be enjoyed."

She touched one of the panels, and it slid open, letting in the air, which was fresh but not pure.

"That's what I wanted you to experience," Jasmine said. "Fresh air, or as fresh as it gets in downtown Los Angeles."

"I can smell impurity in the air, but it is still lovely. Thank you for bringing me here."

Julian, who had gone somewhere with Jasmine's things, emerged and waved at them. "I put everything in the hallway next to your room. I'll see you tomorrow."

"Thank you." Jasmine waved at him.

As Julian closed the door behind him, Ell-rom pushed the walker over the threshold and stepped out onto the terrace.

The air was crisper, and it was noisier outside, but he didn't know where the noise was coming from or what was making it.

His eyes roamed over the terrace, taking in the narrow pool that stretched along its length and the greenery that seemed to sprout directly from the floor in artfully arranged planters.

He moved towards the railing, his gaze drawn to the vista before him. Tall buildings that were covered in glass stretched towards the sky and lined both sides of a broad pathway. Far below, he could see many small conveyances moving along what appeared to be a portion of the pathway that was designated for their use.

"What are those?" He pointed.

"Those are private vehicles," Jasmine explained. "It's how most people get around in the city."

Ell-rom furrowed his brow, trying to recall if Anumati had similar modes of transportation, but his mind remained frustratingly blank. "I don't remember what we used on Anumati," he admitted.

Jasmine put her hand on his arm. "You can ask the gods when they get here. Their information is a little more updated than yours, but they probably know what modes of transportation were available to the Kra-ell seven thousand years ago."

Ell-rom nodded. "Is this considered a large city by Earth standards?"

"Los Angeles is huge, but what you can see from here is just a tiny fraction of it. Later, we can go to the other apartment, which has a better, unobstructed view."

"I would like to see that. I would like to see all of Earth one day."

She chuckled. "Perhaps I can arrange for you to have a virtual tour, but you probably need to get better before they can hook you up to the Perfect Match machine."

Jasmine had told him about the devices that matched compatible mates, but he didn't know what they could do for him.

"I'm not looking for a mate." He leaned over and kissed her cheek. "I found her already."

She grinned. "Perfect Match started as a matchmaking service, but they also offer solo adventures. You can learn how to fly an air transport or jump out of one with a big canvas canopy that will slow down your descent so you can land safely. And that's just the tip of the iceberg. There are so many things that can be experienced from the comfort and safety of the Perfect Match studio."

There was a wistfulness in her voice, and he wondered what was stopping her from experiencing the things she had mentioned.

"Have you ever been hooked up to one of those virtual reality things?"

She shook her head. "It costs a lot of money that I don't have, but Kian promised me a job at the company, so I might get to do some free runs."

Ell-rom's gut twisted. Was Jasmine going to leave him to go work for the virtual studios?

"Are you about to start working there soon?"

"Don't worry." She patted his arm. "For now, my job is to take care of you, and until you are back to how you were before entering the stasis chamber, I'm not leaving your side."

"I don't want you to ever leave my side."

"That's a lovely thing to say, but eventually, you will tire of my constant company, and you will be happy to see me go to work so you can have a break from me and my never-ending chatter."

"Never. I love listening to you, seeing your beautiful face, your charming smile, and just being around you."

"I feel the same about you, my prince." Jasmine cupped his cheek and planted a soft kiss on his lips. "Let's explore the rest of the place in privacy, before the others get here and we won't be able to."

Jasmine led him through the spacious living area, pointing out various features. There was a food preparation section with various cooking and cleaning appliances, a comfortable-looking seating area with big couches that were made from the hide of some animal, and shelving units that were filled with books like the ones Jasmine had shown him. Words printed on pages that told a story. There was a fireplace with a big screen above it on which to watch broadcasts. Works of art with bold colors hung on the walls, sculptures perched on pedestals, and a colorful rug covered some of the floor.

They entered a short corridor, and Jasmine stopped next to a door. "This is our bedroom." She swung it open and motioned for him to go ahead of her.

The large room was dominated by a bed that was piled with pillows and looked far more comfortable than what he had been sleeping on since he had woken up from stasis. More floor-to-ceiling windows offered the same breathtaking view of the city.

Ell-rom stepped inside, his eyes roaming over every detail. He noticed a door off to one side, presumably leading to a bathroom. Everything looked soft and inviting.

"Nice, right?" Jasmine walked over to the other door in the room. "Wait until you see the bathroom. It's not utilitarian like the one in the clinic." She frowned. "There are no grab bars. I hope you will be able to manage without them." She rubbed her temple. "I should have thought about that."

"It's okay." He left the walker and took two hesitant steps toward her. "I will manage." He wrapped his arms around her and dipped his head to take her lips in a kiss.

When Jasmine embraced him back, he had a feeling that she was doing that to make sure he didn't fall over, but as their kiss became more passionate, she began using her hands to caress him instead of to support him.

When they both needed to come up for air, Jasmine looked up at him with a smile on her lips and in her eyes. "I love how tall you are. You make me feel feminine and delicate."

"You are feminine and delicate."

Her smile widened. "I'm considered tall for a woman, and I'm built solidly rather than delicately, but thank you for thinking that."

He couldn't understand why being tall and solid was considered less desirable than being short and delicate, but then he did not understand a lot of things. Maybe it was something specific to humans?

Not that it mattered either way.

He loved Jasmine just the way she was.

He loved her, and suddenly, he couldn't contain the enormity of the feeling without expressing it.

"I love you, Jasmine. I think you are beautiful, kind, smart, charming, and talented. There isn't one thing I would want to change about you."

Looking suddenly shy, Jasmine let out a breath and leaned her forehead against his chest. "There is one thing you should want to change about me."

"What's that?"

"You need to make me immortal."

63

JASMINE

"I will," Ell-rom whispered. "As soon as I can."

Jasmine wanted to kick herself.

He'd just told her that he loved her, and all she could say in return was that he needed to make her immortal.

Talk about lame and unromantic.

Taking a deep breath, she lifted her arms and wound them around his neck. "I love you too, and I wouldn't change a thing about you. I'm not in a rush, so don't feel pressured. It will happen when the Fates want it to happen."

It was still a lame love declaration, but he had taken her by surprise, and she hadn't had a nicely articulated and romantic speech prepared.

Jasmine had recited words of love in many plays, and she had even been moved by some, but now that she knew what love felt like, none of them could adequately express what was in her heart.

Ell-rom nodded. "I know, but I want to be who you need me to be. I don't want to keep you waiting."

She lifted on her toes and kissed him lightly on the lips. "You already are who I need you to be. You are kind, smart, and you love me. The rest will come, and I don't mind the wait. All good things are worth waiting for." She took his hand. "Let's see that bathroom, shall we?"

After exploring the bathing chamber with its luxurious shower and soaking tub, Jasmine led Ell-rom back to the living room.

"Would you like some coffee?" she asked as he parked the walker next to one of the couches. "We have the benefit of the kitchen being right here, so I don't have to go anywhere to make it. That alone is worth the move."

She sounded a little nervous, even to herself.

This was a shift to a new environment, and she didn't know how well they would adjust to it.

"I would love some, thank you."

The low couch did not lend itself to someone with weak leg muscles, and Ell-rom sat down with marked effort.

Heading toward the kitchen, Jasmine heard the front door open, and as she turned to see who it was,

Margo entered with Frankie and Gabi right behind her, all three carrying shopping bags.

A smile spread across her face. "You're back early." She walked over to greet them.

"We got tired of the crowds." Margo dropped her bags by the entry door, embraced Jasmine, and then turned, her eyes lighting up as she spotted Ell-rom. "You must be the prince. Look at you."

Ell-rom rose to his feet, trying to hide how difficult it was for him, and gripped the handles of his walker.

As he headed toward them, Jasmine had a moment of panic, realizing that her friends didn't have the earpieces in.

It wasn't that she was afraid Ell-rom would suddenly discover his compulsion power, but it was a security breach, and Kian would be livid if he found out.

She had to make sure he never did.

"You need to put the earpieces in," she told Margo. "Ell-rom only speaks Kra-ell."

Margo's eyes widened. "Crap, I forgot." She reached into her purse, pulled out the devices, and put them in her ear.

Frankie and Gabi did the same, and by the time Ell-rom made it to where they were standing, they all had the earpieces in.

At least they had the presence of mind to keep the devices in their purses and not somewhere in their rooms. They hadn't known that she would bring Ell-rom to the penthouse so early. He had been supposed to be napping after his hydrotherapy session.

"Ell-rom, these are my friends, Margo, Frankie, and Gabi."

"Hello." He smiled. "I've heard a lot about you. Thank you for accompanying your mates and mine on the search for my pod." He dipped his head. "I owe each of you a life debt for saving me and my sister from an imminent death."

None of them had noticed that he had called Jasmine his mate, perhaps because they had all assumed it already, but Jasmine's heart did a little happy flutter.

Margo waved a dismissive hand. "Oh, don't be silly. We joined it only because it was an all-expenses-paid trip to Tibet." She offered him her hand. "You look amazing. I'm so glad that you are getting better."

"Yeah," Frankie said, giving Ell-rom an appraising look. "Hard to believe that you looked like a corpse only ten days ago."

"Frankie!' Gabi admonished. "That was rude." She turned to Ell-rom with a bright smile. "The doctors have done an amazing job. You look so healthy!"

Regrettably, Frankie had been the honest one.

While Ell-rom looked good in clothes, Jasmine knew the reality underneath. He was still painfully thin, with his ribs not only visible beneath his pale skin but actually sticking out. The memory of Julian and Bridget's concerned expressions each day when they weighed him flashed through her mind.

Being vegan and a finicky eater wasn't helping things, and she made a mental note to discuss protein shakes with the doctors. Perhaps that would help Ell-rom gain weight faster.

"Let's sit down," Margo said. "My feet are killing me after all the shopping. I can't wait to take my shoes off."

"Yeah, me too," Frankie joined in an equally exaggerated tone.

They must have noticed how difficult it was for Ell-rom to remain standing and were making it look like it was them who needed to take the weight off their feet.

When all of them were seated, there was a moment of awkward silence, and then Ell-rom asked, "Where are Aru and his friends? Are they still working on the salvaged parts of the pod?"

"I hope not," Gabi said. "They were supposed to pick up the food from the Golden Dragon."

As the conversation shifted to the descriptions of the dishes Margo had ordered and which of them Ell-rom could eat, Jasmine's thoughts drifted to the bedroom and the big bed in the middle that had made Ell-rom nervous.

He probably expected her to initiate sex, and even though she was very much on board for that, she was worried that he wasn't physically ready yet. Maybe they could take things slow and explore each other but save the main event for when he was in better health.

Heck, maybe she could introduce him to porn so he wouldn't feel like such a clueless novice? Not the cringey stuff that guys like to watch, but the romantic stuff she enjoyed, with actual plot and conversation and not just bodies going at it.

Nah, that was probably a bad idea.

What if he became addicted to it, and it would all be her fault for corrupting the innocent, virginal former priest?

She'd seen how it affected some guys, warping their expectations and attitudes. Ell-rom needed a gentler introduction to sexuality.

The sound of the door opening again pulled Jasmine back to the present.

Aru entered, followed by Negal and Dagor. They were laden with bags from the Golden Dragon, but even without the insignia on the paper bags, the aroma of Chinese food was unmistakable.

Suddenly, it occurred to her that Ell-rom might get nauseated by the smell, and she cast him a quick glance, but he seemed fine, smiling at Aru, who he had met before.

"Ell-rom!" Aru exclaimed, walking over and offering Ell-rom his hand. "You look much improved. How are you feeling?"

Jasmine was relieved to see that all three had their earpieces in.

Ell-rom smiled and shook the god's hand. "Much better, thank you. Supposedly, I'm making good progress, but I wish it was happening faster. I'm impatient." He smiled. "I also wish I had the strength to greet you standing up."

"No worries, my friend. We understand." He motioned for his companions to step forward. "These are my teammates, Negal and Dagor."

"Pleased to meet you," Ell-rom said as he shook Negal's offered hand and then Dagor's.

"I have many questions about Anumati," Ell-rom said. "I was hoping you could tell me about it."

"Hold that thought," Margo interrupted. "Let's get this food sorted out first before it gets cold. There'll be plenty of time for questions over dinner."

"Oh, damn." Jasmine shot to her feet. "I forgot to bring Ell-rom's special meal from the clinic."

"No worries," Aru cut in with a smile. "Margo reminded me to pick up Ell-rom's dinner on the way."

64

ELL-ROM

The dining table was covered with an array of dishes, fragrant and colorful, and as long as Ell-rom didn't know what they were made from, he didn't get nauseous. Perhaps the aversion to animal products was not physiological but psychological, and it was so deeply rooted that even the loss of his memory could not erase it.

Nevertheless, he was grateful for the bespoke meal, which was a carefully prepared blend of nutrients designed to help him regain his strength. It looked bland in comparison to what the others were eating, but he didn't mind. It was tasty and didn't make him feel sick.

As everyone settled in and began to serve themselves, the conversation flowed easily. Jasmine kept a watchful eye on him, ready to jump in if he seemed uncomfortable, but he was holding his own.

"So, Ell-rom," Frankie said between bites, "What do you think of Earth so far?"

"I like the people." He turned to Jasmine. "Human and immortal." He shifted his gaze back to Frankie. "I saw the blue sky today, and I wondered how it compared to the sky over Anumati. It's frustrating not to have even the most basic memories."

"The sky over Anumati has a reddish hue," Aru said. "It's much darker, even in the middle of the day, because our sun is dimmer but much larger than Earth's, and the planet itself is much larger than Earth as well. We have two moons, and that's cool to see at night. But the planet is hot and humid in most locations. It is also quite windy, which is actually helpful as it counteracts the heat and humidity to some extent. The gods prefer to live in underground cities, protected from the wind and the heat, but the Kra-ell are a hardier lot, and they revere nature and its bounty, not technology and its conveniences."

Ell-rom nodded. "What about transportation? Do they use private vehicles?"

"The gods use hovercrafts," Dagor said. "That's a much more efficient mode of transportation because there is no need to pave roads. Instead, the underground cities are connected by large tunnels, and gods can either traverse those in their private crafts or board a fast train."

"What about the Kra-ell?" Ell-rom asked.

Negal chuckled. "Believe it or not, most just walk or run. Their society is organized in semi-nomadic small tribes." He glanced at Aru. "You know how to explain that better than I do."

Aru nodded. "I often think that their diet is what shapes their entire culture. They don't need to grow anything, and they don't need to store food, which are the two main catalysts for societal organization, cooperation, and innovation. Wars are also a catalyst for those things, so the Kra-ell made some progress over time, but they prefer their traditional ways and are proud of them."

As the god described the Kra-ell, Ell-rom thought of Jade and how powerful and proud she'd seemed. She embodied her people.

Aru continued. "Throughout much of their history, tribal wars were a way of life, effectively regulating population growth, but when these were stopped many millennia ago by their then queen, the population exploded, and relying on hunting alone was not enough, especially after a disease killed many of the larger animals on Anumati. They had to come to the gods for help. The gods produced synthetic blood for the Kra-ell to consume." Aru smiled. "I could go on for hours, talking about how that event led to the conflict between the gods and the Kra-ell, but I don't want to bore you."

Ell-rom shook his head. "It's fascinating to me. I wonder how much of this I was told in the temple."

"Religion is also a catalyst," Jasmine said. "I mean for shaping a society in a certain way. I'm sure you were taught a lot about that."

The concept of religion as a societal catalyst intrigued Ell-rom, and he wondered about the teachings he'd received in the temple. Those memories remained frustratingly out of reach, and the one teaching he knew for sure he'd been given was celibacy, which he wasn't going to adhere to.

"You're right," he said to Jasmine. "I'm sure I was taught a great deal about the role of religion in our society. I just wish I could remember it."

On the other hand, maybe it was good that he didn't remember the teachings because he didn't want anything to stand in the way of the life he wanted with Jasmine.

Glancing at her, he took a long moment to admire the way her eyes lit up as she laughed at something Margo had said. She was beautiful and kind, and he felt incredibly lucky to have her in his life, but with that feeling came a sense of pressure.

What if he disappointed her?

What if his lack of experience and his still-recovering body made him inadequate for her?

That wasn't an if but rather a given. He was inadequate, and the real question was how much Jasmine was willing to compromise.

65

JASMINE

The conversation around the table ebbed and flowed, touching on Earth customs, Anumati technology, history, and their different colonies, which Jasmine found the most fascinating. She'd heard some of it before during the trip to Tibet, but it was always fun to hear those wondrous tales again.

By now most of the takeout boxes were empty, and the guys were scraping the leftovers onto their plates, and the gals were watching them fondly. Ell-rom had eaten his custom-made meal and even tasted a couple of the vegetable dishes. He'd loved the eggplant but hadn't been too impressed by the green beans with cashews and tofu.

Jasmine couldn't blame him. It was the one dish she didn't like either.

What surprised her was how well Ell-rom was doing in a social setting. She'd been anxious about this gathering being overwhelming for him, but he seemed fine, and her friends liked him.

The gods had been a little suspicious at the beginning of the meal, but they had gotten over it pretty quickly, each of them contributing information that Ell-rom was drinking in.

Aru knew a lot about Anumatian politics and history, Dagor knew a lot about the tech, but Negal had the best stories. He was the oldest of the three, and he had served on several vessels in the fleet long before Aru and Dagor were born. She could listen all night to his stories about the planets he had visited and the adventures he had experienced, but Ell-rom was getting tired. The excitement of the day was clearly catching up to him.

When he tried to stifle a yawn, Margo noticed. "Well, this has been lovely," she said, standing and beginning to gather plates. "But I think Ell-rom needs to get in bed." She smiled at him. "You've been a trooper, but you need to conserve your energy to heal faster."

Jasmine let out a breath. For a moment there, she'd been afraid that Margo was about to tell Ell-rom that he needed to conserve his energy for other things. He would have been so embarrassed.

Although, given how tired he looked, Jasmine was pretty sure that he would be asleep before his head hit the pillow. Then again, it wasn't late, so he might take a nap and wake up invigorated.

Yeah, that sounded like a plan.

Their first time together should be when Ell-rom was in top shape.

Right. So maybe tonight wasn't a good idea at all, or the next week, or maybe even longer.

Damn, she wanted him now.

That was selfish of her. She needed to let him decide when he was ready and not pressure him into anything.

When Jasmine rose to her feet to help Margo, her friend shooed her away. "We've got it. Take your man to bed. Or better yet, draw him a nice bath." She winked.

Jasmine chuckled. "We shall see." She walked over to where Ell-rom had left his walker and brought it closer to him so he could use it to get up.

"Thank you." He gripped the handles and pulled himself to a standing position. "Thank you all for a lovely dinner. I enjoyed the company and the food."

The others responded in kind, and then they were off, walking toward the bedroom.

"So," Jasmine said. "What did you think?"

"I like your friends a lot. They were so genuine in their welcome." He sighed. "It's nice to have friends. I've never had any."

Jasmine felt a lump form in her throat at his words. "Well, you do now." She opened the door to their bedroom.

"Thanks to you." He leaned over and kissed her cheek. "I owe you everything."

"How about a bath?" she suggested, an idea forming as she spoke. "It's a special treat that you haven't experienced yet. It will help you relax after such a busy day."

"That sounds interesting." Ell-rom followed her to the bathroom. "I just hope I won't fall asleep in there." He eyed the large tub. "That is big enough for two, but not lying down."

"You are not supposed to lie down in the tub. You are supposed to recline. Do you see these holes?" She pointed. "Those release jets of water that massage your muscles."

"I need that." He chuckled. "I'm aching all over."

"This will definitely help." She plugged the drain and started the water. "It's a big tub, so it will take a while to fill up. You should sit down and start undressing." She pointed to the bench where she'd left a stack of towels.

Poor guy. He hadn't complained even once, so she hadn't known. Not that there was much she could have done for him. When her muscles hurt after a workout, she usually popped a pill. Bathing was a rare luxury that she'd enjoyed once in a while when staying in a high-end hotel. The bathtub in her apartment was child-sized, so it hadn't offered much relaxation.

Oh, right. She didn't have that place anymore. Jasmine was glad that she didn't need to pay rent anymore, and she was staying in a luxurious penthouse, so she wasn't homeless, but she felt displaced.

Ell-rom must feel so much worse.

She cast him a sidelong glance to see how he was doing, but all he had accomplished so far was to toe off his shoes. "Do you need help undressing?"

He shook his head. "You said it will take a long time to fill up the tub, so I'm not in a rush."

She smiled at him. "Take your time."

He was no doubt embarrassed to undress in front of her, but that was silly. She had seen him in his swimming trunks twice already. And yesterday, they had even made out in the pool.

A smile tugged at her lips at the memory.

Ell-rom was still skin and bones, but it hadn't detracted from the pleasure she'd felt straddling his hips and rubbing herself over his hard length.

As she added foaming bubbles to the water, a small worry niggled at the back of her mind. What if Ell-rom really fell asleep in the warm water? As skinny as he still was, she knew she wouldn't be able to lift him out of the tub herself, and having to call one of the gods to help her would mortify Ell-rom. He was so proud.

She had to ensure that he stayed awake.

66

ELL-ROM

As Ell-rom unbuttoned his shirt, he hesitated before shrugging it off.

Jasmine had seen him shirtless before, but they hadn't been alone when he had removed his robe and entered the pool, and she hadn't been focused solely on him because Julian had been there to distract her.

Now, that was what a male should look like. Perhaps if Ell-rom hadn't seen the medic bare-chested, he wouldn't have been so self-conscious about the way he himself looked. He was so thin that he could count each protruding rib, and his belly was concave as opposed to the rippling muscles on Julian's midsection.

Jasmine added some liquid to the tub water that created a layer of foam on the surface.

"Most men think that bubble bath is girly, but I think

it does wonders for sore muscles, and the smell is amazing. Right?"

He nodded. "The smell is nice."

The shirt was still on him, just opened at the front, and he hadn't done anything about the pants.

"Do you need help undressing?" Jasmine asked again.

"No, I can do it." He forced himself to remove the shirt and reached for the belt holding his pants up.

Jasmine rose to her feet. "I would leave and give you privacy, but I'm afraid you will slip. The best I can do is close my eyes so you can finish undressing, and you can duck into the bathtub while using my arm like a grab bar."

He wanted to deny that he was being shy, but that would be a lie.

"Thank you. It's just all new to me. I mean, being with a woman, feeling these urges."

It wasn't a lie, but it wasn't the truth either. It was the best he could do.

"No problem. I know what it's like." She closed her eyes and extended her arms. "I'm not peeking."

How would she know what it was like for him? Had she ever been less than perfect? He doubted it.

Ell-rom removed the rest of his clothing much faster than he had done with the shirt, and as he pushed to his feet, doing it fast made him dizzy, and he braced a hand against the wall.

"Are you okay?" Jasmine asked.

"Yes. I just stood up too quickly." He took a step forward, gripped her hand, and used it to stabilize himself as he lifted one leg over the edge of the tub.

The warm water felt wonderful, but the tub was slippery, and he sat on the edge before pulling his other leg over. Now, all that remained to do was to slide his bottom into the tub and lie down.

"I really wish they had grab bars in here."

Jasmine got closer to the tub with her eyes still closed. "Hold on to my hand, and I'll move with you as you slide down."

"Thank you," he murmured, touched by how helpful and understanding she was.

He did as she instructed, and when his butt touched the bottom of the tub, he sighed in relief and let go of her hand.

The layer of foam hid everything except the top of his chest, his shoulders, and his head. The water was the perfect temperature, and the smell was calming, but he was anything but calm.

"Can I open my eyes now?" Jasmine asked.

"Yes. Please, and thank you." Ell-rom sank further down into the water with a contented sigh.

Jasmine turned around and perched on the edge of the tub. "Comfortable?" she asked, running her fingers lightly over the mounds of foam.

"Yes." No. He was sporting a huge erection, and he hoped she couldn't see it.

Jasmine smiled. "How does the water feel?"

"Amazing."

"I'm glad." She looked at the foam. "If I activate the jets, the bubbles will get out of control. There will be mountains of it."

"Is that bad?" More foam would cover more of him.

Jasmine rose to her feet, gripped the hem of her blouse, and pulled it over her head. "You tell me."

Ell-rom's breath caught in his throat. He had seen Jasmine in her skimpy bathing outfit, so seeing her in something similarly skimpy shouldn't have excited him so, but then he had also been excited when they had been in the pool. The tiny top she was wearing now barely covered her breasts, and it was made from a semi-sheer fabric that didn't hide her nipples.

He wanted to grip himself under the foam cover, but there was no way Jasmine wouldn't see that.

Given her satisfied expression, she knew what she was doing to him and was loving every moment of it.

His female was a natural seductress.

Hooking her thumbs in the waistline of her pants, she turned around and bent down as she pushed them off her pert bottom, and Ell-rom nearly choked.

Her underwear was even more revealing than her bathing suit bottoms. The back triangle was missing, and her butt cheeks were on full display.

And what a magnificent display that was.

As she turned around, he half expected the front triangle to be missing as well, but there was one that was also semi-sheer.

He wasn't going to look. He was going to concentrate on her smiling brown eyes with the gold flakes swimming around her pupils.

"You like?" she asked as she entered the tub on the other end and sat down.

"Do you have to ask?"

"Not really, but I like to hear it."

"You are magnificent."

Her smile broadened. "Thank you." She slid under the foam, and a moment later, the top underwear item went flying. "That's much better." She sighed, lifted her legs, slid the bottoms up her shapely thighs, and tossed them as well.

Now she was completely naked under the foam cover, and Ell-rom really couldn't breathe.

"So, do you want me to activate the jets?" She played with the thin layer of soap bubbles barely covering her breasts.

Unable to speak, Ell-rom just shook his head.

67

JASMINE

"Would you like me to wash your hair?" Jasmine offered as she reached for the shampoo.

Ell-rom laughed nervously. "What hair?"

"Okay. The fuzz. It still needs to be washed."

His eyes started glowing. "I would love your hands on me. So, if you want to massage my scalp, you are more than welcome to do so."

Jasmine knew what her prince was thinking, which was exactly what she wanted him to think. She would have to rise above the cover of bubbles, and he would get to see her breasts.

"Turn around." She circled with her finger.

He looked disappointed. "Do I have to?"

She laughed. "How else am I going to get to your head?"

The glow in his eyes intensified. "You could lean over me."

Jasmine canted her head. "Then the game will be over before it begins. Turn around, Ell-rom."

There was defiance in his blazing blue eyes, but after a moment, he did as she'd commanded, giving her his back.

He had a nice back, even though she could count all his ribs. It was broad, with the skin stretched taut over it, and it was starting to look healthy. It had a slightly lighter shade than hers, and it had a natural golden hue that she could only accomplish by rubbing colored tanning oil over herself.

One day soon, though, he would fill out, and this gorgeous skin would be stretched taut over strong muscle. He wouldn't even need to frequent the gym to get ripped. Immortals and gods didn't have to work hard for their perfect physiques.

As she moved behind him, rubbing a little shampoo into his scalp and massaging gently with her fingertips, Ell-rom moaned and tilted his head back.

"You see? I told you it would feel good."

"I knew it would," he murmured. "You have magic fingers."

She chuckled. "You've seen nothing yet, big guy."

He swallowed audibly. "What are you planning to do to me?"

"Only good things. Lots and lots of pleasure."

He tilted his head so far back that he could look upside down into her eyes. "I don't want to be just the receiver. I want to be the giver."

"I know, sweetheart." She pressed a soft kiss to his forehead. "And you will."

"Promise?"

"Yes, I promise."

Jasmine still didn't know how she was going to do that without overwhelming him, scaring him, stressing him out, or embarrassing him. Virgin priests were not her specialty.

When she was done with the scalp massage, she took a fresh washcloth, wetted it with the spray nozzle, and rubbed the suds off.

After dipping it in the water again, she squirted some liquid soap onto the washcloth and ran it over his back, his neck, and his arms, lovingly stroking every part of him she could reach.

It should have been relaxing for Ell-rom, but his shoulders were stiff. She had a good idea why, but there wasn't much she could do about it. If she just looped her arms around him and reached for his pleasure handle, he would come like a firecracker and get embarrassed.

Damn. She had never been with someone so inexperienced.

How was she going to make him feel comfortable? Could she just be herself and do things the way she wanted?

When she leaned over him, flattening her breasts against his back to reach around and soap his chest, he groaned, but he didn't make a move to touch her. He was letting her lead because he assumed that she knew what she was doing.

Well, she did. She could seduce most men and give them a night to remember, but pleasuring a former virgin acolyte with amnesia would be uncharted territory for the most experienced of courtesans.

Her movements were slow, deliberate, appreciative of the raw potential of his big body. One day soon, he would be covered in corded muscles. Leaning over his shoulder, she could see the tip of his erection protruding over the bubbles, and her mouth watered for it.

He hadn't even touched her yet, and she was so damn aroused that if he mounted her right now, she would be ready for him.

Biting her lip, she moved the washcloth lower, soaping his stomach, but she stopped before reaching his bobbing shaft.

His groan sounded pained. "Jasmine," he breathed.

"Yes?"

He shook his head. "Nothing. Just don't stop."

68

ELL-ROM

When Jasmine had massaged Ell-rom's scalp, it had relaxed him and aroused him at the same time. When she'd washed his back, shoulders, and arms, he'd gotten even more aroused, but when she wrapped her arms around him to wash his front and pressed her naked breasts to his back, the arousal became so intense that he felt lightheaded.

Hopefully, he wasn't going to faint from overstimulation and miss out on all that pleasure.

The feel of her hard nipples rubbing against his back made his shaft throb and elongate, eliciting urges he didn't think he had ever experienced. He wanted to turn around, grip Jasmine's waist, and ram the pulsating rod between his legs into her sheath.

He wasn't going to do that, but the image was so vivid in his mind that he wished he could at least grip the erection to assuage the ache.

How much longer could he endure this without doing anything?

Suddenly, she lifted off him, and his back was mourning the loss.

"Turn around," Jasmine said. "I want to soap your feet."

Mother above, he was about to see her breasts.

He couldn't move.

"Are you stuck?" she asked, her voice full of concern. "Do you need help?"

"No, I'm fine. I just need a moment."

He heard the water sluice as she moved back into the large tub. Then she waited. Bracing his hand against the tub's bottom, he turned around, lifting only a tiny distance to do so. His erection was as hard as it ever got, and even the foam was not enough to fully hide it, so he put his hand over it and only then lifted his eyes to gaze at Jasmine.

She was on her haunches, her breasts glistening from the water, her nipples erect, and a satisfied smile blooming on her face.

He was awestruck.

"Lift your foot, Ell-rom."

He obeyed. "I haven't decided yet if this is torture or pleasure."

Jasmine put his foot in her lap and started massaging his arch. "You will discover that delaying gratification enhances the pleasure. Letting the pressure mount makes the climax more explosive."

Ell-rom felt his fangs elongate. "If you keep talking like that, the pressure will erupt whether I want it to or not."

He was getting bolder in the way he talked with her, perhaps because she was not only receptive but seemed to enjoy it.

"As I said before, that's perfectly fine, and it will be very satisfying for me, so don't hold back."

Was she telling him the truth or what she thought he wanted to hear?

"How could it be satisfying for you if I'm not even touching you?"

She leaned down and kissed his big toe. "You will find out that sometimes giving pleasure is more fulfilling than receiving it, and when people are in a relationship, they can take turns. It doesn't have to always be simultaneous."

She put his foot back in the water and motioned for him to lift his other foot onto her lap.

"Tell me more," he asked, trying to keep his tone even as she started massaging the arch of his other foot.

"I'd rather show you." Her fingers continued to

massage his calf, getting closer to where he wanted her to touch him.

Each of her touches made his erection throb and strain, and if not for his hand keeping it down, it would have raised its head above the foamy water and demanded Jasmine's attention.

When her hands reached his knee, he gritted his teeth and crossed his legs.

He was a hair away from blowing, and she'd given him permission to do it, but that wasn't how he wanted it to be.

Scooting closer, she leaned down and kissed one knee, then the other, and then applied light pressure to pry them apart. "Don't fight me, Ell-rom. I'm not going to hurt you."

"I know. I'm not afraid of that. I'm just not used to this. I don't know what to do."

"But I do." She smoothed her hand down the inside of his thigh and then lightly wrapped it around his shaft. "Oh, my. You are a big guy."

He jerked and spread his knees even wider, giving her full access. His fangs were fully elongated by now, so biting his lip to prevent himself from groaning and moaning was not happening. If he cut his lip and tasted his own blood, he was going to get sick. He couldn't stand the taste of blood, not even the smell of it.

The unpleasant thought was enough to cool his fervor, so he didn't explode all over Jasmine's hand.

Never mind that it was what she wanted him to do.

Her touch was gentle, and he wanted more of it, but he wasn't okay with this being one-sided, no matter what she had said about giving pleasure being sometimes more satisfying than receiving it.

Or maybe she was right, and that was why he needed to pleasure her first.

The only problem was that he didn't know how, and he would need her to guide him.

69

JASMINE

Ell-rom put his hand over Jasmine's. "Please. I can't."

He looked so pained that she released him right away. "What's wrong? Did you change your mind? Do you need more time?"

He shook his head. "I need to pleasure you first. Maybe it's an instinct, one of those genetically programmed memories, but it just doesn't feel right for me to be on the receiving end."

It was a little chauvinistic of him, but if she told him that, he wouldn't understand what she meant. Heck, there was probably no equivalent word in Kra-ell. They were a matriarchal society, but that didn't mean the males were pushovers or weaklings. They were the defenders of the tribe, and they were dominant, but they took their orders from the mistress, who was the head of their large family unit.

Still, that wasn't the instinct driving Ell-rom. The male Kra-ell probably needed to compete for the affections of their mistresses, and the need to be good, generous lovers was most likely genetically ingrained in them. Heck, it was natural selection, the survival of the fittest, or, as happened in the Kra-ell society, the survival of the best lovers. The males who got to father the next generation had to excel at sex to get repeat invitations to the females' beds.

Their natural selection favored good lovers.

Jasmine had no proof of that, and the only thing she had been told about their sexual practices was that they were violent and that they fought for dominance, but perhaps Edgar had exaggerated.

Ell-rom was gentle. He would never get violent with her or hurt her in any way. Of that, she was positive.

Ell-rom needed to prove himself to her. Not only that, she had been the initiator in all their exploration so far, and it didn't sit well with him. He needed to take the lead.

"Okay, big guy." She leaned back. "I'm at your command."

"I need guidance," he admitted. "Would you teach me?"

Nodding, she handed him the washcloth. "You can start by soaping me."

"Turn around," he said quietly.

When she did, he put a hand on her shoulder, leaned in, and kissed it, then started running the washcloth over her back, her arms, and her stomach, and as he skimmed the sides of her breasts, she moaned.

Dropping the washcloth, he used his hands to lather her belly, her hips, and the tops of her bottom. And then his hands rested on her waist, and he lifted her and turned her around in a show of unexpected strength.

Jasmine gasped. "How did you do that? You are not supposed to be able to lift me yet."

"I got fueled by passion." He cupped her cheek, then smoothed his hand down the length of her neck and all the way to her collarbone, learning her contours with such reverence that it made her feel like a goddess.

From her collarbone, he smoothed his forefinger down and circled her nipple without touching her needy peak.

"Touch me here." She cupped her other breast and showed him how to tweak her nipple. "Kiss me right here." She arched her back.

He groaned and leaned down to press a sweet, soft kiss where she had shown him, and then moved to the other one and did the same thing.

Apparently, her prince was a literal guy, and she had to explain what she'd meant by a kiss.

"Lick it, close your lips over it and suck. Just be careful with your fangs. Don't nick me. If you do, you will have to lick some more to heal me."

Something passed over his eyes, and if Jasmine hadn't known better, she would have thought it was revulsion.

Had she given him too many instructions?

Too much detail?

She didn't want to kill the mood by being overly bossy or too literal.

But Ell-rom seemed excited to do everything she had told him and did exactly what she had told him to do. To his credit, he was an excellent student.

"Yes, oh, yes." She moaned. "Just like that. More."

Ell-rom must have misunderstood what she'd meant by more and moved one hand to cup her bottom.

Her shy prince was getting bolder, and she was loving it.

Moving his other hand to her hip, he rubbed the heel of his palm over her clitoris as if he knew what it was, and she wondered once more if that was a genetic memory or a normal memory that had resurfaced. Perhaps he had been taught in a purely academic setting about female anatomy, and how a male was supposed to pleasure a female.

After all, if he were to serve as an actual spiritual leader to his people, he would have to answer questions pertaining to sex.

She was writhing under his palm, pressing and rubbing her achy nubbin and bringing herself closer and closer to climax. Ell-rom changed tactics and probed her entrance with his forefinger, beginning to intimately investigate her sex.

How the heck had he not exploded already when she was ready to blow in half the time?

Wrapping her palm around the back of his neck, she pressed her lips to his, and when she licked the seam, he parted them for her, and her tongue darted inside to meet his.

Ell-rom groaned and pressed his finger firmer against her opening, breaching the entrance and slipping it farther in.

She moaned to encourage him to keep going, and as her sheath clamped around the digit, he gasped into her mouth.

The deeper he pushed his finger, the more the heel of his palm pressed against her clitoris, and the more she rocked against his hand.

She was seconds away from coming, but then he suddenly withdrew his finger.

"What are you doing?" she asked.

He looked dazed, his glowing eyes unfocused. He was all instinct now, and she hoped he remembered that she was human and he had to be careful with her.

Somehow, he was suddenly much stronger than he had any right to be at this stage of his recovery.

70

ELL-ROM

Despite the strong flowery smell of the foaming bath bubbles, Jasmine's scent of arousal overwhelmed Ell-rom, scrambling his brain and demanding that he taste her. Could it be that he had been taught how to pleasure females, and the memories were surfacing at the right moment?

Or was it instinct again? The same instinct that assured him that she would love for him to lick her right where that intoxicating smell was coming from?

Nevertheless, he had to ask permission before attempting such an intimate act.

"I have to taste you," he hissed from between his elongated fangs. "Will you allow it?"

Jasmine's eyes widened in surprise and then narrowed. "Did Julian tell you to do this?"

Ell-rom nodded. "He said that I need to seek consent and that consent for one thing did not imply consent for everything, which is why I am asking permission."

"Unbelievable," she murmured. "I would never have guessed that oral was innate."

He needed to do this more than he needed to breathe. "Please, say yes."

"Yes."

There was an elevated area in the bathtub, a seat of sorts that was above the foamy bubbles, and once again, he lifted Jasmine with almost no effort and set her down on that seat.

"How are you so strong?"

"I don't know." He knelt in front of her, suddenly unconcerned about the club jutting out from between his thighs.

Jasmine had her hand wrapped around it only a moment ago, so it wasn't as if she didn't know what was going on. Not only that, she seemed as excited by his arousal as he was about hers.

Even though she was seated on an elevated seat and he was kneeling, they were eye to eye, and as he leaned to kiss her neck, she arched her back, showing him exactly where she wanted him to kiss her next. Leaning back on his haunches, he flicked his tongue over one nipple and then took it between his lips to suck. When she moaned and pressed her breast to his mouth, he licked and sucked before moving to her other breast.

With her being out of the water, he was drowning in the scent of her arousal, and the need to taste her became too strong to deny.

Spreading her legs, he breathed in the scent and then pressed a kiss to her glistening folds. She shivered, but it was the good kind of shiver that meant she enjoyed the kiss. He gave her folds a tentative lick and then looked up at her to see her expression.

"It's good." She put her hands on his head, guiding him back to where he had just been. "Don't stop."

He had no intention of stopping until she climaxed all over his tongue. Licking up and down, he found her most sensitive spot, and as he flicked his tongue over it, she cried out, but again, it was the good kind of cry that meant she wanted more, and he was happy to oblige. The way she rolled her hips and ground into his mouth was further proof that he was doing it right.

Ell-rom's chest swelled with satisfaction.

He was pleasuring his mate, and she was loving it. There was no higher honor.

Well, there might be somewhere out there in the outside world, but right here in this bathtub, there was none.

Well, there was. When she climaxed.

He wasn't thinking straight, but given how scrambled his brain was, it was a miracle he could think at all.

Still, he knew to add his finger to the play and thrust it in and out of her in sync with his licking and sucking.

"Yes," she cried out, throwing her head back. "I'm so close!"

He could feel that she was about to detonate by the way her hips were churning against his finger and his tongue.

Suddenly, she bucked, her sheath squeezing over his finger, and screamed his name. He licked like a male possessed, taking everything she had to give until the last drop.

"Stop." She pushed his head away. "I'm too sensitive now."

He filed that information for the next time.

When her breathing returned to normal, she slid into the water and motioned for him to take her place. "Your turn, big guy."

He could no longer refuse her, nor did he want to. He had pleasured her thoroughly; she climaxed all over his tongue, and now she could do with him as she pleased.

When she kneeled between his legs and regarded his shaft with hungry eyes, he gripped it, holding it for her. "Do you want to taste me?"

Peering up at him to gauge his reaction, she brought her mouth so close that he could feel her warm breath, and when her lips made contact with the sensitive skin, he shuddered and felt his seed rise.

He'd been on the verge for so long that a gentle kiss would have been enough to detonate the explosion, but he refused to relinquish control of this senseless body part.

Not yet.

He wanted at least a few moments of her mouth on him before it was over.

Sensing his struggle, Jasmine leaned back, collected water in her cupped palm, and drizzled it over his engorged male part.

By now, the bathwater had turned lukewarm, but it felt cold against the heat of his erection, and the cooling sensation helped him regain control.

71

JASMINE

Once Ell-rom had regained control, Jasmine flicked her tongue out and lapped at the head, once, twice, three times.

He groaned, and his grip on his erection tightened.

Good. That would help him last longer. If he let her, she could do that for him, keep him on the edge for much longer than he would normally last, but perhaps that was better saved for after he had learned his own body's responses.

If Ell-rom were fully recovered, he could climax and be ready for more in minutes, but he was operating on pure adrenaline fueled by lust, and the moment he ejaculated, she had no doubt he would collapse. Hopefully, she would manage to get him in bed before that.

When he threaded his fingers into her hair, she took the tip into her mouth, and he emitted an anguished groan and threw his head back.

He wasn't going to last even if he strangled his manhood with that grip.

Perhaps she should just let him finish and deal with his embarrassment and disappointment over coming too quickly later.

Sucking him deeper into her mouth was all it took for him to lose control, and as he started coming, his body jerked, and he yelled her name.

As she swallowed every last drop, memories of her time with Edgar suddenly intruded on the haze of satisfaction, and she realized that she had forgotten a very important part of an immortal male's physiology. Ell-rom was going to bite her, and when he did, she was going to black out, and if he also fainted from exhaustion and the drop in adrenaline or testosterone, she was going to drown.

He would survive even if submerged in water because his body would enter stasis, but she wouldn't.

His fingers were still threaded in her hair, holding her to him, but then he lowered his hands and cupped her face, gazing down at her with glowing, hazy and unfocused eyes, and fangs that were fully elongated and ready to strike.

Jasmine lurched back, and he let go of her face, but as she tried to scramble out of the tub, he shot out a hand and clamped it on her shoulder with a bruising force.

"Let go!" She gripped his wrist and pulled. "You are hurting me!"

Shaking his head as if to clear the haze, Ell-rom released her, but she had no doubt that by tomorrow, there would be purple bruises where his fingers had been.

He was freakishly strong despite still looking starved.

"I'm sorry." He looked at her with pleading eyes. "Let me lick where I hurt you to heal what I have done."

"Not here." She jumped out of the tub, nearly slipping on the wet floor. "When we are in bed."

If he managed to stay awake and had the energy to bite her, Jasmine had no problem with him doing that while they were both in bed.

She grabbed a towel, wrapped it around herself, and then unfurled another one and held it out for him.

When he didn't move, she lowered the towel and frowned. "Do you need help standing up?"

He shook his head and didn't look at her.

"Then what's the matter?"

"I'm ashamed." He put a hand over his heart as if

ready to make a vow to atone for a sin he hadn't committed.

"Oh, sweetheart." She sat on the edge of the tub and cupped his cheek. "Don't worry about it. Once you kiss my booboo, it will go away."

He moved his head to avoid her touch. "That's not the only thing I'm ashamed of. I finished in your mouth. I scared you. You were trying to get away from me, and I tried to stop you."

She reached for his chin with a hooked finger and turned his head so he was forced to look at her. "I wanted you to finish in my mouth. It was as satisfying for me as it was for you when I finished all over your face. The reason I tried to get away was that I expected you to bite me. You were so exhausted that I thought you would faint, and since I always black out after a venom bite, I could drown in the tub water, and you wouldn't be present to save me."

"So, you really enjoyed this?"

"Yes, very much so." She leaned over and kissed his forehead. "And if you still want to bite me when we are in bed, I would love it."

He let out a shuddering breath. "We both need to wash away the suds." When she hesitated, he smiled to show her that his fangs had almost fully retreated. "I won't bite you. I promise."

72

ELL-ROM

Later, as Ell-rom lay in bed holding the sleeping Jasmine in his arms, he thought about what had transpired between them, and despaired.

The truth was that he couldn't have bitten her even if he wanted to. The urge had been there, the instinct was strong, and when he had shamefully restrained her to prevent her from running away from him, he was about to do it, but he doubted he could have actually gone through with it and sunk his fangs into her neck.

The memory of the taste of blood was so revolting to him that just the thought of having her blood on his fangs made him nauseous.

What was he going to do?

The venom bite was part of immortal sex, and he

wouldn't be able to induce Jasmine's transition without it.

Perhaps the medics could milk his venom and put it into a syringe so he could inject it into her?

Right now, his venom glands were swollen, and a distant memory of biting a towel pushed itself into his mind. Was that how he had dealt with the urge back on Anumati?

He had assumed that since he had never had sex before, he had never felt the urge to bite either. But perhaps he had imagined being with a female and had touched himself. He didn't know whether it was permitted or not, but he had a feeling that he and Morelle hadn't followed all the rules imposed on acolytes.

If only he could remember more.

As a priest, he had probably never gotten aggressive enough to produce the combative type of venom either, so he also hadn't been forced to bite any males. With how strong his aversion to blood was, Ell-rom doubted he could have done that either.

Perhaps he could have overcome his opponent by throwing up on him.

He chuckled softly so as not to wake his mate, but there was no mirth in the sound.

He was such a failure as a male.

How was he going to satisfy his mate and protect her if he couldn't bring himself to use his Goddess-given gifts?

How would he make Jasmine immortal?

COMING UP NEXT
The Children of the Gods Book 87
Dark Awakening Hidden Currents

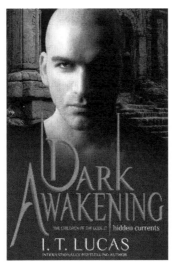

To read the first three chapters, JOIN the VIP club at ITLUCAS.COM. To find out what's included in your free membership, flip to the last page.

As Ell-rom's latent abilities resurface, he confronts an unexpected nemesis – himself. Haunted by emerging memories that paint him as the monster everyone feared, he grapples with a visceral aversion that threatens not only his relationship with Jasmine but her transition into immortality as well. With his sister still comatose, Ell-rom must conquer his inner demons on his own and secure their future.

Coming up next in the
PERFECT MATCH SERIES

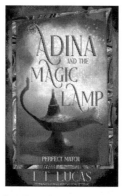

To read the first three chapters, JOIN the VIP club at ITLUCAS.COM. To find out what's included in your free membership, flip to the last page.

ADINA AND THE MAGIC LAMP

In this post-apocalyptic virtual reimagining of Aladdin, James, the enigmatic prince, and Adina, the fearless thief, navigate the treacherous streets of Londabad, a city that echoes London and Ahmedabad and fuses magic and technology. In the face of danger, the chemistry between them ignites, and the lines between prince and thief, royalty and commoner blur.

JOIN THE VIP CLUB
To find out what's included in your free membership, flip to the last page.

NOTE

Dear reader,

I hope my stories have added a little joy to your day. If you have a moment to add some to mine, you can help spread the word about the Children Of The Gods series by telling your friends and penning a review. Your recommendations are the most powerful way to inspire new readers to explore the series.

Thank you,

Isabell

Also by I. T. Lucas

THE CHILDREN OF THE GODS ORIGINS
1: Goddess's Choice
2: Goddess's Hope

THE CHILDREN OF THE GODS
Dark Stranger
1: Dark Stranger The Dream
2: Dark Stranger Revealed
3: Dark Stranger Immortal

Dark Enemy
4: Dark Enemy Taken
5: Dark Enemy Captive
6: Dark Enemy Redeemed

Kri & Michael's Story
6.5: My Dark Amazon

Dark Warrior
7: Dark Warrior Mine
8: Dark Warrior's Promise
9: Dark Warrior's Destiny
10: Dark Warrior's Legacy

Dark Guardian
11: Dark Guardian Found
12: Dark Guardian Craved
13: Dark Guardian's Mate

Dark Angel

14: Dark Angel's Obsession
15: Dark Angel's Seduction
16: Dark Angel's Surrender

Dark Operative

17: Dark Operative: A Shadow of Death
18: Dark Operative: A Glimmer of Hope
19: Dark Operative: The Dawn of Love

Dark Survivor

20: Dark Survivor Awakened
21: Dark Survivor Echoes of Love
22: Dark Survivor Reunited

Dark Widow

23: Dark Widow's Secret
24: Dark Widow's Curse
25: Dark Widow's Blessing

Dark Dream

26: Dark Dream's Temptation
27: Dark Dream's Unraveling
28: Dark Dream's Trap

Dark Prince

29: Dark Prince's Enigma
30: Dark Prince's Dilemma
31: Dark Prince's Agenda

Dark Queen
32: Dark Queen's Quest
33: Dark Queen's Knight
34: Dark Queen's Army

Dark Spy
35: Dark Spy Conscripted
36: Dark Spy's Mission
37: Dark Spy's Resolution

Dark Overlord
38: Dark Overlord New Horizon
39: Dark Overlord's Wife
40: Dark Overlord's Clan

Dark Choices
41: Dark Choices The Quandary
42: Dark Choices Paradigm Shift
43: Dark Choices The Accord

Dark Secrets
44: Dark Secrets Resurgence
45: Dark Secrets Unveiled
46: Dark Secrets Absolved

Dark Haven
47: Dark Haven Illusion
48: Dark Haven Unmasked
49: Dark Haven Found

Dark Power
50: Dark Power Untamed
51: <u>Dark Power Unleashed</u>
52: <u>Dark Power Convergence</u>

Dark Memories
53: Dark Memories Submerged
54: Dark Memories Emerge
55: Dark Memories Restored

Dark Hunter
56: Dark Hunter's Query
57: Dark Hunter's Prey
58: <u>Dark Hunter's Boon</u>

Dark God
59: Dark God's Avatar
60: Dark God's Reviviscence
61: Dark God Destinies Converge

Dark Whispers
62: Dark Whispers From The Past
63: Dark Whispers From Afar
64: Dark Whispers From Beyond

Dark Gambit
65: Dark Gambit The Pawn
66: Dark Gambit The Play
67: Dark Gambit Reliance

Dark Alliance
68: Dark Alliance Kindred Souls
69: Dark Alliance Turbulent Waters
70: Dark Alliance Perfect Storm

Dark Healing
71: Dark Healing Blind Justice
72: Dark Healing Blind Trust
73: Dark healing Blind Curve

Dark Encounters
74: Dark Encounters of the Close Kind
75: Dark Encounters of the Unexpected Kind
76: Dark Encounters of the Fated Kind

Dark Voyage
77: Dark Voyage Matters of the Heart
78: [Dark Voyage Matters of the Mind](#)
79: [Dark Voyage Matters of the Soul](#)

Dark Horizon
80: Dark Horizon New Dawn
81: Dark Horizon Eclipse of the Heart
82: Dark Horizon The Witching Hour

Dark Witch
83: Dark Witch: Entangled Fates
84: Dark Witch: Twin Destinies
85: Dark Witch: Resurrection

Dark Awakening
86: Dark Awakening: New World
87: Dark Awakening Hidden Currents

PERFECT MATCH

Vampire's Consort
King's Chosen
Captain's Conquest
The Thief Who Loved Me
My Merman Prince
The Dragon King
My Werewolf Romeo
The Channeler's Companion
The Valkyrie & The Witch
Adina and the Magic Lamp

TRANSLATIONS

DIE ERBEN DER GÖTTER
Dark Stranger
1- Dark Stranger Der Traum
2- Dark Stranger Die Offenbarung
3- Dark Stranger Unsterblich

Dark Enemy
4- Dark Enemy Entführt

5- Dark Enemy Gefangen
6- Dark Enemy Erlöst

Dark Warrior
7- Dark Warrior Meine Sehnsucht
8- Dark Warrior – Dein Versprechen
9- Dark Warrior - Unser Schicksal
10-Dark Warrior-Unser Vermächtnis

LOS HIJOS DE LOS DIOSES

EL OSCURO DESCONOCIDO
1: EL OSCURO DESCONOCIDO EL SUEÑO
2: EL OSCURO DESCONOCIDO REVELADO
3: EL OSCURO DESCONOCIDO INMORTAL

EL OSCURO ENEMIGO
4- EL OSCURO ENEMIGO CAPTURADO
5 - EL OSCURO ENEMIGO CAUTIVO
6- EL OSCURO ENEMIGO REDIMIDO

LES ENFANTS DES DIEUX
DARK STRANGER
1- Dark Stranger Le rêve
2- Dark Stranger La révélation
3- Dark Stranger L'immortelle

THE CHILDREN OF THE GODS SERIES SETS

BOOKS 1-3: DARK STRANGER TRILOGY—INCLUDES A BONUS SHORT STORY: **THE FATES TAKE A VACATION**

<u>BOOKS 4-6: DARK ENEMY TRILOGY</u> —INCLUDES A BONUS SHORT STORY—**THE FATES' POST-WEDDING CELEBRATION**

BOOKS 7-10: DARK WARRIOR TETRALOGY
BOOKS 11-13: DARK GUARDIAN TRILOGY
BOOKS 14-16: DARK ANGEL TRILOGY
BOOKS 17-19: DARK OPERATIVE TRILOGY
BOOKS 20-22: DARK SURVIVOR TRILOGY
BOOKS 23-25: DARK WIDOW TRILOGY
BOOKS 26-28: DARK DREAM TRILOGY
BOOKS 29-31: DARK PRINCE TRILOGY
BOOKS 32-34: DARK QUEEN TRILOGY
BOOKS 35-37: DARK SPY TRILOGY
BOOKS 38-40: DARK OVERLORD TRILOGY
BOOKS 41-43: DARK CHOICES TRILOGY
BOOKS 44-46: DARK SECRETS TRILOGY
BOOKS 47-49: DARK HAVEN TRILOGY
BOOKS 50-52: DARK POWER TRILOGY
BOOKS 53-55: DARK MEMORIES TRILOGY
BOOKS 56-58: DARK HUNTER TRILOGY
BOOKS 59-61: DARK GOD TRILOGY
BOOKS 62-64: DARK WHISPERS TRILOGY
BOOKS 65-67: DARK GAMBIT TRILOGY
BOOKS 68-70: DARK ALLIANCE TRILOGY

BOOKS 71-73: DARK HEALING TRILOGY
BOOKS 74-76: DARK ENCOUNTERS TRILOGY
BOOKS 77-79: DARK VOYAGE TRILOGY
BOOKS 80-81: DARK HORIZON TRILOGY

MEGA SETS
THE CHILDREN OF THE GODS: BOOKS 1-6
INCLUDES CHARACTER LISTS
THE CHILDREN OF THE GODS: BOOKS 6.5-10

PERFECT MATCH BUNDLE 1

CHECK OUT THE SPECIALS ON
ITLUCAS.COM
(https://itlucas.com/specials)

FOR EXCLUSIVE PEEKS AT UPCOMING RELEASES &
A FREE I. T. LUCAS COMPANION BOOK

JOIN MY *VIP CLUB* AND GAIN ACCESS TO THE VIP PORTAL AT ITLUCAS.COM

TO JOIN, GO TO:
http://eepurl.com/blMTpD

Find out more details about what's included with

your free membership on the book's last page.

TRY THE CHILDREN OF THE GODS SERIES ON <u>AUDIBLE</u>
2 FREE audiobooks with your new Audible subscription!

FOR EXCLUSIVE PEEKS AT UPCOMING RELEASES &
A FREE I. T. LUCAS COMPANION BOOK

Join my *VIP Club* and gain access to the VIP portal at itlucas.com
To Join, go to:
http://eepurl.com/blMTpD

INCLUDED IN YOUR FREE MEMBERSHIP:

YOUR VIP PORTAL

- Read preview chapters of upcoming releases.
- Listen to Goddess's Choice narration by Charles Lawrence
- Exclusive content offered only to my VIPs.

FREE I.T. LUCAS COMPANION INCLUDES:

- Goddess's Choice Part 1
- Perfect Match: Vampire's Consort (A standalone Novella)
- Interview Q & A
- Character Charts

If you're already a subscriber and you are not getting my emails, your provider is sending them to your junk folder, and you are missing out on important updates. To fix that, add isabell@itlucas.com to your email contacts or your email VIP list.

**Check out the specials at
https://www.itlucas.com/specials**

Made in United States
Orlando, FL
25 November 2024

54431011R00252